Praise for Rebekah Crane's

PLA

D1022897

"I love this book as an ad~~~ ~~~ ~~ ~ ~~~~~~~ I would have been obsessed. Rebekah Crane captures perfectly and poignantly the thousands of feelings, thoughts, dreams and desires of that wonderful creature called a teenager." —*Lili Taylor, Actress*

"Hilarious, heartfelt, and edgy... From the first page you'll root for Marty even as she makes the obligatory mistakes that all teens must commit. At its core, *Playing Nice* shows that fighting for true friendship, even through major challenges, is well worth it." —*Rory O'Malley, Tony Award Nominee for The Book of Mormon*

"This book is a must read for anyone who is or has experienced any form of bullying or has ever been a teenager girl... Smashing." —*Meagen Howard Fox, Page Turners Blog*

"I think the mark of a truly excellent young adult novel is when you stop and think, wow, I knew that badass chick in high school; I had a crush on that hot, mysterious musician; I was that girl who always tried to be good even though I just wanted to scream sometimes. It's tough to create teenage characters that are believable, but *Playing Nice* hits it spot on." —*Lindsay Feneis, age 23*

"Quirky, real, emotional and funny." —*Virginia Ryan, age 29*

"I want to read this book from cover to cover over and over

again."
—*Maggie Tugend, age 14*

"*Playing Nice* shows how strong teenage girls can be—through the fun times, the sad times, and the times you fall madly, deeply in love."
—*Allison Williams, age 32*

"I loved *Playing Nice* so much; I never wanted to put it down!"
—*Kaylie Taips, age 13*

PLAYING
Nice

Rebekah Crane

In This Together Media

New York

In This Together Media Edition, January 2013

Published in the United States by In This Together Media, New York, 2013

www.inthistogethermedia.com

BISAC:

1. Girls & Women-Juvenile Fiction. 2. Humorous stories-Juvenile Fiction. 3. Friendship (Social Issues)-Juvenile Fiction. 4. Emotions & Feelings (Social Issues)-Juvenile Fiction. 5. Bullying (Social Issues)-Juvenile Fiction

ISBN-10:0985895659, ISBN-13: 978-0-9858956-5-5

eBook ISBN-10: 0985895640, ISBN-13: 978-0-9858956-4-8

Cover photograph by Tyler Maroney

Cover and Interior Design by Steven W. Booth, Genius Book Services

For Anna and Emmy, who share their greatest gift with me—
Laughter.

CHAPTER 1

My mom likes to tell everyone that from the day I was born she knew I would be a nice person. According to her story, I emerged from the womb with a smile on my face.

"You didn't even make a peep. I thought you were dead," she always says. The doctor told her I came out shaking his hand, like I was trying to introduce myself.

"How nice!" he announced at my arrival. At least, that's what my mom claims.

Last year, I was voted The Nicest Person in Minster High School. I got an entire page dedicated to me in the yearbook. I waited until I had a copy in my hands to tell my parents. I wanted them to see what all their hard work had accomplished. All the years of practicing manners at the dining room table and forced conversation with old ladies at church about their bridge games. It all paid off with a full-page spread of their daughter, describing all the nice things she does.

I came home and placed the yearbook on our kitchen counter, open to that page, across which were splattered in glossy color pictures of me starring in the school's production of *Guys and Dolls*. I played Sarah Brown. It was my dream roll: the do-gooder Salvation Army girl who helps a bad-boy gangster become a better person. And I got to have my first stage kiss.

There were also pictures of me tutoring after school and

picking up garbage on the weekends with the Clean Air Club. All the things that make people like me.

When my mom went to make dinner, she saw it and screeched, "My daughter, the nicest person in Minster High School! I knew you could do it!"

I smiled from the couch as I watched TV, knowing I'd made them proud once again, that I had lived up to the expectations, set at my birth, that I would be a nice person.

When the photographer came to school to take pictures for my page, he sat me down in a seat and said, "Smile and don't move." I pulled my shoulders back, the way my mom always taught me, and posed, chin up, chest out. Posture shows people how you view yourself. The pictures came out great. My teeth look as white as snow next to my mahogany hair and hazel eyes. I look pretty, but not overdone. *A lovely lady a man will want to marry one day*, my father said.

Smile and don't move. Whenever someone makes me mad or a bubble rises in my gut that makes me think everything I've been working for, everything I think I am, is a lie, I remind myself: smile and don't move. Doing that got me an entire page in my high school's yearbook and it's going to get me into a great college and find me a wonderful man to marry. And when it becomes my turn to have a baby, that girl is going to come out smiling, just like I did. The nicest baby that doctor has ever seen.

ɔ

I signed up for the Welcoming Committee at the beginning of the year because I needed more things to put on my applications for college.

"Junior year is the most important. Don't get off-track,"

my mom told me. She has a way of singing the end of her sentences so they don't sound too harsh. She can make a demand seem melodic and uplifting. *Clean your room or you're grounded*, sounds better chirped out like a Disney character. Once she heard about The Welcoming Committee, my mom insisted I join and run for president. She even made posters with glitter that said, "Vote for Marty. A welcome face."

In the end, I was the only candidate. Ms. Everley didn't even make a ballot. She just stood up at one of our meetings and said, "Looks like WelCo has its first Margaret Thatcher." I didn't really like that she compared me to an old English lady, but I reminded myself that it didn't matter because I'd won, even if I was running against me.

The Welcoming Committee was formed to help freshman adapt to high school. We show the new kids around to their classes, make sure no one ends up duct-taped to the football goal posts, stuff like that. It's been easy and I won't complain about another opportunity to show the University of Michigan that I'm a well-rounded person.

I've had an application to U of M sitting on the desk in my room since I visited Ann Arbor two years ago. I knew from the moment I set foot on the campus that it was where I was meant to go. A prestigious university four hours away from my parents' house in Minster, Ohio. Close enough to go home for the weekend. Far enough away that they can't come knocking on my door at any moment. I've even picked out what dorm I want to live in freshman year and what sorority I'm going to rush. All I have to do is pack my transcripts with so many great things that U of M can't possibly turn me down.

"Thanks for coming in early this morning," Ms. Everley says as I sit down at one of the desks in the Welcoming

Committee office. It's really just the Special Ed classroom, but we've decorated with happy posters and motivational signs to make it our own.

Ms. Everley is the teacher in charge of WelCo, as we like to call it. She's also my English teacher, one of the hot ones who makes teenage boys confused and sweaty, who flip their hair and put on too much perfume and make-up. She usually wears tight black pants that crease at the butt because they're too small and some lacy top, except today her pants are beige and her red silky top has ruffles around the boobs. I don't think she's married, so there must be something wrong with her. My mom says any woman over the age of thirty who isn't married probably pays too much attention to her job and not enough to what's important. And it does seem like Ms. Everley loves teaching.

"No problem. I like getting here early. It helps me focus." My mom always says I should act appreciative even if I'm not. The truth is that I stayed up late last night watching TV and I'm tired. I had to put on an extra layer of makeup to cover the bags under my eyes. "Is this about what happened last week?"

When Ms. Everley emailed me late yesterday, I was worried that our meeting had to do with a freshman girl who got busted having sex in the boys' locker room with a senior. Our principal found them with their pants down mid 'thrust,' as he called it. Just thinking the word 'thrust' makes my palms sweaty. Everyone in school knows. The girl's life is totally ruined. I heard her parents are thinking of moving to Finley. You can't do things like that in Minster. You just can't.

"Actually, we have a new girl coming to school today, and I thought you'd be the perfect person to show her around, being president of WelCo and all."

"A new student?" I ask, a bubble of anticipation rising in my stomach. No one ever moves to Minster. It's in the middle of nowhere. The last person who did was Phillip Knasel, and he came from Wapakoneta, a town twenty miles away. His parents died in a car accident and the courts said he had to go live with his grandma. Sometimes I think he still has a hard time fitting in. Or maybe he's just sad because he doesn't have any parents. I don't know what I'd do if mine died.

"We are the Welcoming Committee, after all." Ms. Everley shrugs and her boob-ruffles bounce.

"Of course, I'd be happy to help." I smile widely at the thought of meeting someone new, of being their first impression of Minster High. They'll always remember the day they met me. I'll be a shining star in their high school career. The nice girl with bright eyes and a strong handshake, who offered them guidance and friendship when they needed it most. I smooth down the front of my dress. I was born for stuff like this.

"Great. She's a junior, like you, and she's in your English class."

I nod. I'm in Honors for English, along with every other subject. If the new girl's in my class, she must be smart. I like smart people. They have goals and expectation, just like me.

Ms. Everley keeps talking for a few minutes, but I tune her out. My eyes hurt right where the bulb meets the socket. I shouldn't have stayed up last night. My dad told me to go to bed, but I was engrossed in an episode on the Discovery Channel about animals who mate for life. Their dedication to each other fascinated me, the way a father penguin will stand in the bitter cold for months holding an egg on its feet, all because he loves the mother and wants the baby to survive. I've never been in love, but if a penguin can find a soul mate, I'm sure I can, too.

I'm lost in thoughts about penguins and love and how I need to remember to talk slowly and smile when the classroom door opens and a girl walks in. Her heavy boots on the linoleum shock me out of my trance. Each step sounds like her feet are tied together with chains.

I look up and see a girl so covered in black I think she might be the goddess of night.

"You must be Lily Hatfield," Ms. Everley says, rising to greet the new girl.

"Don't call me Lily. It's Lil." The new girl speaks as if she's correcting a peer, not a teacher. She takes off her gigantic red sunglasses and places them on top of her black hair.

"Okay, Lil," Ms. Everley says, accenting the new girl's name. The pleasantness that coated her voice seconds ago is gone. Now she sounds strained, like she's swallowing the words she really wants to say. She points to me at my desk. "This is Martina Hart, the girl who'll be showing you around today."

I blink and stand up. *You're being rude*, my mother's voice whispers in my ears.

"Hi Lil. I'm Marty," I say, extending my hand for her to shake.

"Marty? And I thought Lily was bad." She doesn't take my hand, but shakes off her black leather jacket and slings it over the back of a chair. I stare at her right hand, waiting for her to reach out to me. Every finger is covered in a silver ring; the biggest is a huge skull on her middle finger. I force myself to look at her face and clasp my hands behind my back. I don't want her to feel bad if she doesn't want to shake.

"It's a family name," I smile.

My dad named me after my grandmother. Our family is seven generations deep in Minster. My great-great-grandfather has a plaque dedicated to him in the town hall for saving six barns during the great fire of 1903. We live in the same farmhouse my dad was raised in, though my mom insisted on updating everything. *We're not farmers. Your father is a dentist, for Pete's sake,* she said when she tore up the kitchen and made the entire bottom floor open-plan.

"Marty can help you find your classes and make sure you're acclimating. I have no doubt she'll do a stellar job," Ms. Everley says as she makes her way to the door, walking backwards and almost tripping. She's probably escaping from any more awkward moments. That, or she's fleeing the uncomfortable tingle in the air from so much black in a room this early in the morning. "Just let me know if you need anything."

And then we're alone. I wait for Lil to say something or show me her schedule, but she only picks at the dirt under her black-painted nails.

"Where did you move from?" I ask, remembering the importance of generating conversation through questions. My dad once said that people who only talk about themselves are dicks. It's the only time I've ever heard him use the word, so I knew it was an important life lesson.

"Florida," Lil says. She twists her aquamarine nose ring, spinning it around before picking something out of the inside of her nostril and flicking it on the ground.

"Where in Florida?" I gulp. This is not going as planned. I thought Ms. Everley said she was in my English class. People who know how to read and write usually know how to form sentences and talk. I wait a few more seconds, and then decide maybe I need to show Lil we have something in common. "I went to Florida last year with my parents on spring break. We stayed in a condo right on the beach in Siesta Key. It was amazing. I didn't want to leave."

"Do you smoke?" Lil asks, finally looking at me. The color of her eyes matches the nose ring, and I can't help but think that without so much black eyeliner, Lil might be pretty.

"I tried it once, but it's not for me."

"Are you a virgin?"

"I..." The question throws me. Did she just say *virgin*? I wring my hands together, wondering what to say. I can't admit I've never had sex, but I don't want to lie and say I have, either. It's an un-winnable question. If I say yes, I'm a prude. If I say no, I'm a slut. And what if Lil tells everyone in school my answer? I think about that poor freshman girl who got caught 'thrusting' a senior and choke. I can't believe she asked me that. She's ruining the way this is supposed to go. I ask the questions and she answers; her somewhat lengthy response leads us to further conversation.

I play with the front of my dress, running my hands down the smooth cotton. I picked it out specifically for today's warm weather. It's Mod-style and shows off my legs in a non-sexy, non-nun like way. Just how I like it.

"I'm kidding. Of course you are. No boy could get past those tight thighs," Lil says and points to my crotch. I pull my legs even closer together. She digs into her black, silver-studded purse, but I can't stop looking at her face and gaping at how casual her eyes are as she asks me such personal questions.

"Do you need me to show you to your first class?" It's the only thing I can think of. I've never felt more awkward. Not even the time Robby Sumter accidentally grabbed my boob diving for a basketball in gym class and got an erection.

I remind myself to smile. A smile makes everyone happy.

"What I need is a cigarette, so if you don't mind, Polly-anna, I'm going to find a tree outside where no one can see me and have an early morning nicotine breakfast. I'd ask you to come, but I'm afraid your virgin stink will rub off on me and, since there's nothing else to do in this town, I plan on getting laid while I'm here. See you in English."

My mouth falls open. In one sentence, she's admitted to having sex and wanting to have more. Doesn't she know you can't do that here? Was she raised in some sort of hippy commune in Florida where people walk around naked and talk about sex like it's the weather?

"Wait," I say, not realizing my mouth is moving. My skin tingles with little poking needles and a bubble rises in my gut, screaming to be released. She should need me. Instead, she's blowing me off like I'm not good enough because I'm a virgin and I care about my lungs. This is the only oppor-tunity I have to make my impression. And it's going wrong.

Lil looks at me, eyebrows raised. Her eyes are so clear, like a summer sky in the middle of the day. The color is so different from the rest of her black-covered self. It's mesmer-izing.

Words come out of my mouth that I don't expect. May-be it's because it's my duty to make sure Lil does well to-day. Maybe I'm worried she'll contact U of M and tell them I failed her. Or maybe I don't want to sit in the Special Ed classroom, thinking about penguins and sex and waiting for my first class to start. Maybe I want to be outside instead of stuck inside the four walls of this school.

"Can I come with you?" I ask.

She doesn't respond at first, just keeps staring at me with

squinted eyes, like she's scanning me for possible diseases.

"Fine," she grumbles.

I don't know why I want to go anywhere with Lil. Based on the black clothes and skull ring alone, I'm pretty sure she's a one-way ticket to hell, but I grab my backpack and make for the door nonetheless.

I just hope she doesn't ask me about sex again.

CHAPTER 2

Lil doesn't say a word as we sit on the ground next to a large oak tree across the street from the school. She takes long drags on a cigarette, holding it in her mouth, and then exhaling a smooth line of smoke into the air.

I stare at the skull ring. It has a red rhinestone for a tongue and two black eyes. It looks like a Halloween costume accessory. Except I'm pretty sure Lil wears it every day, because her finger indents around the silver base like the ring has grown into her skin.

On closer look, she's not fully covered in black. Her hair is actually brown. Deep, dark, brown. Like soil after you dig a few feet into the ground. With her blue eyes and red lipstick, she looks like Snow White. A smoking, combat boot-wearing princess.

The whole time we sit there, I try to think of what to say, but what's appropriate when she's already said "tight thighs," "virgin" and "getting laid" in our first five minutes together? And I'm entranced at how her hand holds the cigarette like it's an appendage and her mouth curls around the end, making out with the filter, as if she's been smoking for years.

I wonder if her parents know. The one time I tried a cigarette, I hid next to the dumpster in the alley behind Rite Aid on Main Street so no one in town would see me. When I went home, I covered myself a layer thick in plumeria lotion and mouth wash to mask the odor. I was worried my parents would be able to tell. My mother scolded me for smelling like a hooker and told me to stop buying that lotion. I haven't worn it since.

Once Lil finishes, she puts the cigarette out, sizzling the lit end into the earth. My hand reaches out to pick it up and put it in the trash can. Cigarette butts take forever to biodegrade. But I stop myself. It wouldn't be kind and Lil needs to know that I'm nice.

The second before I decide to start a conversation, she gets up and walks away, the chains on her black combat boots clanging with each step. Nothing is spoken between us. I watch her cross the street back to school, her fresh smoke smell lingering in my nose, and a weight hangs in the air. It presses on me, like each word I thought about saying is a boulder on my shoulders. I realize I'm disappointed. No one has ever talked to me like that before; no one's ever been so honest and brash. Now that Lil's gone, I'm left sitting on the ground, dirt on my favorite pink dress and an annoying pinch in the back of my chest reminding me how foolish it was to follow her.

I get up and look around. Until this moment, I hadn't thought about what people would think if they saw me sitting with Lil while she smoked. I was too focused on her mouth. Luckily the first bus is just starting to unload a pack of students and no one's looking.

I dust off the back of my dress, giving it an extra wipe clean. I wear a dress to school every day but Friday. My mom says people know the type of person you are by what you wear. Some weeks I'm so tired of crossing my legs so no one can see my underwear that I can't wait for Friday to roll around. But then I remind myself that boys like dresses, probably because it's easy access to my lady parts, and leg cramps are just the price I have to pay.

Brushing out the wrinkles that have formed, I look for my best friend in the crowd of students exiting the busses. If Lil doesn't want my help, I can't force her. That's another thing we talked about in WelCo at the beginning of the year. If someone is lost and they don't want help, it's not our job to save them. I tell myself that over and over until the uncomfortable jabbing in the back of chest eases to a dull poke. I decide it's better that Lil walked away silently. My mother always says, if you can't say something nice, don't say anything at all.

I find Sarah lingering at the back of the crowd, headphones plugging her ears. She's always listening to classical music. Beethoven, Bach, Tchaikovsky. I tried to get her to listen to a musical once, one of my favorites, but she covered her ears. *This shit is terrible*, she screamed. Sarah plays flute in the Minster orchestra. First chair, of course. We've been friends since kindergarten, when her parents moved from one side of Minster to the house directly across the street from us. My mom and I brought a cherry pie over as a welcoming present. Sarah came running to the door, her hair pulled into a tight bun on the top of her head, like a ballerina.

"Do you want to play Barbies?" she asked, waving around a blonde-haired Barbie and a brunette.

"Sure," I said, grabbing for the blonde one.

"You can't have either of these." Sarah yanked her hand away. "You can be Ken."

I looked at my mom. I really wanted to be the blonde Barbie. She smiled and whispered through her teeth, "Don't be rude, Marty."

I forced a grin and grabbed Ken.

Sarah never did get better at sharing her dolls, but that's just her. Eventually, it was all about Ken and Barbie lying naked on top of each other like they were having sex, and it didn't matter anymore. Sarah's planning to attend U of M with me, but as a Music Theory major. We've been friends for so long; I couldn't imagine doing anything without her. It just seems right to go to college together.

"You smell like cigarettes," Sarah says as I approach. She pulls the headphones from her ears; a screech of violin music blares from the speakers. "Why weren't you on the bus?"

"Ms. Everley wanted me to come in early and meet a new girl," I say, pulling vanilla perfume from my backpack and spraying it on my wrists.

"A new student at Minster High? That hasn't happened since, like, third grade. Is she pretty? Please tell me she's butt-ugly."

My brain scrambles for the right words to describe Lil, to tell Sarah about our awkward conversation and the skull ring and the way Lil knew I was a virgin just by looking at me. How she kind of makes me want to confess things I would never say out loud, but I don't know why.

"She's different."

"Different in a hot way or different in a gross, smells-like-cheese way?"

"I don't know. Neither." I play with my hair like that might focus my thoughts. "She's dark."

"Dark? What the hell is that supposed to mean?" Sarah says as we walk into the school building.

"She likes the color black," I say.

"She sounds weird. Thank God. I thought you didn't like smoking?" Sarah asks.

"I don't. But I didn't want to leave her alone."

"Well, where is she now?"

"Alone," I shrug. "It didn't go as planned."

We head for the bathroom to do our normal morning routine. Sarah always spends a few minutes fixing her hair, making sure every curl is properly placed. Last year in psychology, we learned that what people find most attractive in a person are a large forehead, big eyes, and a small mouth. It's why people always love babies. Sarah's face has all those features. A clear forehead, big brown eyes, and a rosebud mouth. She complains about her curly red hair, but I've come to realize that most people don't like their hair. Curly people want straight, blonde people want brown.

I'm an exception to the rule. I love my hair. *God's blessing,* as my mother calls it. Not too thick, not too thin, and cut right below the shoulder blades. I blow it dry every morning, brushing each piece with a round brush that curls it ever so slightly at the bottom.

"Did you hear that Jamie is going to the Hot Shot Dance with Josh Harper?" Sarah says, puckering and applying clear lip gloss.

"That's surprising." Sarah and I live for dances. It's the only thing that ever happens in Minster, and we have one almost every other month. The Hot Shot dance celebrates the opening of hunting season. It's kind of a big deal, and this year WelCo is in charge. Being president and all, I'm taking it on as my biggest high school challenge. I want everyone to walk into the gym and think *Marty Hart has done it again. This is the nicest dance Minster High has ever seen!* Next to playing Sandy in this year's spring musical, *Grease,* the Hot Shot dance will be a defining moment for me.

"I think he thought it would be okay since Cody's off at

college, but it is so not okay." Sarah emphasizes the *so*, dragging out the O. Jamie dated Josh's best friend for over a year. Once you date someone in Minster, you're off-limits for the rest of your high school career, especially with their friends. It's unwritten dating law.

"We're still going stag together, right?" I don't think I can handle the stress of finding a date and planning the dance. For Homecoming, Sam Higgins waited until three days before to ask me. I couldn't eat for a week I was so nervous. Finally, he sent me a text. *Want 2 go 2 dance?* Not the most romantic thing, but at least I wasn't alone.

Sarah nods and fluffs her hair.

"Have you decided what you're going to wear?" I ask. The dance isn't for weeks, but I can't stop thinking about my dress.

"Ugh, I'm so sick of all my clothes. I think we should go shopping." Sarah blows herself a kiss in the mirror. "So what's her name?" she asks as she screws the top back onto her lip gloss.

"Whose name?"

"The new girl."

I powder under my eyes, making sure no bags are showing, and wonder why it's so hard for me to talk about Lil. Why can't I just tell Sarah she'll notice her when she sees a creature like the Grim Reaper approach?

But there's something about Lil, her blunt questions, her smoking, and the way she talked to Ms. Everley, as if she didn't care what anyone thought about her, that I want to keep to myself.

"Lily Hatfield," I say, zipping up my backpack.

"Lily. Sounds pretty." Sarah frowns in the mirror. "Seriously, Marty, I don't know how you live with your boy name. It's like your parents have been trying to torture you since birth."

"Right," I say. But I love my name. It was my grandma's and now that she's gone, every time someone says it, I picture her standing beside me in her plaid apron, flour on her hands. It's like she's still here on Earth.

I take one last look in the mirror before heading out of the bathroom. Carefully, I force a smile. Maybe it's the cigarette smoke still lingering in my nose or the dirt I can't seem to brush out of my dress, but something in my reflection looks off. I'm just tired, I tell myself. It's the bags under my eyes that make me look different.

❧

I search for Lil all morning, but can't find her anywhere. Every time I hear someone whisper about the new girl, I get anxious, wanting to see her again. Then a pit of guilt drops in my stomach. How could I let her walk away without saying a word? It's my job to make people feel welcome, and all I did was enable her bad habit of smoking, which by every doctor's standards, is horrible and leads to cancer.

By the time I get to English, I'm starting to worry. What if her day has been terrible and I've failed? What if Lil told Ms. Everley I shouldn't be president of WelCo anymore? What if she wrote on the bathroom wall, "Marty Hart has a rotten, never-been-used vagina that stinks"?

I walk into the classroom, hoping Lil is already seated, but she's nowhere to be found. Butterflies flutter in my stomach as I play out terrible scenarios of what's happened in my mind. My mom would say my imagination is one of my worst attributes. I make up crazy scenes, like Lil getting arrested for smoking and the principal suspending her and at the last second she screams my name and tells everyone I was responsible. It's irrational, but I like to think it helps me perform onstage. I don't have a problem getting into character. I let my mind become someone else's and pretend life is different than it is and POOF! I'm no longer me.

"How did the rest of this morning go?" Ms. Everley asks as I take my seat.

"Great," I say with a little too much enthusiasm. "I think she's adjusting well. I mean, she's quite interesting. Florida and her nose ring and her love for all things black." I'm babbling, trying to act like our conversation was fruitful, when all I really know is the intimate way Lil makes out with a cigarette and her plans to get laid.

"I knew I could count on you." Ms. Everley smiles and turns toward the chalkboard. With every letter she writes, her butt shakes in her painted-on beige pants. It almost looks like she's wearing nothing from the waist down. I take a deep breath and pull out my homework. We're reading *The Catcher in the Rye*, and last night I had to write a personal letter to Holden Caulfield. I couldn't write what I really wanted to say, about how stupid I think he is for leaving prep school in the first place and how he should've kept his head down and not bothered Stradlater. I ended up pretending I was Phoebe and wrote the letter from her perspective. I just signed it with my name. I'm sure Ms. Everley will love it.

I'm digging through my backpack when I hear the boots and the smell of cigarette smoke wafts in my direction. I sit up quickly and see Lil taking a seat at the desk next to mine. Every kid in the classroom is staring at her, but she doesn't seem to notice. Or maybe she doesn't care. The only time I want people looking at me with eyes popping out of their heads is when I'm on stage. Staring is rarely a good thing, unless you're a super model or famous and Lil is definitely neither one.

"It's good to see you again," I decide to say. It's the line I usually use when I talk to the old ladies at church. The ones that smell like mothballs and spearmint gum. I have to yell just so they'll hear me. I'm never *really* that happy to see them, but with all the people staring at Lil, this is my opportunity to be a shining example of a nice girl.

"Don't say things you don't mean," Lil says in a flat, no-nonsense tone. I blink, shocked at being called out so easily, and look around to see if people heard. Pippa Rogers giggles two seats behind me and my face burns raging hot. My mind fumbles with how to recover, but it's as if Lil's words have made everything go blank.

"I'm sorry, but that's my seat," Alex Austin says to Lil, saving me a response. I take a deep breath and push down the bubble in my gut that makes me want to scream at Lil and smack Pippa.

"Marty said I could sit here." Lil says it even-keeled and direct. Her tone makes the statement sound true.

"No, I didn't," I say, and now I'm calling Lil out on her lie. I gape at her, partly mad because she put words in my mouth and partly because she's acting like we're well acquainted. Other than a few curt words and sharing her second-hand smoke, I barely know her.

"That's okay. She can sit there." Alex grins at me. I don't know if he can sense the tension and he's trying to help, or if he just likes smiling, but seeing his mouth turn up into a rosy-cheeked half moon makes the anger coursing through my veins settle.

Sometimes I look over at Alex during class and notice

he's staring at me. Last year, he came to see *Guys and Dolls* and told me afterward that I looked beautiful. It's the only time a man has called me beautiful, except for my dad. I'd say Alex likes me, but other than smiling and calling me beautiful, he's never done anything to show interest.

Sorry, I mouth to him. He shrugs and takes a seat in the back of the room. In a way, I think Alex might be perfect for me. He's strong but not too muscular, his smile is straight with only a slight gap between his two front teeth, and even though his wardrobe consists of way too many flannel shirts, he's a pretty good dresser. But he's a jock, and I just can't date a jock. I hate the smell of sweat.

I turn my attention from Alex back to Lil and breathe. I decide to take another stab at conversation. It might be a kamikaze mission, but I can't have her walking around school telling people I'm a liar.

"How has your first day been?" I ask.

"Just peachy," she says.

I wait for her to continue. Silence. Lil starts to twist her nose ring again.

"Did that hurt?"

"Not compared to my other piercings."

"You have other piercings?" I say, a slight wobble in my voice.

Right after I ask the question, Ms. Everley stands up to start class. My mom would kill me if I pierced my nose or anything other than my ears and something tells me Lil probably has a hidden tattoo somewhere that she got at one of those seedy joints I saw littered all over Florida.

I force my eyes off her and onto the front of the classroom. I can pretend all day long that I should get to know Lil, but the truth is that tattoos and skull rings and piercings and people who speak exactly what's on their mind scare me.

"I'd like everyone to welcome a new student to our class," Ms. Everley says. "Lil, would you come up here?"

Any eyes that weren't on Lil are now. She groans, shaking her head, and mouths the word *fuck*. I look at Ms. Everley, mouth hanging open, to see if she's noticed but she's too busy fluffing her hair and checking out her reflection in the window. Lil gets up from her seat, boots clanging as she walks to the front of the classroom.

"Would you like to share anything about yourself?" Ms. Everley asks.

"No." Lil stares at Ms. Everley like she daring her to ask another question. Chuckles ripple through the classroom.

"Nothing?"

Lil stares at Ms. Everley, her blue eyes intense, and then it happens. Someone whispers *freak*.

"What was that?" Ms. Everley asks.

No one in the room says a word. A feather could drop and we would hear it.

My heart pinches, uncomfortable. It's an instinctive reaction when someone does something mean. I can't help it. It's the nice in me. I turn around to see who said it, and everyone stops giggling and looks down.

Lil stares forward, not even flinching, and walks back to her seat. By the lack of emotion on her face, I'd assume she didn't hear, but both of her hands are balled into such tight fists that her knuckles have turned white.

She plops back down in the seat and slouches. I turn and smile at her, hoping that one single act of kindness will wipe away the bad moment. I figure it's the least I can do.

"Let's get back to *The Catcher in the Rye*." Ms. Everley turns to the board and starts writing the word PHONY in capital letters. A line of chalk residue runs across her rear, making it impossible not to stare at her ass.

For a second, I think I feel Lil's eyes on me. I sit up straighter in my desk, chest out, shoulders back. After all, this is Honors English.

જ

For the rest of the day, I keep my mind focused on school. The only time I let myself drift to my awkward conversation with Lil is after gym, when I put on an extra layer of perfume because I'm worried my virgin stink has grown stronger with physical activity. It's irrational, but I can't stop myself.

By the time the final bell rings, I'm anxious to go home, even if that means riding the bus. It's the only thing I would change about high school. It seems criminal that I have a license, but I still have to ride next to freshmen who forget to put on deodorant and talk too loudly about stupid things. I guess one good part is that it's the only time Sarah and I have to us. Her schedule is the exact opposite of mine; we don't even have lunch together. It's the orchestra's fault. It takes up two periods in the morning. I don't want to be needy, but by the end of the day, I'm dying to talk to someone.

Even though I'm the nicest person in Minster, I don't have a gaggle of friends. I've found that most people like to be associated with me and the things I do, but very few actually want to get to know me. That's okay. My mother says you make your best friends in college anyway.

On the bus, Sarah and I usually sit all the way in the back and try to ignore the armpit smells and squeaky voices. At least once a day, one of us will mention that we're in desperate need of a car.

I'm waiting for Sarah when a blue car like something my Grandma Martina would've driven, a long boat-looking thing that eats more gasoline in one block than a modern car would in a hundred, pulls up in front of me.

Lil leans over the passenger seat and rolls down the window. "You want a ride, Pollyanna?" she asks. Her voice is loud to compensate for the blaring music coming out of the speakers, and her skull ring glints through the windshield.

I can feel people's eyes on me, waiting to see what I'll do. I bite my bottom lip; the anxiousness from earlier rumbling in my stomach, like Lil planted a seed and something foreign is growing inside me. If I say no, I'm being mean. I'm the president of WelCo and it's my job to make her feel good.

"Sure, but I need to tell my friend I won't be on the bus," I say, smiling and swallowing my apprehension.

"Whatever." Lil waves her hand through the air like she's brushing away my words.

I find Sarah just walking out of the school building. *I'm a nice girl*, I repeat in my head. This is why I'm getting in the car. If I say it enough, maybe I can convince myself it's the truth. Maybe I can squash the feeling Lil brings out in me, a crazy new feeling that makes me want to scream and burst into a million pieces.

"Um, I'm going to catch a ride with Lil," I say, wringing my hands together.

"You're what?" Sarah snaps.

I bend into her to whisper. "She's new and I feel bad."

"More like suicidal," she scoffs.

"It's one ride. I'm WelCo president, for Pete's sake."

"Getting in a car with that," Sarah points at Lil's boat and cringes, "is taking your job too far. She looks like a vampire, Marty. You don't even know her."

"I'll text you later, okay?"

"It's your funeral," Sarah says.

I gape at her. This isn't that big a deal. People give rides to people all the time, I tell myself. And again I push down the rumble that tells me otherwise, that's quietly screaming at me that Lil is new. Uncharted territory. A blank slate who speaks her mind and wears a dead person's face as an accessory.

"I'll text you," I repeat as I walk toward Lil's car.

I open the door and slide into the seat. Old Taco Bell wrappers and empty cigarette cartons litter the floor. A pine tree air freshener hangs from her rearview mirror; it's stinking up the car, so I keep the window rolled down. Outside feels like September instead of November.

"Seat belts for safety," Lil says.

I reach behind me and snap the belt into place. For some reason, even with it on, I don't feel like Lil is safe. Almost everything in my body is telling me to get out of the car, like this one singular moment is going to change my life forever.

Everything except some small part of me, hidden behind layers of skin and bones and manners and rules, a deep part that goes all the way to the back of my soul where things turn black and light never shines, a part that begs me to stay put.

I look out the window and see Sarah just making it to our bus. She's carrying her flute case and a water bottle. Everything about her looks right. Her hair's half pulled back so her cheekbones show, and her short brown skirt falls exactly mid thigh, not too short, but not too long. Sheet music sticks out of her backpack. She's the exact person I've known for twelve years.

Sarah looks at me and shakes her head. I know what she's thinking. That I look ridiculous in Lil's car. That the music coming from the speakers is horrendous. That I need to get out now before it's too late.

Lil pulls the gear shift down into drive, her tires screeching on the asphalt, and peels out of the parking lot. Too late.

CHAPTER 3

"My house is on Washington Street," I say as Lil pulls away from the school.

"Who said anything about going home?"

"But you offered me a ride?" I ask, panic rising in my throat. This doesn't feel comfortable, like the part in a scary movie before something pops out all bloody and dead.

"I offered you a ride. I didn't say I would take you home. I need to go somewhere. Do you think you can handle that?"

I nod and gulp down the lump in the back of my throat. Lil's just a girl. The new girl, to be exact. So what if she's dressed all in black, like some sort of gothic Johnny Cash? Instead of judging, I should be getting to know her, like I was supposed to do today.

"What band is this?" I ask. I attempt to make my voice sound comfortable and inquisitive. Showing someone you're interested in what they like makes conversation flow, even if you're totally faking it. The truth is that as much as I try to act like I know about popular music, I know nothing. Musicals are more my speed.

"The Violent Femmes."

"Interesting." It's the only word I can think of to describe the noise coming out of the speakers, like monkeys on cocaine singing.

Lil lights up a cigarette. I don't want to be rude, but I lean my face closer to the window. I may have put up with it this morning, but right now my eyes hurt and it's taken all day to get rid of the stale smell on my dress.

"Is this bothering you?" she asks, looking at me sideways.

"My mom has the nose of a drug dog."

"Do you care that much what your mom thinks of you?"

I nod and speak the truth. "Yes, I do."

Seeing disappointment on another person's face is the worst thing I can imagine. Last year, my mom found out that Sarah and I stole liquor from Sarah's parents' cabinet and got drunk. I just wanted to try it and see what all the fuss was about. I figured doing it in a contained environment with no danger of taking off my shirt and letting an entire party see my boobs was a good idea. We learned in Health that alcohol lowers your inhibitions and makes you do impulsive things. The last thing I need is a rumor spreading around Minster that I'm a lush.

Sarah poured water in the vodka bottle to cover up the amount we took. We drank in her basement until the ceiling was spinning and both our heads were in the toilet. It was a terrible feeling, but worse still was my mom's blank expression when I went home the next morning, plagued with a headache and green-faced. It was like all the expectation drained from her eyes and I was a stranger. She didn't talk to me for a week. She still gets skeptical when I sleep over at Sarah's.

Lil throws the barely-smoked cigarette out the window and turns the music up. I don't ask her where we're going. I doubt she'd tell me. I just sit back and look out the window at the passing fields.

I've always liked living in Minster, where fresh food grows all around us. My grandma used to say that farming reminds us about the circle of life. That people are born and blossom and shrivel and die. *You can't stop the seasons from changing*, she'd say, *so you'd better enjoy the summer before you end up looking like me, a dried-up raisin with fake teeth and an adult diaper.*

Lil drives, letting the wind push her hand through the air like a wave. She'd almost look innocent, if it weren't for the nose ring and the dead face on her finger. I move closer to the window and let the sun warm my cheeks. The sun's starting to shift, hanging low on the horizon, a sign that the seasons will eventually change, even though the air is warm with remnants of Indian summer.

Some days, I wish I could force myself to blossom, like my grandma said, instead of constantly feeling like I'm encased in a bud.

We pull into Minster's town square and drive past Bob's Barber Shop and the wedding dress store that's only open two weekends a month and has had the same dress in the window since 1999.

"This place is like a fucked-up Mayberry," Lil mumbles and shakes her head.

"Where?" I ask.

She looks at me, sunglasses propped on the top of her head. "Have you ever even seen a penis?"

I blink, shocked. *PENIS!*

"Sure," I mumble. I've seen lots of penises in Health class.

Lil parks on Main Street in front of Vinyl Tap, the only record store in town. It stands out from all the other establishments like a hippy at a cocktail party. I've never actually been inside. Sarah dared me once, but I refused. I was worried everyone would start laughing the moment I walked in, like a sign would go off over my head that said 'poser.' Plus, they don't carry the stuff I like to listen to.

"This is where we're going?" I ask as Lil cuts the engine.

"Do you have a problem?"

"Can I just wait in the car?"

"No." She gets out and slams the door behind her. I want to stay put in protest, but it was my decision to get in the car when I could've just gone home on the bus.

Vinyl Tap smells exactly like I expected, like rotten cardboard and incense. Tapestries hang on the walls beside posters of Jimi Hendrix and Bob Dylan and the Beatles. I may not be into rock music, but I know the big guys when I see them.

Lil heads straight to the back of the store, disappearing into a sea of records and old cassette tapes, while I stand by the front door, arms crossed over my chest, trying to make myself as small as possible. I debate walking around and scanning the music, but I'm afraid someone will ask me a question. I'd look foolish, stumbling through an unintelligent response. Instead, I stay still like a statue and wait for my ride.

If I'd gotten on the bus, I'd be home by now, finishing my homework and watching TV before dinner. It's my favorite time of day. With my dad at the office and my mom at her afternoon volunteer work, I have the house all to myself. My mom visits Shady Willows Retirement Community and Nursing Home, heading their bingo games and changing their sheets. *I'm not built for bedpans and vomit, but making a bed with properly tucked sheets I can do*, she says.

In the afternoons, I get to walk around the house singing at the top of my lungs or watching whatever I want on TV. Once, I spent an entire afternoon practicing kissing. I watched myself in the mirror and analyzed my technique and proper head position. I even snuggled with a pillow, imagining what it would feel like to have a boy put his hands on my face and gently touch his lips to mine.

I've only been kissed once, not including the stage kisses I had to do with Jim Parker last year in *Guys and Dolls.* It was in eighth grade at a birthday party. We played Seven Minutes in Heaven and I went into the closet with Brandon Schulz. We stared at each other for six minutes before he said I was the kind of girl he hoped to marry some day, but for right now, he was looking to date someone with bigger boobs. Ten seconds before the door opened he leaned in and kissed me. It was a fleeting, slightly off-center peck that was so quick I thought I imagined it. He walked out shouting that it was the nicest kiss he'd ever had. I couldn't be mad after that. At least he didn't lie and tell everyone he touched my boobs.

I think about kissing all the time lately, like my body is begging to be touched. I tell myself to wait for the right person because that's what girls like me do. I can't just go around groping anyone I want. But some days I worry that maybe I'm not good enough to have someone love me. To have someone want to place their lips on mine and know the taste of my skin, the way I know the taste of theirs.

The door dings, announcing a new customer and breaking my thoughts into pieces. I blink and realize I need to find Lil so I can go home. It's getting late.

"My Hart in Vinyl Tap. Never thought I'd see the day."

I turn around and come face to face with Matt James-Morrison-Walker, the guitar-playing, free spirit rock God of Minster High School. He's the only person that every girl would die to date, even though he comes from a broken home and it's rumored his mom is a pot dealer. For some reason, none of the girls care. I think it's the way he's always speaking slowly and squinting, like he's searching your soul and melting your heart in the same glance. Or maybe he's just smoking his mom's pot and it takes his brain a long time to process things. Either way, he might be the coolest person I've ever met. Plus, he has three hyphenated last names, which only adds to his mystique.

"Matt," I say unsure of how to get my mouth to keep forming words. I tutored him last year in Algebra, even though I'm a year younger than him. I got all mixed up inside every time he looked at me with his brooding green eyes and surfer blonde hair. When he found out my last name is Hart, he started calling me My Hart. That was about the time I started daydreaming about kissing him and writing *Marty Hart-James-Morrison-Walker* all over my notebooks. My mom would kill me if I ever dated him. He is so *not* acceptable and yet, my lips always seem to angle themselves toward his when I'm in his presence. I gulp and choke at the same time, my mind pummeled with visions of making out, only this time Matt is the star.

"Suddenly into good music?" he asks, flashing his famous lopsided grin. He looks goofy and gorgeous in the same beat. He tucks a loose piece of hair behind his ear, displaying the leather armband with brass buckles decorating his wrist. On his other wrist are stacked black jelly bracelets, the kind you put in your mouth when you're younger and pretend are retainers. They haven't changed since last year.

I used to stare at Matt's hands when he wrote down algebraic equations and wonder what his fingers would feel like tangled in my hair. He's the only guy I know who can wear something other than a watch around his wrist and get away with it.

"Just here with someone from school," I smile and play

with my hair, twirling it around my pointer finger like a toddler. My mother would tell me to stop fidgeting and stand up straight. "What are you doing here?"

"I jam in the back room on Thursday nights. You should come listen to us sometime."

I blink and stare at the Wonder Bread vintage t-shirt he has on before my eyes flutter down to his tight jeans. Did I hear him correctly? Did he just invite me out? More kissing images cloud my brain, but before I can say anything Lil reappears.

"Ready to go?" She's carrying a brown shopping bag and doesn't even acknowledge Matt.

"Lil, this is Matt James-Morrison-Walker. He goes to our school."

"Hey." She waves her hand through the air like she's shooing away a fly and says again, "Ready to go?"

I nod and say to Matt, "It was good to see you. I hope math is going well this year." The second the words come out, I cringe. Couldn't I have thought of something cooler?

"Think about Thursday. I'd love to see you here more often." And then Matt winks at me. A deliberate, slow, supersexy wink that makes his hair fall in his face again.

I don't realize until we're out on the street that I'm holding my breath. The cooler night air shocks my senses and I exhale, but my mind can't stop repeating his words. Matt Three-Last-Names just said I and love and you in the same sentence—a sentence directed at me.

"Are you going to get in?" Lil asks as she puts on her red sunglasses.

"Huh? Oh, yeah," I say as I fumble with the door handle.

"Oh my God." Lil stops and pulls the glasses down to the end of her nose. "You like that guy."

"I don't know what you're talking about," I say. The door won't open even though I'm tugging on the handle to a near-violent extreme.

"You like that guy, Matt. It's written all over your baby face."

"I don't have a baby face." I rub my hands over my hot cheeks, praying they aren't as red as I think they are.

"You're a liar."

The second Lil says the words, fury rises in my throat so high I couldn't choke it back if I tried.

"You don't even know me! You say you'll give me a ride and then you make me go to some stupid record store. I try to be nice and all you do is smoke cigarettes and play bad music. You won't even tell me where you're from in Florida!" I smack my hand over my mouth, shocked. What I've just said is out of character for me. I never lose my temper.

At first, Lil doesn't flinch. She just stands still, staring at me. I wonder if she'll get in the car and drive away, leaving me alone outside of Vinyl Tap. I've completely failed as Wel-Co president. Rule number one is be friendly at all times.

And then her face breaks into a huge, teeth-showing grin.

"There you are, Marty Hart. I knew a real person existed under all that politeness."

"What are you talking about?"

She pushes her sunglasses back up. "Just get in the car. I'll take you home."

"You're not mad?" I ask, finally getting the passenger's side door open.

Lil slides into the driver's seat. "You said Washington Street, right?"

I nod. We pull away from Vinyl Tap as the sun begins

to set over the western horizon. I've missed any chance of freedom from my parents today.

❧

We make it to my house five minutes before my parents pull into the driveway. I'm nervous the entire ride that Lil will take a wrong turn and refuse to drop me off, but she drives straight to my house without saying a word. I don't even need to give her directions.

"I'll see you tomorrow," I say as I climb out of the car.

"Tampa. I'm from Tampa, Florida." She keeps her eyes forward as she speaks. I can't help but smile.

Once through the front door, I drop my backpack on the ground and put on the house slippers my mom insists everyone wear to protect our bamboo floors. My limbs hurt from exhaustion. The day has been long and I want to curl up in bed and sleep. I plop myself on the couch and stare at the quote my mom painted on the wall above our mantle. *Where can a person be better than in the bosom of their family?* She put it there after the construction was completed to remodel the main floor.

I know my dad misses the way the house used to be. He always tells stories about my grandma and how happy she was in her simple kitchen, making jam from berries in her garden. She moved into Shady Willows Retirement Community and Nursing Home right before I was born. My mom updated the house with fancy cabinets that don't make a sound when you close them and stainless-steel appliances and no walls right at the same time Grandma died.

During dinner, I push around my potatoes and chicken, not saying much and taking little nibbles here and there as my mind swims. I can't believe what I said to Lil. How mad she made me, how it made her smile, how I don't feel bad for saying it because it was the truth.

"How was your WelCo meeting?" my dad asks. He's still in his baby blue scrubs. My parents spent the last fifteen minutes discussing a difficult root canal he did at the office today, and the question catches me off guard.

"It went good."

"*Well*, honey. It went *well*," my mom says, dabbing the corners of her mouth with a cloth napkin.

I nod, having heard my grammatical mistake the second it came out. "There's a new girl in school. Ms. Everley wanted me to show her around."

"That's nice. What's her name?" my dad asks.

"Lily Hatfield."

He swallows the chunk of chicken in his mouth with a huge gulp. It makes a weird sound, like I just dropped a rock off a cliff and it landed in deep water.

"Did you say Hatfield?"

I can tell he's trying to keep his face straight, but there's tension in his throat, like when he told me my pet guinea pig died.

I nod. "Why?"

"It's nothing." My dad shakes his head back and forth and smiles, like he's clearing away the last few seconds. I can smell the mint mouthwash on his skin.

"I thought Lil was new in town." I say, looking from my dad to my mom. Seconds pass while I wait for an answer; I don't understand how, with one name, I've managed to bring dinner to a grinding halt.

Neither looks up from their plate. Then, in a causal move, my mom lifts her glass of Chardonnay to her pursed lips and sips the slightest bit of wine, leaving a peach lip-stick ring around the top. I know the look. It's the same one she gave me when I asked her about sex in seventh grade. In one movement, my mother has told me to drop it.

"I just hope you were nice to her," she says.

CHAPTER 4

That night, I have a dream that I'm running down a hallway, fleeing something. My heart beats out of my chest, echoing in my ears, *thump, thump, thump,* and I keep falling down. I'm terrified of what's chasing me. The second before I reach a door to escape, I look back, but the only thing behind me is me.

I wake up in a sweat. My skin and hair smell like mold and salt mixed together and I cringe. It's the worst smell in the world, next to maybe the rotten fish stink that sticks to the air after my mom cooks salmon. Even my pillow is wet. Gross.

I look at the clock, sitting on the nightstand next to my favorite picture of my grandma. She's standing in an empty cornfield in the middle of winter, thick work boots on her feet, wearing an ugly brown barn coat. Grandma wasn't much for fashion. Her silver hair is streaming out behind her because the wind is so fierce and she's laughing, a smile as big as the moon on her face. She was really pretty.

The picture was taken before I was born. Before Grandma went all crazy and couldn't remember how to put on underwear or take care of her personal hygiene.

The clock says 5:45 AM. It's that time of morning when I could go back to sleep, but chances are I'll only scrape together a few extra minutes and I'll end up way more tired than if I just got up. Plus, I don't think I can sleep with the disgusting sweat smell tingling in my nose.

Some days, I actually like getting up early. I can watch the sun rise through my window and be quiet with my thoughts. Being an only child, you'd think I'd be alone a lot. It's not true. My parents are constantly on me. Did you do your homework? Have you shaved your legs? (My mom has a thing about prickly leg hair.) Did you brush your teeth and floss after lunch? I hate flossing. It hurts. But I do it anyway because my dad's a dentist and it's important to him.

But early in the morning, when they're still in bed and I don't have to worry about what my breath smells like, I can just be.

I get up and walk over to the antique wooden desk that sits in front of the only window in my room. My U of M application is laying next to a picture of Sarah and me from last year's Spring Fling dance. I touch it and remind myself of what I want in life. I picture myself reading something sophisticated, like Lord Byron or Emily Dickinson, under a tall oak tree on campus next to a handsome young man with an anatomy textbook. He's pre-med, of course, and not dentist pre-med, real pre-med. But this morning, somewhere in the back of my daydreams, Matt is strumming his guitar and swerving his hips all sexy-like and the picture goes fuzzy. Then I hear Lil's coarse voice say, *Have you ever even seen a penis?*

I shake my head and look out the window. The sun is starting to crest the flat horizon of farmland that stretches for miles to the east. I read once that the sun's going to fizzle out and die in five billion years. Scientists know this for a fact. I'm glad I'm here now. I'd hate to be alive in five billion years and know that any day the earth was going to go dark. Without thinking, I grab a sheet of paper and write:

Yellow is the morning,

Like the first petals of spring's early flowers,
I open my heart to daylight,
The panoply of rays spraying the night's sky with color,
And hope its sunshine will seal my cracks,
But worry I'm ridged so deep,
Nothing can fill the void.

I stare at the paper, as if the words appeared there by themselves. I even managed to use one of my English vocabulary words for the week. *Panoply: a wide-ranging and impressive array or display.*

This happens some mornings when I'm lying in bed and staring at my pink walls or looking at the picture of my grandma, wishing I could talk to the four-inch image and hear her talk back. My brain feels like it needs to expunge the thoughts roaming around in my head, so I write a poem.

I keep the poems locked in a box in my desk. I would hate for anyone to see them, but I can't bring myself to throw them out.

Now I take out the box from the bottom drawer. The stack of papers always surprises me. Thousands of words scribbled on paper and locked away. I add this morning's to the pack. Now that the sun is up, I need to get the sweat off my skin.

❧

"So did she want to suck your blood?" Sarah asks in her best Transylvanian accent as I meet her at our bus stop. It's Friday, so she's dressed in her red and white band uniform, the kind with gold tassels on the shoulders and large buttons over the pockets that look like nipples. To Sarah's chagrin, the orchestra performs at every football pep rally and game.

Minster would be nothing without football; I have an array of 'school color' shirts that I wear every Friday throughout the fall. Today, I went for my red and white striped boat-neck shirt and jeans. I even had my mom tie a red ribbon around my ponytail.

"No." I roll my eyes.

"Seriously, you never texted me last night. I almost called out a search party."

I don't realize until this moment that I didn't text Sarah like I said I would. My mind was too wrapped up in Matt and his arm accessories and the way Lil knew I liked him just from looking at my face. I tried to hint to Sarah about my crush all last year while I was tutoring Matt, but she never once asked me about it.

"I'm sorry. I totally forgot."

"So..." Sarah raises her eyebrows.

"So... what?"

"Come on, Marty. That girl is a total crazoid. She's like a vampire, and not the kind that sparkles and eats animals. You can NOT hang out with her anymore." Sarah grabs my arm and looks me directly in the eyes, her pupils wide and rimmed with deep brown. "You've done your good deed, and now there's no need for anymore interaction."

I nod, even though inside I don't know if that's what I want.

"So, for real, what did you do with her?" Sarah asks.

"Nothing, really. We went to Vinyl Tap and she bought a record." I shrug, but wonder if I would really call yesterday nothing. It felt like something. "I ran into Matt James-Morrison-Walker there."

"Of course he would be there." Sarah shakes her head, red curls bouncing. They match her band uniform spot-on.

"Did you tell him that it's totally stupid to have three last names? I mean, what was his mom thinking? That's, like, so hippy-feminist."

She rummages around in her purse. I wait for her to say more, to ask me about Matt, for her to see like Lil did that I'm interested in him so I can get her advice. Instead, Sarah pulls out a tube of lip gloss and says, "Do you think this matches my uniform? If I'm going to be forced to wear this gross thing, my face better look pretty."

I nod, disappointment creeping up in my stomach as the bus rounds the corner.

When we pull up in front of the school, I can't help but look at the tree Lil and I sat under while she smoked yesterday. She's there.

"Look Marty, it's your *girlfriend*," Sarah jokes. "God, what is *up* with the combat boots? This is Ohio, not Afghanistan."

I shrug her off and look away from the window. "She's not my girlfriend," I whisper almost to myself. "Hey, did you tell your parents about Lil being in school?"

Seeing Lil reminds me of last night. Something about Lil is familiar to this town, and for some reason my parents don't want me to know about it.

"No. We try not to talk about the living dead at the table. So, are you going to meet me tonight after the game?" Sarah continues speaking without waiting for my answer. "Thank God football season is almost over. I don't think I can stand this uniform much longer. Polyester does nothing for my figure."

It's what we do every Friday. Sarah plays in the halftime show and I wait for her either in the stands or at home, depending on the weather. I hate sitting in the rain. It makes my mascara run. We usually watch a movie or paint our nails or pick out wedding dresses on the internet until my eyes get clouded over with white Vera Wang's.

If I didn't have Sarah, I'd probably spend every weekend in my bedroom just waiting for college. Sometimes that scares me, but my dad says it isn't a big deal. That you don't need a lot of friends, just a few good ones. And Sarah's a good one, most of the time.

"Sure. I'll meet you at the east entrance after the game."

As we walk away from the bus, my eyes find Lil across the street again. She's wearing a deep purple t-shirt and black jeans today. Her red sunglasses are propped on top of her head, even though so many gray clouds have rolled across the early morning's bright sky that it looks like it might start raining at any moment.

My insides feel pulled, with one leg wanting to walk over to Lil, while the other knows I need to go into school and do what I do with Sarah every day.

And I can't get the eerie look on my parents' faces last night out of my mind. It should propel me closer to Sarah. It should make me never want to talk to Lil again. Instead, it makes me want to know more.

❧

My mom and I planned all week to go to Hobby Lobby on Main Street on Saturday to pick out decorations for the Hot Shot Dance. She got so excited when I told her I was in charge; she pulled out her old Youngstown High School yearbook and showed me pictures of when she was senior class president and planned what she called: *the best prom my high school has ever seen.*

"I spent months sewing fake flowers that fell from the

ceiling during the last dance," my mom said, laughing. "By the time prom rolled around, my fingers were so covered in calluses that I had to soak them in a vat of cocoa butter the night before so my date wouldn't notice!"

Then we went page by page through the entire year-book, and my mom told me about every single person in her graduating class. *I saw her eat a tomato like an apple once. Ugh, he was in my Math class and picked his nose.* She turned to the page with the Homecoming King and Queen. *Last I heard, he's working at a car plant and weighs 300 pounds ... she got pregnant in college.*

I kept staring at the pictures and thinking how young everyone looked and how old they are now. If my mom's right, life is basically downhill from the second you graduate; I started freaking out about how I'm living the peak of my life, but so far it consists of watching *Sweet Home Alabama* for the seventh million time with Sarah and daydreaming about kissing Matt without actually doing it.

"Do you have a date yet?" my mom asks as we walk into Hobby Lobby. "Please tell me it's not Sam Higgins again." She rolls her eyes. Along with asking me out in a text, Sam broke my parents' three cardinal rules of dances. 1) Be on time. 2) Bring a corsage. 3) Don't smell like your father's cow farm.

I have few more secret rules. 4) Don't wear boots. 5) Hair gel is meant to be used in small amounts. 6) All undershirts must have sleeves. 7) No camouflage, flannel, jersey, or pink shirts. And finally, and this is the most important, 8) Slow dance.

When I'm slow dancing, I like to pretend we're in some romantic movie, like *Dirty Dancing* or *Step Up*, and we're doing something dangerous and sexy. Plus, I get to press myself against a boy and lately that's all I want to do. I blame it on my hormones and lack of sexual encounters. Plus, it's safe. Everyone in town expects kids to slow dance. It's a completely acceptable activity.

"Sarah and I are going stag," I say.

My mom stifles a laugh. "If one of you doesn't get a boyfriend soon, this town is going to think I have a lesbian for a daughter."

"*Mom.*" I look around to see if any of the old ladies perusing the store at nine in the morning heard her. I can't believe she just said *lesbian* on a Saturday in Hobby Lobby.

"I'm just saying: my daughter is beautiful and smart and deserves the best boyfriend Minster has to offer." Mom smiles at me and tucks my hair behind my ears. "Maybe if you pull your hair back and show off those gorgeous cheekbones, a boy will notice you."

I force a laugh; really, the comment stings. Sometimes when my mom thinks she's being funny or kind, she's really hurting me. But I know she means well and only wants me to be the best person I can be, so I swallow the lump in my throat and leave my hair behind my ears.

"So, what've you come up with?" she asks as we grab a cart at the front of the store.

I take the piece of paper with my dance decoration ideas out of my purse. It looks more like an architect's blueprint. Last week, I went to the gym and copied down all the dimensions I'd be working with. I almost made a diorama, like the ones you build in elementary school out of an old shoebox, but I thought that might be taking it too far.

"The theme I've come up with is, 'Two is Better than One'," I say as we push down the first aisle. It's crowded with different spools of yarn arranged by color.

My mom walks over to the pink section and picks up a

magenta-colored spool. "Um-hmm," she says, closed mouth. "This color is pretty, don't you think?"

A rock drops in my gut. *Oh crap.* "It is pretty. I love magenta."

Mom puts it back and walks farther down the aisle, running her hand over the different yarns, not saying a word. I follow behind her, my mind racing with what to say.

"The theme has a double meaning. Two people are better than one, and the second amendment allows people to bear arms." I look at her, hoping for eye contact.

It doesn't happen. My mom rubs a fuzzy aqua spool against her cheek.

"Um-hmm," Another closed mouth response, her eyes on the yarn. "This feels great on the skin. Maybe I'll buy it for Mrs. Schneider. She's a great knitter. You know those wool socks I wear all winter? She made those."

This is worse than I ever could have imagined. Mom's talking to me about Mrs. Schneider, a mean old lady from church who smells like mothballs and foot cream. I start to fidget, wringing my hands, as my stomach flip-flops over and over.

"I figured we could decorate the gym in fake trees and leaves with Cupid hiding in the branches." My heart pounds as my mom places the blue yarn in our basket. I clutch my sketch, a physical representation of all the hours I've spent thinking about this dance, of the seventeen pieces of white paper I covered in different theme ideas until they turned black with words.

"I think I'll ask her to make you a sweater. Blue is a great color on you. Would you like that?" My mom still won't look away from the yarn. Yarn that I'm sure is pokey and uncomfortable when made into a sweater that will make me sweat in the dead of winter. A sweater that will constantly remind me of this moment, and how awful my mother's icy answers felt.

"That would be nice," I say. I take a deep breath, one that pushes all the oxygen I can suck out of the air into the deepest part of my lungs. And then I ask the question I know I have to. "What do you think of my idea?"

My voice curls up on the ends with extra sugar, as I hope against hope that my mom will hear my plea.

She pushes the cart down the aisle, moving away.

"I think it's fine, dear."

Fine.

The world's worst word. It doesn't mean what the dictionary says. Fine should be a synonym for good, but it's good's ugly, pimple-faced younger brother who smells like B.O. and could never get a girlfriend. Fine is terrible. I close my eyes and stuff my drawing back in my purse, weeks and weeks of work crushed with one word. *Fine.*

We walk in silence for a minute, rounding the corner into the colored cardboard aisle. The green and brown paper practically screams at me, broadcasting what could have been. All the fake leaves and trees that would have been designed for the dance are going to stay in Hobby Lobby for someone else to buy.

I swallow my disappointment, a rock slowly choking its way down my throat, and ask the question I know my mom wants to hear. "What would you do?"

She stops the cart and finally looks at me. Her eyes are twinkling. I can practically see the wheels spinning in her head. She's gone into senior class president mode. She had the same sparkle when she remodeled our kitchen, like she could barely contain her joy as she bashed down the walls of my grandma's house.

"Do you really want to know?" she asks, voice in full-blown Disney character mode.

I nod, even though I want to cry. I remind myself that her idea is going to be good. My mom would never want me to fail, so it's probably best I do whatever she says.

"If I were in charge, I'd use the theme, 'Shot Through the Heart'." Mom's eyes get big as she expands on the idea. "I would hang red heart bull's-eyes all over the gym and have little Cupids holding shotguns."

"What about the fake trees?" I ask, hoping one of my ideas will survive.

"Marty, no one thinks a forest is romantic." My mom starts loading the cart with red and pink cardboard. "You want to be remembered, right?"

I nod again, moving my head without thinking. *Smile and don't move. Smile and don't move.*

"I do," I say.

"'Shot Through the Heart,'" Mom repeats. "It's going to be great."

⁂

We get in line to pay, our cart full of all the things my mom has picked out that will make the Hot Shot Dance a night to remember. Pink and red paint, big sheets of white paper on which to write out her theme: "Shot Through the Heart". Glitter and glue and sequins to make the gym come alive.

I push the cart up to the cashier, trying my best to be excited about what's in the bin.

"We forgot the glue gun," my mom says. "Run and grab

one, please."

I walk back down the yarn aisle, taking my time. *The dance will be great*, I remind myself. And my mom means well. She really does. She has a knack for these things; she can't help it if her creative mind takes over.

A black spool of yarn with silver specks intertwined in the thread catches my attention. It reminds me of something Lil would like. It's weird that even though I don't know her, I feel as though I do. Maybe it's because she wears who she is right on her skin and in her words.

Lil didn't speak a word to me in English yesterday. She didn't even look in my direction.

"You can't have your seat back, Jock Strap," is all she said when Alex walked down the row toward her. He didn't respond, just smiled at me and went to his new seat. Lil stared forward and picked at her nails for the rest of class. By the end, she had stacked a huge pile of black polish in one corner of her desk. She didn't even throw it out when she left.

Just looking at the yarn makes a bubble of frustration rise in my stomach. Not at Lil. At myself. It makes me want to tear off my skin and crawl into someone else's. Someone like Lil, who says what she wants, who can sleep with any boy and not care and smoke cigarette after cigarette out in the open for the whole town to see. Who can say *you smell like virgin* and *I want to get laid* and '*Shot Through the Heart' is a terrible theme because no one cares about Bon Jovi anymore!*

I take a breath. And then another. And another. Once my blood pressure eases back to normal, I put the yarn down, grab the glue gun, and find my mom at the front of the store. She's talking to Mrs. Rogers, Pippa's mom, when I walk up behind them.

"Did she honestly think changing her daughter's last

name would make a difference? We all know she's back," Mrs. Rogers whispers.

My mom leans in closer. "Poor Marty had to show the girl around school." She shakes her head. "I just hope she stays far away from us."

Lil? I hold my breath, wishing I were invisible so they would keep talking; but at that moment, my mom turns and finds me standing there, glue gun pointed directly at the two of them.

"Found it." I shrug and smile.

"Marty." My mom tucks my hair behind my ears and smiles. "We were just talking about you."

"Hi, Mrs. Rogers," I say.

"Your mom was telling me how spectacular the Hot Shot Dance is going to be. It was always my favorite when I was in high school." Mrs. Rogers grabs a basket and hooks it over her arm. I grit my teeth, squeezing my jaw so tight I feel like enamel might chip off.

"I'm excited," I squeak out.

"It was good to see you, Marilyn," my mom says as she ushers me toward the door.

"You too."

They eye each other for a second before Mrs. Rogers takes out her cell and turns toward the scrapbooking aisle.

"What about the glue gun?" I ask.

My mom places it on one of the cashier stations. "We'll get it some other time."

CHAPTER 5

Back in my room, I sit on my bed next to the Hobby Lobby bag full of decorations and rub the ear of the gray stuffed rabbit my grandma gave me when I was a baby.

We never named animals on the farm when I was younger. Harder to eat a burger when you'd named the cow Sally, Grandma would say. So I never named him.

I replay my mom's conversation with Mrs. Rogers over and over, trying to understand what they meant. Did Lil change her last name? And they said *back*, which means Lil's been here before?

But every few seconds, out of the corner of my eye, I'll see the pink and red cardboard sticking out of the top of the bag and start singing, Bon Jovi's song "You Give Love a Bad Name". Then I picture Jon Bon Jovi's gigantic blonde-highlighted 80's hair and the way he dresses like an eighteen year old when he's really, like, eighty, and I get distracted. When my brain gets too clouded over, I decide maybe I need to write some words down and get them out of my mind.

What's in a name?
Rose by any other word would smell as sweet,
Except that's not true.
A rose is a rose because we call it so,
Year after year,
A rose can never be anything but a rose,

Unless people decide to name it otherwise.

When I'm done, I pull my dance design out of my purse and tear it into scraps of paper so tiny it can never be put back together. I throw them into the garbage and flop back down on my bed.

I'm staring at the glow-in-the-dark stars I put on my ceiling in junior high when my computer dings with an email.

> From: RPMcMurphy@o-mail.com
> To: marty.hart@o-mail.com
> I can practically smell u thru this computer.

I look around my room, bubbly nerves shooting through me. The email address is one I've never seen before. I check my armpits. They don't smell. I put on two layers of deodorant today and vanilla perfume.

> From: marty.hart@o-mail.com
> To: RPMcMurphy@o-mail.com
> I don't mean 2 b rude, but who is this?

> From: RPMcMurphy@o-mail.com
> To: marty.hart@o-mail.com
> Why do u always say things u don't really mean? Of course, ur being rude. I just sent u a weird email. While we r on this topic, what person under the age of 30 uses email?

I gape at the response, my stomach twisting in all sorts of contorted positions, tangled partly with anger and partly with intrigue: who could possibly email me like this? I want to type back that email is underappreciated by young people. If I can't live in a time when actual letter writing is cool, at least I still have email. Plus, how else is my future husband going to send me love letters? I'm sure not saving text messages from him to show my kids. Then it clicks. Only one person makes me feel this way.

> From: marty.hart@o-mail.com
> To: RPMcMurphy@o-mail.com
> Lil?? How did u get my email?

> From: RPMcMurphy@o-mail.com
> To: marty.hart@o-mail.com
> Ms. Everley thought I might need it. Ur coming to a
> party with me tonight, Pollyanna.

A party? I sit back in my seat and stare at the email. The clock ticks on my nightstand; my favorite DVD, *West Side Story*, leans against it. My Saturday night plans. I love when Tony and Maria sing 'Somewhere'. It always makes me cry. Romeo and Juliet put to song. Could there be anything better?

Two days ago, I would have said no. Now, I don't know the answer. I look at my no-name rabbit and the patch of material I've worn down to the stuffing. Why do I always rub in the same place? Because it's safe? Because my fingers automatically go there? It's worn so thin almost nothing is left, yet the rest of him is fluffy, practically new. My computer dings again; another email.

> From: RPMcMurphy@o-mail.com
> To: marty.hart@o-mail.com

Matt will be there.

A gulp and a choke and I almost throw up on the keyboard. And then my fingers type the response my heart, not my brain, knows I should say.

> From: marty.hart@o-mail.com
> To: RPMcMurphy@o-mail.com
> Okay.

> From: RPMcMurphy@o-mail.com
> To: marty.hart@o-mail.com
> Pick u up on the corner of Washington and Forest in 30 mins.

> From: marty.hart@o-mail.com
> To: RPMcMurphy@o-mail.com
> What does RPMcMurphy stand for?

Lil doesn't respond. I sit back in my chair and scroll up through our conversation. My stomach tickles with butterflies. I can't believe I agreed to go to a party with a girl my parents don't want me to have anything to do with. And Matt will be there. MATT WILL BE THERE.

I look at the bag of decorations sitting on my bed. My gaze moves to the torn up pieces of paper in the garbage can beneath my desk.

My mind is already made up. I just need to pick out what to wear.

❧

I come down the stairs twenty minutes later dressed in a black cotton long-sleeved shirt and my favorite dark jeans that hug my legs clear to my ankles. I tied a red scarf around my neck; I look Parisian, maybe, and artistic. *French* kissing, I say to myself and picture Matt. I stood in front of my mirror and practiced my "surprise" face, eyebrows arched and eyes twinkling, for when I see Matt and say, "I had no idea you'd be here." I even practiced touching his arm nonchalantly.

With my makeup redone and fresh pink lip gloss shining on my mouth, I walk into the family room. My mom and dad are watching *Dateline*.

"I'm going to meet some people at the movies," I say, trying to keep my voice steady.

"Who?" my mom asks, tilting her head over the top of the couch so that she can see me.

"Um," Stumbling over words, I say the first name I can think of. "Alex Austin."

"A boy?" My mom sits up and smiles.

"It's not a date," I snap. "He's just a friend from English class. I mean, he wears sleeveless undershirts under his football jersey." Panic is rising in my veins. I'm used to little blemishes on the truth. *You look pretty today*, even though it would take a blowtorch and plastic surgery to fix the person's problems. *I love foreign films*, even though reading subtitles while watching a movie makes my head hurt. I even lie to myself sometimes. *Everyone likes you for you. You're pretty even when you cry. A boy hasn't kissed you because he's waiting for the exact right moment to fall head-over-heels in love.*

Some days, the white lies work. On others, I want to scream from the top of a building and cut all my hair off.

My mom slouches down on the couch and goes back to rubbing cuticle cream on her fingernails. I think I see a flash of disappointment in her eyes. "Just be home by midnight."

"I will." I head toward the door and almost run into the wall.

"And don't forget you're a Hart," my dad yells after me.

Ugh. *The dreaded line.* I hate it when my parents remind me I'm a Hart. It's like they're placing the world on my shoulders and telling me to run a marathon. Or clamping a chastity belt around my waist so no boy can ever get close to my lady parts. Some days, I have a hard time being seventeen, let alone a girl with perfect posture and the vagina of a saint.

"I will," I repeat, grabbing my black pea coat out of the closet.

And then I'm out the front door and standing on the porch, the cold autumn air circling around me. I take a deep breath, letting it clear my mind, and realize I just lied to my parents. I'm meeting the one girl they would never want me to hang out with.

Something swells up in my gut. It's the same feeling I get when words come from the back of my mind and I have no choice but to put them down on paper. An uncontrollable giggle slips from my lips. This might be the most exciting thing I've ever done.

∞

Lil pulls up five minutes late. I hear angry guitar music blaring before I ever see the car. Taking a breath, I force the door open.

"Hi," I say.

"Pollyanna," she nods.

"Why do you call me that?"

"You just answered your own question."

"Huh?" I ask thoroughly confused. "Well, if I asked you to stop, would you?"

"No."

I slouch into the seat and cross my arms over my chest.

"Fine, *Marty*." Lil rolls her eyes. In the moonlight they're still bright blue, almost glow-in-the-dark colored.

"I like your shirt," I say appraising the gold sequined tank top she has on over black jeans. "But aren't you going to be cold?"

"Are you my mother?" she asks.

"No, I just thought you might want a sweater or something."

"I'll be fine." Lil grabs her black leather jacket out of the backseat and places it between us.

"So where are we going?" I ask. As the words come out, it dawns on me that this one answer is important. That I've agreed to go to a party with a girl I don't know, whose name sends my dad into a chicken-choking fit, who prompts Saturday morning gossip sessions in Hobby Lobby. My earlier excitement wanes and I realize the heaviness of what I've done.

Lil lights a cigarette, pulls the gear shift into drive, and smiles at me. "Lake Loraine."

☙

"Lake Loraine," The words get caught in my throat.

"Do you have a problem with that?" Lil asks.

I can only gape at her. During the day, Lake Loraine is a huge reservoir on the outskirts of Minster. But at night, it becomes a breeding ground for bad decisions. I've heard stories of huge bonfires with psychedelic hippy drugs and sex tents where people trade partners. A boy from the next town over drowned in the reservoir four years ago. It was rumored that he was at one of those parties, but no one would come forward and say it was true.

Worried Lil might say something else about my virgin stink or tight thighs or lack of penis knowledge, I shake my head.

The sky is velvet black with clouds blocking any light from the moon. The perfect night for an illegal party with a bunch of random people in the back woods.

We pull up to the remote side of the reservoir and drive down a barely-there path covered with overgrown grass. The car bumps and shakes, making my stomach even more upset. My parents would kill me if they knew I was here, like, murder in the first degree. Drinking vodka at Sarah's is nothing compared to partying at Lake Loraine. My parents would probably have me automatically tested for an STD if they knew I even touched a cup of beer.

"How did you hear about this?" I ask as Lil parks the car.

"You need to open your ears more. You'd start hearing a lot of things."

I get out of the car without asking another question.

"Follow me," Lil says. I take a breath and straighten out my jeans. *I'm a Hart*, I remind myself. My amazing social skills allow me to adjust to any situation. *Be a leader, Marty*, my dad's voice rings in my ears. *No one follows a follower.*

But how can I be a leader when I've never seen a mushroom or smoked pot? And I have no choice but to follow Lil. At Lake Loraine, I'm blind.

We walk for what feels like a mile in silence. I trip over branches and jump every few feet, terrified that some crazed, hallucinating person is going to jump screaming out of the trees. In my head, I start to sing songs from *West Side Story* to keep myself calm.

I should have stayed home. I should have curled up in my comfortable pink fleece pajamas with my no-name rabbit and watched Tony and Maria fall in love.

But then what if Tony didn't meet Riff that night of the dance? What if he decided to stay home and watch *Leave it to Beaver* on TV, or whatever people watched in the 50's? He never would have seen Maria. He never would have fallen in love with her.

And then I hear it. Music. Real music, not the songs in my head. Smooth melodic tones with a heavy bass beat waft through the air; they get louder the closer we walk. I actually like what's being played, and it calms my jitters. It sounds like sunshine bouncing around the black forest.

"Who is this?" I ask.

Lil doesn't miss a beat. "Bob Marley."

I picture his poster on the wall at Vinyl Tap. His dreadlocks and smoked-out eyes. *A pothead*, my mom would say. But the music is peaceful and fresh. Way clearer than the man in the picture.

"I like it," I say, and bob my head to the beat.

Lil rolls her eyes. "Can you try not to be so green? It's Bob Marley, not an orgasm."

I stop and cross my arms over my chest. "You're the one who invited me in the first place. If you don't like the fact that I've never seen a penis or whatever, I'll just go home." I pretend to turn on my heel, hoping Lil stops me. I don't really want to walk away from the party and Bob Marley and Matt, but Lil needs to lay off.

"Fine, I'm sorry." She groans, and then smiles. "I knew it."

"What's the big deal if I've never seen a guy's *thing*?"

"Do you want to see Matt's?"

"I..." I pause. In a way, I do, and in a way, I'm scared to my bone-rattling core. "I don't know yet."

Lil turns without saying anything. We walk into a clearing in the woods and finally find the party. People are everywhere, chatting and dancing and smoking substances I've only read about in Health class. Someone has driven their pick-up truck all the way out here and set up a stereo on the bed. It's like I've stumbled upon a hidden population that only comes out at night. Drunken vampires that feed on pot and sex. I look around at the nameless faces, all the people I never knew existed, and see a couple making out in the distance against a tree trunk. The girl's shirt is practically off and the guy has his hand down her pants. It's not how I've envisioned making out at all. It's coarse and hurried, like they know their time might expire and they want to get as much out of each other as possible.

Lil walks over to one of the many kegs propped up against a tree. "You want some?"

"No, thanks. I don't really like alcohol."

"Suit yourself." Lil pumps the keg like an expert, tilting her cup so the beer doesn't get foamy. I gather this isn't Lil's first time, and I wonder if she has any of those left.

I play with my scarf and bob my head, trying to look like I know the song playing, but it's no use. Sweat starts to prickle the back of my neck and my stomach turns inside out. Maybe I will take a beer. I remember my Health teacher, Mr. Spencer, saying alcohol is a depressant. I could use something to depress the anxiety creeping up under my skin.

"Did you like living in Tampa?" I ask Lil, rubbing my

sweaty hands on my pants.

"No. I hate hot weather."

"Is that why you moved to Ohio?"

"No." She turns away from me and takes a long gulp of beer.

I wait for her to say more, but she just bites the top of the red plastic cup. I undo my scarf and rewrap it around my neck. A girl dressed in a full-on fairy costume comes up to the keg and pours a beer. I think about grabbing a cup before my knotted insides burst free from my chest and spill my truth on everyone here. That I'm a phony in a red scarf. That in seventeen years, this is the first time I've ever heard a Bob Marley song.

And then I see him. Matt Three-Last-Names. GULP.

He's carrying his guitar strung over his back, like I've seen him do so many times at school, but here he looks different. Sexier, if that's even possible. In the dark, his blonde hair glows like a halo and his body seems to curve around the guitar. He has on a navy blue hoodie zipped up to his neck, but he's pulled the sleeves back to expose his arm accessories. I catch my breath, so much excitement dropping in my veins that I wonder if I'll explode.

"I'm just going to hang out over there," I say toward Lil, trying to keep my voice calm and flat. When she doesn't answer, I look over at the place she was standing and realize she's disappeared. "Of course," I whisper to myself.

Not sure what to do, I find a seat on a picnic bench and wait. *Patience is a virtue and very rewarding if you know how to use it*, my mother always says. Some days, it feels like I've waited an entire lifetime for things to happen. It took forever for me to finally sprout boobs. I was the only freshman still wearing a training bra. And I've waited seventeen years and counting to be kissed. I mean, really kissed. My father says girls who get kissed too early turn ugly in college. But do girls who've never been kissed in high school turn into the Virgin Mary at graduation? I don't want to be known around Minster as a slut, but being a prude is just as bad.

Needing to keep my hands busy and my mind focused on something other than the gorgeous rock god standing across the way, I take my cell out of my purse and check my messages. I want to look casual, like I come to Lake Loraine all the time, like watching people making out against a tree is just another Saturday night.

I have one message from Sarah.

Hey, loser. Want 2 come over 2morrow?

I wonder what Sarah would say if she knew where I was right now. If she knew I was with Lil and that Lil had already ditched me. That Matt Three-Last-Names is here with his guitar, exuding a sexiness that makes my heart beat erratically.

Sarah'd probably shrug her shoulders and say Lake Loraine is for potheads and she hopes I don't catch any STDs.

I know Sarah and I have a plan for U of M and most days I'm happy with it. But on cloudy days, when the rain beats on my windows and I want to curl up in bed or write a thousand poems, I wonder if I'm wrong. I start to picture a different person, one who lives in California or Seattle or anywhere that isn't flat and humid, who marries an artist or never gets married at all and writes line after line of poetry all over the walls and doesn't care who reads it.

I usually feel better when the sun comes out and I know that U of M and marriage are for me. If I can have a life like my parents, I know I'll be happy.

"Be still My Hart. First Vinyl Tap, now Lake Loraine?

Has the world started spinning backward?"

My breath catches in my throat at the mere sound of his voice, like a purring cat, and I look up from my cell, cheeks instantly on fire.

"I thought it was about time I saw the better side of Minster," I say. I'm surprised I can get the words out without jumbling them up. In my head, all I see are a mixture of letters that make no sense at all and Matt's lips.

He sits next to me on the bench, placing his guitar behind us, and takes a sip of beer. His hair falls over his forehead at just the right place and every few seconds he has to tuck it back behind his ear. I have to clasp my hands in my lap so I don't reach out and touch him.

"Are you going to play tonight?"

"Maybe," he winks. "Are you going to sing tonight?"

I laugh a breathless giggle that comes through my teeth and makes my eyes go splotchy. I don't think the songs I know are good material for this party, but my heart gets light at the realization that Matt knows more about me than I thought. That he actually paid attention when I was tutoring him.

"Maybe," I flirt back. Inside, I'm shocked at how steady my voice sounds and the fact that his leg is touching mine and it isn't sending my mind into a crazy montage of sex scenes.

We sit for a few moments, not saying a word. Matt leans back on the table and takes another sip of his beer. I stare at the jelly bracelets on his wrists, black stacked on top of black, and then my gaze travels down to his hand resting in his lap. Without thinking, I look at his crotch and the way his jeans wrap tightly around his man parts.

Do you want to see Matt's? Lil's voice rings in my ears. I look up quickly, my cheeks even hotter than before. Matt's still staring straight ahead. Thank God.

"If you ask me, people don't sing enough anymore, " I say, not really understanding that my mouth is moving and words are coming out that mean something. "All we do is listen to music. We never really experience it."

"What do you mean?" Matt asks, turning to look at me and cocking his head to the side. A strand of hair falls into his eyelashes and I swallow hard.

"Well..." I blink and try to focus my thoughts past the part of my brain that's imagining all the places I want to touch on his body. Double gulp. "Listening locks the words inside of you. But when I sing, I feel every word, like I'm living in it." I stop. I've just said something I've thought a million times, but I've never shared it with anyone else. "I'm sure you feel the same way about playing the guitar, like if your fingers didn't pluck the chords you couldn't truly understand the song."

Matt doesn't say anything at first, just takes long sips of his beer, almost like he's chugging it. I start to play with the bottom of my shirt, worried it was a bad idea to say anything at all. Why did I do that? I want him to think I'm pretty and nice and kissable. Not a jumbled mess of illogical words. I should keep those to myself. Lake Loraine isn't the place for existential thought. It's for making out and getting drunk.

When the silence drags on longer, I wish I could grab what I said out of the air and stuff it back in my mouth.

"Would you like to dance?" he finally asks.

I stare at him, not sure what he means. "Here? In front of all these people?"

"Do you think anyone cares what we do?"

I think back on the couple practically having sex against

the tree.

"I would love to dance with you," I say.

Matt grabs my hand and lifts me off the bench. His fingers have calluses on the tips from years of playing guitar. *The mark of a true musician*, he once said when I was tutoring him. And now his hands are going to touch my back, the part that divots in the center, a part very few people have ever touched on me. My toes start to tingle and I hope I don't faint.

"Do you like this song?" he asks.

I'm glad Bob Marley is still playing and I don't have to lie. "I do," I say as he pulls me closer and puts his one arm around my back. Slow dancing. My favorite. I close my eyes for a second and tell myself to keep cool, that I've danced with a lot of boys. But this is the first time I'm pressed against a boy I would take my shirt off for. A boy I would let touch me in all the ways I've dreamt of in the back of my mind.

Matt keeps my other hand held in his and places it on his chest. His sweatshirt is soft cotton and my mind races, imagining what's underneath.

"Your hand is on my heart," he says.

It's beating, slow and steady. The rhythm juxtaposes with mine, which threatens to jump out of my chest at any minute.

Matt sways back and forth to the rhythm of the song, guiding my body with his hips and holding me close. He's a good dancer, and I think he must be good at sex. He leans down and whisper-sings into my ear, "One love, My Hart, let's get together and feel all right."

My knees buckle as I feel his warm breath in my hair. The lyrics bounce around my head and I decide right now, at this moment, Bob Marley might be my favorite singer ever.

I rest my forehead on his shoulder and smell his skin. It's earthy, like he showered in a bath of dried leaves. I can't believe this is happening. I can't believe this is happening right now! It's a dream and I'm floating in ecstasy.

"One love, My Hart, let's get together and feel all right," Matt says as the song ends.

I'd give anything for the music not to stop, for the song to be on repeat over and over and over again so I could stay locked in Matt's arms with his hushed, sexy voice in my ear and our hips touching. Why can't life be one long slow dance?

But Matt pulls back once the song shifts to a more upbeat tune. My skin goes cold the moment his body isn't against mine, and I shiver. If I could rewind time, I would.

"You're a pretty good dancer," he says as he lets go of my hands. They feel empty without his and I clasp them together, hoping to warm the cold chilling my veins.

"My mom made me take ballet when I was younger." I can feel the moment coming to a close, like a scene in a musical when everything fades to black and a new set is brought onstage. I search my mind for anything to say that will keep it going. "Do you come to these parties a lot?"

"It was nice dancing with you, My Hart." He winks as he grabs his beer and guitar off the table and walks away.

I watch him leave, and my entire body feels different, tingling, more alive than ever before. I know it's not an official kiss, but dancing with Matt felt like the most intimate thing I've ever done. *One love, My Hart, let's get together and feel all right*. I quietly sing Matt's lyrics to the cold night air, letting the words encase me from head to toe.

I think I might need to go to Vinyl Tap and buy a Bob Marley record.

CHAPTER 6

Once I can get my feet to move, I decide to find Lil. I don't recognize anyone else, Matt having disappeared into the woods. Now it's just a bunch of random people tucked in corners blacker than night. I want to go home and relive dancing with Matt over and over until I fall asleep with Bob Marley in my head.

I walk a little farther into the woods, peering around trees, whispering Lil's name like we're playing hide and seek, the grown-up version with beer and pot and boys who stick their hands down other girls' pants in public. Everything about this party feels awkwardly open. No one seems to care what other people think, and I don't know whether I want to embrace it or run screaming into the dark.

I find Lil standing on the bank of the lake, talking to a guy I don't know. Her gold shirt shimmers in the moonlight and almost reflects on the water. It's the first time I've seen her actually bright. I watch the scene for a second, trying to decide if I should politely interrupt or wait for their conversation to be over. My mom always says I need to be better at picking my moments.

The guy leans into Lil's face, kissing her on the cheek. At first, I'm jealous. Even Lil, Mrs. Grim Reaper, the goddess of night, emo-goth-hate-the-world chick, gets kissed. WHY? Am I lacking a gene or something, maybe a kissing chromosome doctors haven't discovered yet, and I'm destined for a spinster life like Jane Austen and Queen Elizabeth? I'm about to turn around and wait for Lil on the picnic bench, but then I realize that the cigarette in her hand looks weird, like her fingers are having a hard time holding on to it.

Then Lil smacks the guy's face away, and I freeze.

"Get the hell away from me, Grandpa!" Lil yells, her shimmery shirt blowing in the breeze off the lake.

But he doesn't. He grabs her around the waist and pulls her hard to him, this time kissing her mouth and neck and shoving his hand up her shirt. It isn't nice, but forced. He even pulls her hair. When Lil's cigarette drops from her hand, I know she's in trouble. I don't know Lil well, but I do know she loves to smoke.

I walk up to them, a weird fluttery feeling in my stomach, like an internal motor propelling me forward even though my mind has no idea what I'm doing.

"I want to go home now," I say to Lil, practically stomping my foot into the ground.

The guy holding her drops his arms and looks at me. He has a creepy goatee, one that's pencil thin, and black eyes. I stand with my two feet in the sand, knees locked. I want to appear strong, so he won't try to kiss me the way he did Lil.

She looks at me with glazed, bloodshot eyes.

"Well, if it isn't the nicest person in Minster High." She slurs her words together so they sound like one big word.

"I want to go home." I say the words again with more force, so Lil knows she doesn't have a choice and the guy next to her will leave.

"I think she wants to stay with me," the guy says, grabbing Lil's arm and tugging her close to him. Lil barely reacts, slumping into his side, her head bobbling like it's on a stick. It's *so* not like her and I think in this moment I know Lil better than I thought because never once have I seen her take a single step that she doesn't mean. And I don't like the way the guy holds her arm, like she might have a bruise tomorrow from his strong grip. I stomp over and yank her away.

"She's my ride and I have a curfew. Clearly you don't because you are, like, 35. I suggest you find someone else at this party as geriatric as you and make *them* kiss you." The words come out smooth and steady without me even thinking. A verbal punch in his slimy gut. I pull Lil away from the side of the lake, making sure to keep my back straight. *Posture tells a person exactly how you feel about yourself.*

Even though I don't know how I feel right now. My body is floating above me in a panicked, excited way.

It's hard to get Lil's feet to move; she's all gimpy and heavy, so I hook my arm around her waist and use everything I can muster to hold her up. I heard once about a kid who picked up a car when his mother was stuck underneath it. They say he was able to do it because of adrenaline. As I walk away, that's exactly how I feel. A hot rush of something I'm not used to is coursing through my veins. I don't stop walking until we are at her car.

Grabbing keys out of Lil's pocket, I unlock the door and plop her into the passenger seat. "Are you okay?" I finally ask, out of breath, my arms shaking from fatigue and nerves. Sweat beads have gathered on my forehead and I wipe them away.

"Am I ever okay?" Lil slurs.

"How many beers did you have? I left you for, like, a millisecond."

"Two." Lil holds up her fingers, then drops her hand into her lap like it takes too much energy to hold it up.

"Two? Either you have the tolerance of a toddler or

you're lying." I sound like Lil, but a fireball of anger is nesting in my gut. I'm mad that she's not telling the truth and mad that Matt walked away and mad that she's blocking my mind from singing the Bob Marley song over and over with her mess.

"I'm not a liar!" Lil leans across the seat and shouts the words in my face. Her breath is coated in beer and I think I can smell the guy's Axe body wash on her skin. "I had one and that guy gave me another. Now here I sit. How did we get here?"

Everything clicks together, like a scene from one of those movies we watch in Health class about anorexia and crystal meth and date rape, but it's real and I can't believe I'm living in it. "He drugged you," I say, almost to myself. The moment feels unreal and something deep inside of me wants to take a shower and wash all these dirty people and the dirty things they do off my skin. I force myself to remember dancing with Matt and how good it felt. If I erase tonight then that's gone, too. "I need to get you to the hospital."

"No!"

"Why not?"

"Because hospitals cost money, Pollyanna." Lil closes her eyes and rests her head on the seat, her arms and legs limp. She looks so helpless; for the first time, I feel bad for her.

I walk around to the driver's seat and start the car. "Where do you live?" Lil doesn't respond, only shakes her head back and forth. "I can't take you home if I don't know where you live."

"But then you'll know," she wags her finger in my face, "and you'll tell everyone."

"This isn't really the time for you to get all 'cryptic-goth-girl' on me. I'm trying to help. So tell me where you live or

I'm taking you to the hospital." I bang my hand on the steering wheel to get her attention.

"Is that anger I detect?" Lil slurs. "Doesn't it feel good?"

"Darn it, Lil! I had a great time tonight with Matt. We danced and he sang in my ear and it was beautiful. Now you're messing it up. So either tell me where you live or I'm leaving you here for goatee guy. Your choice." I cross my arms over my chest, my heart beating wildly. I'm so mad at Lil and so scared something might really be wrong with her. What will I do if it is?

After a few moments of silence, in which the only noise in the car is the fury pounding in my ears, Lil says, "The Addison Farm. That's where I live."

I stare at her for a second. The Addisons have been in Minster as long as my family has. If she's an Addison, Lil is most definitely not new to town.

I reach over her, buckle the seatbelt snug around her chest, and pull away from Lake Loraine, my stomach in knots and my head swimming. I hope Lil doesn't die on the way home. I don't know how I'd explain that to my parents.

℘

The roads are dark as I drive back toward Minster. Lil sits in the seat, her head rolling back and forth, and every few seconds, I stare at her gold sequin covered chest to make sure she's still breathing.

"Lil, I need you to keep your eyes open," I repeat, hoping maybe she can still hear me.

"You need to keep *your* eyes open."

"You think you'd be more appreciative of the fact that I just saved you," I say, thinking even in a drug-induced stupor, Lil has bite. I've thought about these exact situations before, me saving someone and the glory that comes with it, like giving someone CPR or the Heimlich, but it doesn't feel the way I thought it would. My stomach is in knots and I'm worried I might puke. My hands shake as they grip the steering wheel just thinking that someone who would drug a young girl is still at that party and probably doing it to someone else right now. I want to turn the car around and warn everyone or cut off his penis. I won't let my mind go to what he wanted to do to Lil. I can't or I'll cry. I just want to be back at my house in my room, safe.

"Don't you ever wonder why people made these roads so straight? Like it's against the rules to take a curved path. But nobody ever does, because then they'd end up with cow shit on their wheels and the whole town calling them a murderer." Lil says. She's talking crazy now. The drugs have messed with her brain. She might even be hallucinating. I just want to get her home so she can sleep it off.

"What are you talking about?" When Sarah and I got drunk, I said things I would never say out loud, like how she has bad breath in the afternoon and that I think sometimes she's mean because she's insecure. Sarah said I was a prude with a mediocre voice who's destined for a life in the community theater chorus, before she stomped upstairs and left me to sleep on her basement couch.

"Haven't you ever wondered why you stay on this straight boring road, when you can just turn the wheel?" Out of the corner of my eye, I see Lil move. At first I think she's just going for a cigarette or adjusting her pants, but then I see she's coming toward me, toward the steering wheel!

My mind races, but before I can push her back, she yanks it down. DAMN IT! The car turns in a quick jerk and my stomach drops to the floor. I'm going to die doing something nice with a never-been-used vagina!

We skid on the dirt, the car careening toward a deep, dark ditch filled with water and certain death at the bottom. Why does she hate me? Why did I come tonight? How did I forget that Tony ends up dead at the end of *West Side Story*? And now, my decision to come to Lake Loraine means I'm going to die with a drugged-up Lil! Our bodies will be found at the bottom of a creek and people will always remember me as the girl who bit it with a druggie. I won't get a plaque or one of those flowered wreaths on the side of the highway, just a dedicated PSA about the dangers of drug use!

I slam on the brakes, my hands clenched so tightly I think the paramedics might have to pry my lifeless fingers one by one from the steering wheel. A cloud of dust encases the car, and seconds before we disappear over the edge, it stops.

"What the hell are you doing?! Are you stupid?!" I yell as I push her hand away.

Lil doesn't even flinch, just plops back in the seat, eyes half-closed and empty. "You tell me. We're in the same English class."

"You could have killed us!" I think I'm having a panic-induced heart attack. Everything is fuzzy and numb and hot. Angry tears prickle my eyes, begging to be released.

"You should scream at me." Lil looks at me. Her eyes are clear for the first time since I pulled her away from the lake and the guy with the tainted beer. "Go on; do it."

I shake my head back and forth. What good would that do in this moment? I need to get her home before she tries to do another crazy thing, like pull out all her hair or cut herself. That's what nice people do. They help and smile.

"What are you so afraid of, Pollyanna?"

"Don't call me that," I bark. But the nagging pinch in my chest is back and growing with every moment I spend with Lil. It's a balloon expanding in my lungs, pushing me to my breaking point, and I just want to pop it.

"Go on, Marty, do it."

I look at Lil with her crystal blue eyes and fire in her voice, like a match dangling over a pile of wood drenched in gasoline. All she has to do is drop it.

"Why?" My voice wobbles.

"Do it!" Lil yells, jerking her head, her dark hair swishing chaotically.

I don't know why I roll down the window, why I stick my head out, why the weight of seventeen years is pressing on every speck of my being and screaming, at this very moment, feels like the only thing in the world that will ease the pain. I suck in a gulp of air and open my mouth. I don't know what will come out. A weak meow. A short staccato bark.

And then a yelp releases from the bottom of my gut, like a corked champagne bottle popped and everything inside of me is spewing out uncontrolled, covering the air and ground. Seventeen years of holding my tongue, of standing up straight, of only speaking when spoken to bursts from my throat in a giant exhale of noise.

When I'm done, I slump back into the seat, pulling the red scarf from around my neck, my shoulders and chest lighter.

"You're different than this town. You're better," Lil says, the glaze returning to her eyes. Her shoulders slump forward as she sits in the seat. It's like whatever that guy put in her beer is a truth serum; I'm finally seeing the real Lil behind all the black and she's exhausted.

73

"But you hate me," I say.

"I don't hate you. I hate this place."

I wait a second to see if she'll say more. Nothing.

"Lil? Lil?" I shake her, panic spreading in my veins. Oh my God. She's dead. She's DEAD! How do I explain this to my parents? I'm going to jail. U of M will never accept me and I'm going to have to wear a jumpsuit. I've never even seen a cell.

Then Lil's gold sequin shirt rises and she breathes. *Shit.* I collapse my head onto the steering wheel. Taking a deep breath and filling my lungs to capacity, I pull Lil's dirt-covered car back onto the road. My hands rattle on the steering wheel, not from almost dying, not from Lil lying next to me practically comatose, but from the surge of energy still pulsing through me. Lil was right, it felt good to scream. So good, I might have to do it again. But what would happen to my voice if all I did was walk around screaming?

As I drive down the road, Lil passed out next to me, I keep imagining the different paths I could take through the fields. How I could knock down row after row of corn and replant new, curvier lines. And then I think how mad everyone would be if I messed with their perfect crops and how they'd never let me plant anything ever again.

⁊

I pull up to the whitewashed house and matching picket fence and red barn. Up until now, I haven't thought about what to say to Lil's parents or about what will happen when they call mine. I close my eyes and tell myself it's not important. Getting Lil to bed is what matters. My dad once told me that if I was ever in trouble to call him and he wouldn't be mad; he just wants me to be safe. I thought he was bullshitting me at the time. It's like all those moms who want their daughters to tell them once they have sex so they can put them on the Pill. All the mom really wants to know is if some scumbag boy has stolen their daughter's innocence. I convince myself that this situation fits the bill and my parents can't be upset at me, even if it came out of a lie.

"I need you to try and sit up," I say to Lil.

She grumbles in the seat, shifting back and forth, and then rests her head out the window.

I walk around to her side of the car. Lifting her the same way I did to drag her away from the lake, I start toward the front door. This is not going to be good. Remember to smile and say that you had nothing to drink, I tell myself. *Be polite.*

"This isn't where I live," Lil says as we get closer to the house.

"You said the Addison farm. That's where we are."

"I don't live here. I live *there*." Lil picks up her arm like it weighs a ton and points to a silver trailer next to the red barn on the side of the property. It's small, like one-bedroom small, and rusted around the bottom. It looks like a meth lab someone would ditch on the side of the highway.

"You live in that trailer?"

She nods, silent. I can't believe anyone could live in something like that. I don't even know if it has running water.

I walk Lil to the door; unsure of what to do, I knock and wait. The trailer rocks back and forth as someone makes their way to the door, and butterflies rumble in my stomach. Who might it be? I always pictured Lil living in a house with parents and maybe a cat, but not this. Never this.

"Who is it?" a female voice asks from inside.

"It's Martina Hart," I say, "I'm friends with Lil."

The door bursts open, and a woman stands in the trailer door. She's tall, slim and striking with dark brown hair and crystal blue eyes. In her hands is a beat-up copy of *East of Eden* by John Steinbeck. I recognize the cover from our bookshelf at home. I look back at her face. She *is* Lil, just older. "I'm sorry. I didn't know what to do." They're the only words I can think of to say. Lil's head hangs down over her chest and I stumble, trying to hold up her weight.

"What happened?" the woman says, grabbing Lil under the other arm.

"We were at a party and I think she was drugged."

The woman looks at me, her eyes connecting with mine like she's trying to see past the surface and into my brain for the truth. I can't seem to wrap my head around how much she looks like Lil. There's no doubt in my mind; I'm staring at her mother.

"Did you say your name is Martina Hart?" I nod, frozen. The woman sighs and grabs Lil's car keys from my hands. "I'll take her from here."

The door slams in my face before I even have a chance to say goodbye.

೧

I walk the three miles home and make it to my door five minutes before curfew. As I stand in the clean kitchen with my mom's gourmet appliances and the smell of cinnamon and fresh apples in the air, I can't feel the pain in my legs and arms, but I know it's there. I lug myself upstairs and poke my head into my parent's room. They're asleep, tucked under the pristine yellow quilt my mom bought earlier this year in Columbus. She'll switch it out for a blue one once the winter comes and bright colors are no longer appropriate. My parents never wait up because they trust me.

"I'm home."

My mom rolls over and opens one eye. "Make sure to turn off all the lights." She's back asleep before I even shut the door.

In my room, I'm so tired I feel like I could fall to my knees. My brain can't wrap itself around the night, and all I want to do is scream again. Dancing with Matt feels like a lifetime ago. Deciding only one thing will make me feel better, I open my laptop, hook up my iPhone, and download all the Bob Marley songs I can find.

In bed, I plug my ears with headphones and put one song on repeat. I want to remember what it felt like to dance with Matt, how I wanted to melt into his skin and let him feel me all over. *One love, My Hart, let's get together and feel all right.* I fall asleep replaying that moment and blocking out the rest.

CHAPTER 7

Searching in the night for a path unmarked
Clouded by fog so thick no one could see through
Rain on my dashboard pounding like fists on a drum
Ever clear my soul
Awake
My life drowned in a lake of murky black only to find the light.

Sitting at my desk, I remember the night. The good and bad parts. The touching and screaming and row after row of straight lines. I thought I would feel like myself again with the sun in the sky, but instead my mind is more confused than ever. It's like I've fallen off a tight rope and now that I'm bouncing on the trampoline, I don't know if I want to get back up.

On the walk home last night, I imagined a thousand things going wrong. Lil choking on her own vomit. Her mom driving down to the police station and telling them I was responsible. Lil and her mom leaving in the middle of the night and me never seeing Lil again. That thought made me sad, so I started singing the entire score of *Wicked* to myself.

I open my computer and e-mail Lil.

To: RPMcMurphy@o-mail.com
From: marty.hart@o-mail.com
R u okay? I couldn't sleep last night. I'm worried.

As I wait, hoping Lil will respond and tell me she's not dead or in jail and that her mom isn't going to bang down my door and scream that I'm a liar to my parents, I stare at the U of M application collecting dust on my desk. The day I got back from visiting, I asked my mom at what point in college she knew she wanted to marry my dad.

"He was going to be a dentist and that was the type of man I wanted to spend the rest of my life with," Mom said as she set the table, placing the knife and fork and spoon in their proper spots.

It wasn't what I expected. It was so mathematical, like she had an equation. If she was X and my dad was Y then they equaled Z.

"Did you fall in love with him right away?" I asked.

"There are lots of layers to love, Marty." Mom breathed into a spoon and wiped away the spots left from the dish-washer. "I have to go make dinner."

She walked out of the dining room and we never talked about it again. But I watched them for days, waiting for a sign that my mom was making light of the story, being modest about her love for my dad.

It took four days for them to touch. It finally happened when Mom cut her finger slicing tomatoes.

"Let the doctor see it," my dad said. She stuck her finger out and he kissed it. She blushed, and all my worries washed away. I told myself in that moment I was an X and if I found my Y, I would have a good life, just like my parents. Like so many people in Minster.

Now I can't stop thinking about dancing with Matt and how my parents wouldn't approve of his shaggy hair and bad grades and pothead mother. How my mom would complain that she couldn't monogram Hart-James-Morrison-Walker on anything. But I still want to dance with him again and have his hips press against mine and kiss his fingertips until they're silky smooth. Maybe Lil is right, maybe I'm different. Maybe I'm not an X. Maybe I'm not a letter at all.

But if I think about that, panic starts to gurgle in my stomach and everything goes blank. I don't know how to define myself. I go from:

Marty Hart: Noun. Nicest Person in Minster High School, WelCo president, musical theater goddess, U of M graduate, future Mrs. _____ to hot Dr. _____.

to

Marty Hart: Noun.

I place my hand on the application and wait for the surge of rightness I usually get when I think about my future. Nothing comes. *You're different than this town. You're better.*

What does that even mean? I don't know anything other than Minster, and I'm not sure I want to. I stare out the window at the crops surrounding my house, the straight rows of corn plowed year after year. My grandma's fields. Why is it that this morning I keep finding holes, like one of the corn plants was bad, so it was torn from the ground and thrown out?

I email Lil again.

> To: RPMcMurphy@o-mail.com
> From: marty.hart@o-mail.com
> Seriously. I'm scared. R u dead? If u r, I'll never forgive u.

I wait ten more minutes. Nothing. Finally, succumbing to my grumbling stomach, I head downstairs.

"How was the movie?" my mom asks. She's in her pink

eyelet bathrobe and holding the mug she uses every morning, one with pink, red, and orange polka dots, filled with English breakfast tea.

"Good." I stuff my head into the refrigerator and pretend to look for orange juice. *Good*? How about terrible and wonderful and scary all rolled into one?

"So is Alex a good kisser?" She smiles behind her mug.

I slam the fridge closed with a thud. "Mom!" I bark, and look at my dad who's trying to act nonchalant, spatula in hand behind a griddle full of blueberry pancakes.

"What? All the boys in Minster should want to kiss my daughter." My mom walks over to me and tucks my hair behind my ears. "You're a catch."

"I told you; it wasn't a date. We're friends."

Mom sniffs like she doesn't believe a word I just said and walks back over to her seat. "Fine. If you want to be a spinster for the rest of your life..." She sings her words, but they still hurt. I force myself to remember Matt's hips on mine, his breath in my ear. My hand on his heart. *One love, My Hart.* Shivers cover my skin.

"Do you want some pancakes?" my dad asks. He flips one with the spatula and it lands on the ground. "Okay, maybe not that one."

Can Mom and Dad tell I'm different? Not the kind of different I'm sure I'll feel when I finally have sex for the first time, but the kind someone feels when they've dyed their hair or cut bangs where there were never bangs before.

"Eat them quick. We need to leave for church in an hour," my mom says, her eyes now fixed on the Sunday edition of the *Columbus Dispatch.*

"Why do we go to church? We don't even pray before dinner."

The words fall out of my mouth and splatter onto the floor before I can think better of it. Both my parents look at me, eyes bulging out of their heads, like I've transformed into a three-headed atheist monster who believes in abortion and gay marriage.

I take a breath and hold it. My mom's verbena lotion is all over my skin. She hasn't changed it in seventeen years. I even know her morning routine, how she starts by applying it to her face, then moves to her legs and arms and stomach. In the end, she's covered in a layer so thick nothing from the outside world can reach her.

Mom pulls the newspaper up to cover her face and smacks it open. "Wear the blue dress I got you a few weeks ago. The one with the black belt. It's a good color on you."

The headline on the front page reads: ONE PERSON DEAD. ONE STILL MISSING. I can practically feel Lil's lifeless body in my arms and my knees gets wobbly, like I might not be able to stand for much longer. I force my legs to move and walk back to my room, no longer hungry. Still no email from Lil.

Taking the blue dress out of my closet and placing it on my bed, I get in the shower. Black and white words flash in my head: ONE PERSON DEAD... ONE STILL MISSING.

છ

My stomach hurts all through church. We sit in our usual pew five rows from the front, not so close that the Reverend will stare at us the whole time, but close enough that everyone knows the Harts are in attendance. I fumble with the hymnal, dropping it twice.

"What's wrong with you today?" my mom whispers.

I'm worried I'm an accessory to murder and an orange adult onesie is going to be my new signature outfit.

"I'm just tired," I say.

The rock of worry is slowly working its way into a solid wall of panic. Every hour that Lil doesn't respond to me, it grows.

My mom gives the yarn she bought yesterday to mean old Mrs. Schneider and asks her to make me a sweater. My neck itches just looking at the blue wool.

At home, I strip off my dress and go directly to my computer. Nothing. I want to scream. For a second, I contemplate going over to Lil's to check on her and wring her neck for getting me into this situation in the first place, but then I decide that if she's dead it won't do me any good to return to the scene of the crime. Plus, her mom looked at me last night like I might give her bird flu or something.

Instead, I type into Google: R P McMurphy.

A book—*One Flew Over the Cuckoo's Nest* by somebody named Ken Kesey—is the first thing that pops up. I skim the Wikipedia entry, distracting my mind so I stop visualizing Lil, dead in the trailer where I left her. I even download the book onto my Kindle and read the first fifty pages. Finally, I can't stand it any longer.

> To: RPMcMurphy@o-mail.com
> From: marty.hart@o-mail.com
> Randle Patrick McMurphy,
> From this point forward, I'm going to assume u r dead and I don't care.
> From,
> The Chief
> PS- I figured out what ur email means.

I wait. It's five in the afternoon. A police car should be pulling into my driveway any second. A Minster cop with a mustache will walk up to my door and politely ask for Marty Hart. My mom will cry. My dad will shake his head. The front page of the *Columbus Dispatch* will read: MINSTER'S NICEST PERSON NOT SO NICE.

The computer dings.

> To: marty.hart@o-mail.com
> From: RPMcMurphy@o-mail.com
> Don't say things u don't mean.

I breathe for the first time today. Thank *God* she's not dead.

♋

"Did you go to a movie with Alex Saturday night?" Sarah comes up behind me as I wait for the bus on Monday morning. I turn and find her, straight-lipped, hair pulled into a ballerina bun on the top of her head. Just like the first time I met her. *Shit.*

"Did my mom tell you that?"

"Duh," she raises her eyebrows. "Your mom told my mom."

"He asked me last minute. It's no big deal." I spin my hair around my finger, trying to act calm.

"I thought you were against boys who wear jerseys."

I shrug my shoulders. "I made an exception." The answer comes out more like a question, the last word rising upward in hopes of Sarah buying it.

"Whatever," she says. Sarah takes a compact out of her

backpack and checks her hair, running a hand along the top of her head to make sure no curls are loose. It's cold and humid, the weather finally turning into typical Ohio in November. Rain, sleet, cold, wind, repeat. "We have more important things to discuss."

"What?" I say.

"Like what we're going to wear to the Hot Shot dance. Should we go casual, dressy, hunting glam?"

"What's hunting glam?"

"I don't know. Maybe sparkly camouflage? Whatever we decide, we need to go shopping pronto," Sarah says as we climb onto the bus.

We sit in our regular seats and she keeps talking, going through every item of clothing she owns and explaining why it's inappropriate. *My boobs look flat in that shirt. Those pants give me muffin top. That dress looks like something a drunk hobbit would pick off the sale rack at Kohl's.*

At my locker, I pull out books like a pre-programmed robot. A collage Sarah made me in art class earlier this year hangs on my locker door. The words *musical, pretty, great hair,* and *dork,* all glued together with different colored letters from magazines. Two girls' heads, one with brown hair and one with red, are pasted next to each other in the center of the paper with the letters *BFF* in bold underneath. Under the collage is the poster from *Guys and Dolls.* Why does it all look so fake today? Like a different person has been living in this two-foot by one-foot space for the past few months and I'm stuck looking for something that isn't there.

I jot down on a loose piece of paper:
Lost in a sea of pretty,
As deep as the shallow end,
Of a pool frozen with a layer of glass,

One step and I fall through.

"Pollyanna?"

I almost drop my math book as I stuff the paper into a folder.

"Lil?" My voice squeaks. She cocks her head at me and I worry she saw what I wrote. Dark brown sloppy hair is pulled into a messy ponytail on top of her head and her big red sunglasses shade her eyes. Her white skin is almost translucent and one word pops into my head: vampire. "You look terrible."

"Thanks, ass wipe."

"I'm sorry. What I meant was, how are you?" I try to smile, but the scared feeling from Saturday night comes rushing back to me and I want to punch someone.

"Fucking fantastic. Now that we've established that." She turns to walk away.

"Wait." I grab her arm. Her skin is clammy. "Why do you live in that trailer?" I ask. They aren't the words I want to say. I want to ask her if she remembers anything, if she knows she could have been raped, if her head hurts and she wants me to get her some water, if she was telling the truth when she said she doesn't hate me.

"Because my grandpa's an alcoholic bastard with a one-track memory and he won't let my mom inside his house." Her eyebrows rise above the top rim of her glasses.

"Why?"

"Why do you care, Pollyanna?" Lil says it like it's a challenge, like she's daring me to feel for her.

"I was scared Saturday night. Like, really scared," I say. Those are the words I wanted to start off with but couldn't find.

"Well, I survived ... though this two-day hangover makes

me wish I hadn't."

"You look just like her, you know. Your mom. She's pretty." Lil doesn't say anything, just spins her skull ring around her middle finger. "Matt asked me to dance with him Saturday night," I say, a bubbly, uncontrollable giddiness rolling through me. It makes me want to throw up or burst into a million pieces.

"At least one of us had a good time." I can tell Lil wants to say something else because her lips purse and her nose pulls up into the snort face people always make when they're holding something back. Instead of speaking, Lil takes off her sunglasses and puts them on her head. Black eyeliner is smudged around her red-rimmed eyes. She takes a breath. "Everyone in town hates my mom, but they're wrong about her."

"Why do they hate her?"

"Just tell me you believe me," Lil says. She grabs my hands, her eyes fixed so strongly on mine that there isn't a chance of wavering.

"I believe you." I whisper.

Putting her sunglasses back on, she says, "Thanks for saving my life," in a muffled voice. The words are so quiet I'm not sure if Lil actually spoke them.

☙

That afternoon, I almost faint when Matt Three-Last-Names walks up to me in the hallway on my way to a WelCo meeting. My heart drops to my knees, my body remembering every moment of ecstasy, every fingertip on my back, the way my hand pressed against his heart.

"What are you doing here?" I say. Shit. Shit. Shit. *What*

are you doing here?! That's a terrible opener!

"It's school. Aren't we supposed to be here?" Matt says in a husky, sexy, oh-my-God-I-want-to-grope-you way.

"Right," I whisper. I'm losing it. He's wearing a tight white undershirt with sleeves and jeans. I scan his whole body before deciding his simple outfit is the most delicious thing I've ever seen. It makes my limbs turn all gooey, messy like Jell-O.

"Did you have a good time Saturday night?" Matt asks.

"It was interesting." I twirl my hair around my finger and force myself to blink. If I look into his green eyes for too long, I'm worried my entire brain will turn to mush and I'll scream: *touch me, please! Kiss me, please! Have sex with me, PLEASE!*

"Interesting is a good way to describe Lake Loraine." Matt smiles and tilts his head. I can't stop looking at his mouth. His lips are so round. The top makes a perfect heart-shape and he licks them ever so slightly after sentences. "I want to give you something," he says.

"Okay." I might faint. *Breathe, Marty.*

"Here." He takes off one of his black jelly bracelets and slides it onto my wrist. When his fingers touch my skin, everything in my body explodes into one massive shiver. He reaches his hand up and cups my cheek in his palm. OH. MY. GOD. I say it over and over, trying to block out the voice in my head that's telling me good girls don't think about sex, just kissing and holding hands. I might die right here on the gum-encrusted school floor from holding my breath and I don't care.

"Well, it was good to see you, My Hart," Matt says.

I stare at his butt as he walks away, his jeans hugging his hips with just the right amount of tightness so it looks like a shelf. A shelf I want to rest my hand on. I sink back on the wall and stare at my wrist, not sure if my legs can move.

I'm late for WelCo.

ᴄⱭ

Sitting in the Special Ed room, my mind topples over the many hurdles that have come up in the past few days. I can barely wrap my head around everything. I don't even hear Ms. Everley until her voice starts to get louder.

"Marty, are you paying attention?"

I blink and look at her. The v-neck of her red dress dips so low I can see the divot between her boobs. "Did you get the decorations for the Hot Shot dance?"

"Um..." I shake my head clear. "I did."

"Great. What theme did you settle on?"

My mouth sputters for a second while I try to form the words. Bon Jovi plays on repeat in the back of my head, a montage of bad 80's hair. "Shot Through the Heart". My mom was the one who suggested I sign up for WelCo in the first place. Another activity to add to the list. But I hate shaking sweaty palms. And walking next to smelly freshman. But it's all a part of the plan and it makes me a better person to suffer through the sweat.

"Shot Through the Heart," I say. "That's the theme."

Ms. Everley smiles. *See, it's a great idea*, my mom's voice whispers in my ear.

"That's very nice."

I swallow, fighting the strangulation I feel around my neck. Why is it becoming so hard to breathe in my own skin? Why is it I want to scream and tear the Hobby Lobby bag stuffed under my bed to pieces, like I did my original design?

"Thanks," I choke out.

"Moving on to the new girl. I think it's our responsibility to make her feel extra welcome. Does anyone have any ideas?" Ms. Everley asks.

Giggles pepper the room and whispers start to fly like a thousand wings flapping in the breeze. Soon the classroom is abuzz with so much chatter Ms. Everley can't control it.

Kathryn Harris leans toward me. "I heard the new girl got kicked out of her old school," she whispers.

Kenton Studier leans into Kathryn. "I heard her mom is a stripper in Lima."

I picture Lil's mom. A stripper? She wasn't even wearing a booby shirt on Saturday night, and something tells me thongs are strictly forbidden in Lil's household unless they're black and say Up Your Crack. If I was going on appearance alone, Ms. Everley would be the highlight act of the Crazy Horse out on Highway 81—and she's an English teacher.

"I heard she got pregnant and was forced to leave town," Pippa Rogers says, leaning back in her chair and almost falling over.

"Who got pregnant, Lil or her mom?" I ask.

"I don't know," Pippa scoffs, and sit up.

I slouch back in my seat. *Everyone hates my mom, but they're wrong.*

No one comes up with a way to make Lil feel welcome. Instead, every single person in the classroom gets up and walks out before the meeting is formally adjourned. I stay in my seat, staring at one of the posters I made when I ran for president. For some reason, it's still hanging on the wall.

Vote for Hart. A girl with a heart for Minster High.

"Is everything okay, Marty?" Ms. Everley asks, collecting

papers from the desk and shoving them into her black bag.

"I'm fine," I say.

The world's worst word.

CHAPTER 8

As the week passes, words start to fall out of me at weird times, like my internal cup is overflowing and I'm trying to catch everything before it spills on the ground for people to see.

One day after gym class, I feel so overwhelmed to get them down that I scribble everything on the bottom of my tennis shoe. By the time I get home, all that's left are the words *sifted*, *cacophony*, and *bad ass*. I write them down and stuff them in my box anyway. It's getting packed, the crinkled papers stacking up, and I think I might need another one for all my words.

How is it possible that for seventeen years I thought I knew *me*? Now an alien has crept to the surface and I can't decide if it's going to eat me alive or help me breathe better. Part of me knows what I'm writing is wrong, that if my parents saw everything I thought they'd be so disappointed. But the other part of me, the part deep down that bubbles and wants to erupt and coat myself over until I'm born into new skin, knows I might explode if I don't.

Some days I even have a hard time looking at my parents, seeing them in all their X and Y glory and knowing that maybe I want something different. I'm scared that if my mom knew all of me, she might not like me. She said once that a person can love someone they don't like.

I didn't particularly like your grandmother, Marty, but I will al-

ways love her.

It was weird when she said it because it was at Grandma's funeral and all these people kept telling me I was just like her. I cried that night, thinking my mom might not particularly like *me*. Is it better to be liked or loved? And what's the difference? Do you tear up the house of a person you like or does every corner remind you of the good times and the thought of ruining those memories makes your heart hurt?

But on other days, I'll see my mom cooking a healthy dinner and I'll know that saying *this tastes fantastic,* even though it really tastes like feet, will make her feel good. And then my inner voice that wants to scream disappears. On those days, I remind myself that being an X joined with a Y is a good life.

Most afternoons, I find myself hiding in a patch of forest behind our house. My dad calls it "No-Nana Land" because my grandma refused to sell the trees before she died. *Someday that wood is going to be worth more than the soil it's rooted in, mark my words,* she would say. No one ever goes back there, but even now that my dad owns the land, he won't cut down the trees. When I was younger, I used to spend every day here, pretending I was a princess locked in a castle or Laura Ingalls Wilder exploring the frontier. I would get lost in my imagination; it all felt so real, like I'd become someone else for hours at a time.

I never thought about the girl who walked out of the forest and back into her pink bedroom. What she believes in. Who she wants to be. I thought my parents would tell me because they know best. And maybe they do, but even when I think that, the boulder keeps pressing on my chest.

Lil doesn't say much to me, just sits in class listening to Ms. Everley and picking at her nails. One day, she rubs her pen over the same spot on her desk until a long groove forms. Then she gets up and leaves when the bell rings.

I stare at the black mark, my brain screaming that she's just vandalized a desk and walked away, and how could she do that? But then I think, *it's just a desk*. Someone carved the word FUCK into the right-hand corner of mine. At least all Lil did was leave a line.

I know I should lean over and talk to Lil, but I don't. For some reason, her not saying anything doesn't bother me. I have a feeling Lil has said a lot of words in her life and maybe not saying something means more to her than actually talking.

Why does a leaf change?
Its color shifting from constant green,
Into so many colors,
Like it no longer knows what it wants to be,
Maybe the entire time it was green,
It felt like red,
It had to wait for the seasons to change.

I write that one afternoon after I see Matt in the hallway at school. I replay our moment together, running my fingers over the black jelly bracelet he gave me, until I'm tangled in thoughts of him. My stomach gets tight, like I might be sick, the most wonderful sick I've ever been. Sick with love or like, I can't decide. If you don't always like the people you love, I think I want to like Matt. My parents love each other and they don't kiss very much and all I want to do is kiss Matt.

But then I'll see him and he'll walk straight past me like I don't exist and I get all mixed up again.

Maybe the stupid leaf should just stay green
And wait for college to have sex.

❧

Ms. Everley takes the entire English class down to the computer lab to work on our final assignment for *The Catcher in the Rye*. We have to write a literary critique of the book citing previous reviews that support our conclusion.

I'm still not sure how I feel about Holden Caulfield and all his swearing and hookers. But a part of me is beginning to understand how it must have felt for him to be lost in a world he didn't like and how sad he was that his brother was gone. I'm beginning to think that literary heaven is a mess, all full of insane characters like Holden and Randle Patrick McMurphy, guys who really know the meaning of life, who get that we're all just crazy.

"Can I ask you something?" Alex says as I take my seat in the middle row behind an ancient computer that hasn't been replaced since the 90's. The room smells like melting plastic.

"Sure," I smile. He's wearing his red and white Minster High football jersey with a sleeveless undershirt. I force my eyes to his face, away from the hair sticking out of his armpit.

"Did we go out last Saturday? Because that's what I'm hearing."

My jaw drops open and I stumble over my words. "I... umm... well."

"I'm not opposed to it. I mean, you smell really good. I just feel like I would remember something like that." Alex scratches his chin.

"I am so sorry." It's all I can think of to say.

He leans down toward my ear, his usual scent of Old

Spice and freshly-cut grass filling my nose. He smells good, too.

"Whatever we did or didn't do is okay with me. As far as I'm concerned, we went to a movie and I stared at you the whole time because you looked so beautiful."

I smile and exhale. *Beautiful.* There's that word again.

"Thanks," I say to Alex, my cheeks getting hot just like last year when he said "beautiful" to me after my last performance of *Guys and Dolls.*

"Are you going to the Hot Shot dance?" he asks.

"Of course. I'm in charge of it," I pull my shoulders back and sit up straighter. *President Hart at your service.*

"Well..." Alex runs his fingers through his curly brown hair. His blue eyes sparkle even in the dim computer lab. "Since we did go to a movie last Saturday, and you let me put my arm around you, maybe we could..."

"Nice jersey, Jock Strap." Lil cuts him off and casually takes the seat next to me. Alex blinks, surprised. He looks at Lil, and then back at me, a deer-in-headlights kind of look on his face. His shoulders fall a bit.

"Thank you, Lil. You look nice today as always," Alex smiles at her and says in a bold voice, "Thanks for going out with me last Saturday, Marty. I hope we can do it again." He winks and walks over to his seat.

I giggle, the nervous bubble in my stomach deflating. I think kissing Alex would be nice. He probably tastes like apples and his lips are never chapped and I bet he'd run his fingers through my hair just like I've always wanted. We could go out on dates and he'd hold my hand and kiss me on the front porch while my parents peered from inside the house, thinking, *Marty's finally found the perfect boyfriend.*

But what if that's not what I want anymore? I touch the

black jelly bracelet Matt gave me. Insta-goosebumps.

"Oh my God, could he have a bigger boner for you or what?" Lil turns on her computer. I look at her out of the corner of my eye. Her red sunglasses are propped on top of her head, even though it's raining out, and she's looking straight ahead.

Did she just say the word *boner*?! You can't just say things like that out loud!

"Be quiet," I whisper, my heart picking up speed.

"What? Would you prefer I call it a chubby?" Lil speaks even more loudly. Pippa Rogers turns around and rolls her eyes. My face heats up a thousand degrees. I can't believe Lil is saying this. To ME. I breathe, trying to calm my insides.

You are in a class, Marty Hart. Eyes on the board.

"Lil," I bark through my teeth.

"Or maybe purple-headed yogurt slinger!" Lil's voice is on the verge of yelling now and half the class is staring at her.

My mouth has fallen open, a gaping hole the size of the Grand Canyon. I can't believe her ability to say things that should never be spoken aloud.

And then I feel it. It starts with a sniffle that moves to a hiccup that becomes a giggle that explodes into an all-over, body-convulsing fit of laughter I can't control that makes me want to scream BONER at the top of my lungs.

"Is everything okay, Marty?" Ms. Everley asks. I've caused such a commotion that she can't start the lesson. I stare at her and the white line of chalk across the crotch of her black pants. *Is everything okay?* I'd like to know the answer to that question myself. For the past few days, I haven't felt right in my own skin and all of a sudden Lil says some inappropriate words and I'm free and laughing and utterly embarrassed at the same time. What's happening to me?

"It's just a tickle in my throat," I say, and cough.

"Why don't you get a drink of water."

I walk out of the computer lab and breathe. It felt good to laugh, but my mom would be appalled.

When I come back to the classroom, I keep my eyes focused on the computer. But I smile in Lil's direction, just a little bit.

༄

Halfway through class, my phone dings with a text message. We're not supposed to text in school. It's the rules and as my mom would say, it's *highly rude and inconsiderate. Those teachers spend hours developing lesson plans and I expect you to pay attention.*

My mom studied education in college, even though she hasn't worked a day in an actual school, and she considers herself an expert on teaching. I have a hard time believing Ms. Everley spent hours on today's lesson plan about how to Google.

So when my phone buzzes in my purse, I pull it out, worried there's some sort of emergency. Sarah has been in full-blown disaster mode after hearing about a girl in eighth grade who plays the flute like Bach or Mozart or one of those other classical music people. I can't keep all their Germanic names straight.

I glimpse at my phone's screen and my stomach falls to my toes. This is not happening. This is not happening. Pulling the phone ever so slightly away from me, I glance down at it again. Oh no. This is happening.

A text waterfall has only occurred one other time that

I can recall in Minster High School history. Someone got a picture of Kevin Paterson, captain of the football team, making out with McKayla Ernie, a girl who knew the entire baseball team's balls too well—and was definitely *not* Kevin's girlfriend. They were behind the football shed after a game. His mouth was all over hers. It spread like wildfire, everyone forwarding the picture to their friends until there wasn't a soul left in school who didn't know what happened. Kevin was branded a cheater, but people forgot about that a few months later and his girlfriend, Lisa, took him back. McKayla was branded a slut and transferred schools after Lisa keyed her car and etched the word CUNT so far into the paint it couldn't be fixed.

My heart pounds as I look at the picture that just popped up on my cell phone. It's a forward from Sarah.

Looks like ur gf is cheating on u :)

Above her text is a picture of Lil and creepy-pencil-thin-mustache guy at Lake Loraine. His hand is up Lil's shirt and from the look of the picture, Lil doesn't care.

I gape at it. All the fear I felt that night, seeing him yank Lil's hair and bruise her arm, floods to the surface. The caption on the photo reads: *slut ... just like her mom.*

"That's not what happened," I whisper.

"Did you say something, Pollyanna?" Lil's face is fixed on the computer screen.

My foot taps under my desk as I look around the classroom. Half the students have their cell phones in hand. This is bad. This is really bad. I want to scream that it's not the truth. That Lil was drugged. That she was almost raped!

"What is it?" Lil looks at me, the intense blue in her eyes reflecting off her black shirt. She wasn't back to her pale normal self until yesterday. It was like a sheen of sweat covered her skin for days. I see the bruises on her wrist, his fingerprints, and want to throw up.

"Nothing," I say in a high-pitched voice. It doesn't work. I should know better than to lie to Lil. She sees through me every time.

"Give me your phone." The words come out through clenched teeth.

"No," I whimper.

People in class are turning to look at us. Some smile with wicked grins; others are waiting to see what Lil will do, like she's a caged lion and we've thrown her a slab of meat.

"Give it to me."

I place my phone on the desk, screen down. My heart races as Lil picks it up and looks at the picture. A picture that's inaccurate. A picture that makes her something she's not. A picture that captures a moment in her life I'm sure she wants to forget. Now she never will.

Lil's eyes get huge and a darkness I've never seen on anyone before creeps into the bright blue. She looks around the room. Everyone's staring at her. Pippa Rogers and Eliza Moore giggle through their perfect teeth. Teeth my dad cleans every six months. I clutch my stomach, the urge to vomit slowly choking its way up my throat.

Lil slams the phone down and storms out of the computer lab. I stare at her empty seat for twenty seconds, counting in my head as I try to calm down. Then I decide better and run after her.

 co

It takes me ten minutes to find Lil hiding in the bathroom in the second-floor Math wing. Black combat books with purple tights stand inside the stall, unmoving.

I turn on the water and wash my hands, taking time to lather the soap and sing my ABC's to make sure all the germs are killed, just like my dad taught me.

"What did your mom do?" I ask over the running water.

Lil doesn't answer.

"It's only a text." I turn off the faucet and look past my reflection to the stall behind me. My words are lies and Lil knows it.

"Leave me alone, Pollyanna." Her voice is flat.

I run my fingers through my hair, pulling all the way to the end and letting it fall back down to my shoulder blades. So pretty. I lift it up again and look at my reflection. What if I cut it all off? Sarah would tell me I looked terrible. My mom would insist I grow it back. But Lil...

I realize in this moment that if Lil didn't have a nickname for me, I'd be sad because that would mean I wasn't important to her. And I want to be important. To her. I want to know her, the her underneath the dark clothes and curt words.

"I'm not leaving." I say it with as much force as I did when I saw her on the edge of the lake Saturday night. "I want to be your friend."

An eternity of silence follows. My words hang in the Clorox-mixed-with-poop-mixed-with-cigarettes air. I wring my hands together, worried Lil might not believe me. Years of niceness are backfiring; the one time when I mean it, every word I say will be seen as a lie. This must be what breaking up feels like. Someone taking themselves out of your life when things are incomplete and all you want to do is make them stay.

The stall door creaks open an inch at a time and Lil steps

out. Her eyes are clear. No tears have cracked the surface. I have a feeling it would take a lot more than a text message to make her cry.

"Even if the whole town thinks your friend prefers to make out with crusty, old Parisian-looking guys who dabble in date rape?" she asks.

I nod. "Even if."

CHAPTER 9

Lil and I stare at each other. I don't know what to say.

"Well, now that we've had our Thelma and Louise moment, I'm gonna get the hell out of here." Lil nods at me.

I want to ask her who Thelma and Louise are and if she thinks the gross smell in the bathroom will stick to my clothes, but I don't. Instead, I say, "Do you want me to walk you to your car?"

"Do you ever want to be by yourself?" Lil asks, a grayness still filling her blue eyes. I nod and think to myself: *almost every day, and yet, it's my biggest fear.*

She walks out of the bathroom, head up and chest out. I don't move. Instead, I stare at myself in the mirror again. At the purple dress I have on, the one my mom bought me for Christmas two years ago. *It makes your eyes pop!* she yelled, and clapped her hands together when I held it up to my chest. I smiled and wore it all day, thinking I was pretty.

I lean in closer, widening my eyes and searching them for something more. Do my eyes pop solely because purple goes with hazel? Or do they pop because every word that swarms in my heart sparkles in their reflection? If my mom bought me a dress that matched my insides, it would be a tangled mess, every color of the rainbow swirled together. Then she'd complain that nothing matched me and make me take the outfit back.

The bathroom door swings open and three girls walk in,

laughing. I pull back from the mirror and blink.

"I heard she flunked out of her last school," one with dirty blonde hair says. I think her name is Katy or Kathy or Missy. Something with a Y that matches the flouncy tone in her voice.

"What's the saying?" the other girl laughs, pulling a paddle brush out of her bag and running it through her long black hair. "You can take the girl out of Dicksville, but you can't take the dicks out of the girl? I'm sure this isn't the first dude over the age of eighty she's slept with. She should be arrested."

"Statutory rape works the other way," I butt in, fire rising in my throat. "The older man is the one who goes to jail."

The three girls stare at me, eyes bugging out of their heads.

Katy or Kathy or Missy says, "Whatever."

The black-haired girl goes back to brushing. The mute girl adjusts her bra so her boobs pop further out of her v-neck shirt. I just stare at them, wondering if they even know that moments earlier the girl they're trashing was standing in this bathroom. If they would even recognize Lil when they saw her.

I leave as the final bell rings, making my way to my locker. My head and my heart hurt, both pounding like an alarm waking me up for the first time.

And then my phone buzzes. *Not again*, I think.

Sarah: *Not taking the bus 2day. Still on for shopping 2morrow?*

I glare at the text. Anger at Sarah rolls through me. My fingers hover over the N and O on the keypad. I want to press down so badly. Instead, I scroll up to the picture text of Lil and gross-out guy. Clicking on the image, my phone asks what I want to do. Save or delete? I press so hard my fingerprint might never swipe off the screen. DELETE.

But I can't ditch Sarah. She's my best friend. She didn't start the text waterfall. She just forwarded it. It's not her fault. My head gets it, but my heart wonders if what I'm thinking is true. Guilt by association is still guilt, right? Or is it?

Marty: *Sure.*

I press my temples and try to clear my head. Homework for tonight. Math. I grab my Pre-Calc book and shove it in my backpack. Physics. Already done. English ...

"You forgot your purse in the lab." Alex is standing next to me, holding out the purple clutch that matches my dress.

"Did you look through it?" I snap, grabbing it from him. Instantly, I feel guilty. "Sorry, that wasn't very nice."

"Don't be. Purses scare me too much to open."

"They scare you?" I zip up my backpack and close my locker.

"Well, tampons scare me and they're usually in purses." Alex shrugs. I try not to be grossed out by the fact that he just said tampon. "Aaaand I just said tampon in front of you. My brother would be so disappointed."

"What?" I ask.

"He has a list of things you never say in front a girl. Tampons, PMS, periods, poop, babies, wedding, panties." Alex looks at me, eyes wide. "Now I've said them all." He's turning tomato red. "My brother's not very smart."

"Actually, I think he might be on to something," I smile.

Alex looks at his feet and runs a hand through his hair. "Is she okay?" He asks.

My eyes follow his glance down to the red Converse he's wearing. I clutch my phone tight to my chest. "Why red?"

"I have this weird thing about matching clothes with

shoes. I know I shouldn't care because I'm a guy, but I do. I can't help it. The red matches my jerseys."

I nod. I don't know what else to say because Alex is so nice and he brought me my purse and he says things like, you look beautiful. But I can't talk to him about Lil.

"I better go. My brother's waiting."

"The one with the list?" I ask.

"No, that one's off at college making love to a tube sock or something." My mouth falls open and Alex's eyes get big again. "I'll add tube sock to the list," he whispers.

"Good idea." I smile at him.

He turns to walk away but stops. "Tell her I don't mind that she calls me Jock Strap. I do wear one. Oh, and Ms. Everley wanted me to tell you that Margaret Thatcher would be proud, but you're still way cuter than she was. I added that last part." Alex winks at me, a smile as big as the moon on his face.

I laugh and feel bad at the same time as he walks away, his matching shoes bright in the hallway. I wish I could be into Alex. My parents would like him.

Everyone on the bus is talking about the text. I plug my ears with headphones and listen to Bob Marley on full blast. *One love, My Hart, let's get together and feel all right.* I force myself to remember the good parts of Lake Loraine. The hips and sweet whispers.

At home, I concentrate on my homework, but it's no use. Giving up, I pull out my box of poems and leaf through them before adding another to the pile.

In kindergarten we learn to get in line,
Walk straight,
Follow the leader,
Earn a yellow star,

But where does that line lead?
To the same place everyone else goes,
What if I went in another direction?
Would I find new people to follow,
Would I be the leader then?
Or would I be alone.

☙

"I cannot believe you got in the car with her," Sarah says as we stand in the changing room of Kohl's, a stack of dresses piled high on the ground. "Please tell me you burned that outfit."

I pull a yellow knee-length dress over my head so she can't see my face. Our relationship is changing day by day, word by word. Like every time I look at her, I see another flaw. Sarah's morphing in front of my eyes and no matter what I do, I can't stop it. Right now, everything inside of me wants to scream at her and tell her she's being shallow and bitchy. But that would be mean and she's my best friend.

"Rachel Magers told me her mom's a stripper. A stripper! You probably have an STD. I might talk to your mom about getting you checked." Sarah appraises the dress I just put on. "No way. You look like a lemon."

I peel the dress off and drop it on the ground. I almost cancelled on Sarah last night. I stared at my phone and wondered why a person would press send on a text when they know it's going to hurt someone else. But then I remembered how in fourth grade Sarah was the only person to stick up for me when I came to school after a skunk sprayed our house. She washed my hair with tomato juice until her hands were dyed red. *It's my color*, was all she said.

And I remembered how she turned down Kyle Travis for Winter Formal freshman year because I didn't have a date and she'd promised to go stag with me. Or how she let me cry on her lap after my grandma died, the way she stroked my hair until I fell asleep.

Can you forget the past even if the person sucks in the present?

Sarah puts on a short pink dress and steps back to look at herself in the mirror. Pouting her lips, she does her best model pose, knee popped out, elbows back.

"I love this. I look awesome," she says.

Every time Sarah says 'me' or 'I' these days, it's like an invisible pimple appears on her forehead. POP! And the morphing continues. "*I'm* totally getting this one. Look at *my* boobs! It's like this dress was made for *me*." Pop, pop, pop.

I turn away from the mirror and grab a hunter green dress off a hanger. The small space is getting tinier by the minute, and I wonder if there's enough oxygen in here for both me and her. I pull the dress over my head and look in the mirror. It hits mid-thigh, not too short, but not too long, and cinches right below my rib cage, making my waist look extra small. I twist my hips, swishing them through the air. Perfect. It even goes with Matt's jelly bracelet. Sort of.

Just thinking Matt's name sends my groin into a frenzy, like all my pent-up sex thoughts are rumbling around in my lady parts, dying to escape. I've never felt like this before and I don't know if it's right or wrong or if I'm going to hell, but I do know I can't wait to see him at the dance.

"Marty, are you even listening to me?" Sarah flicks my leg.

"What? Oh, I'm sorry." Programmed reaction. I'm not really sorry.

"What's with you lately? It's like you don't even listen to me anymore."

"I was actually thinking about Matt," I say, and smile at myself in the mirror.

"I'm your best friend, so I'm going to tell you this. It might sting, but it's for your own good. You're totally wasting your time. I mean, he's a senior and super gorge and *so* not into geeks like you," Sarah says matter-of-factly.

Wait? What?

"But you don't even know him." I touch the bracelet around my wrist.

"Like I need to. He's got the face of a Greek god. He probably has sex in weird positions with college girls. And I know you, like, better than anybody on this planet. He's way out of your league. You've never even kissed anybody."

Sarah's covered in so many pimples now that I can barely see her face. Shouldn't she support me? Be a shoulder to cry on? Instead, all I get is that I'm a geek and Matt has sex with college girls. I want to squeeze her head until it explodes in a mess of puss.

"By the way, that dress is, like, made for you. You look *so* pretty. You have to get it." Sarah smiles at the two of us in the mirror and wraps her arm around me. Her in her pink dress and me in green. It's the picture we'll take the night of the dance. The one that will replace the Spring Fling photo on my desk.

I force a smile and beat back all the words Sarah just said about Matt. All the words she said about Lil. My phone buzzes in my purse and I break our pose, peeling Sarah's arm off my skin.

Lil: *Wanna come over 2nite?*

I breathe in, stealing my air back. Just seeing Lil's name makes me feel better. She put on an extra layer of black eyeliner and walked down the halls today like a statue that wouldn't break. A sophomore football player with bad teeth whispered *whore* as she went by. Lil pretended to go at him and he flinched, almost falling into a locker.

"Fuckwad," Lil said and smiled.

She looked so calm and collected, but I know that even statues weather. Eventually, they succumb to the beating of time, no matter how badly the artist wants them to stay intact.

"So, you want to watch a movie tonight?" Sarah asks.

I look at my phone, then up at Sarah in the mirror. Her hands are on her hips and she's smiling, trying to coat everything over with a nice candy shell. It doesn't work. Her words are floating in the air around us, and I don't want to stand under them anymore.

"I'm pretty tired. I think I'm just going to hang at home."

Sarah shakes her head, her red hair bouncing with the movement. "Whatever, loser."

She pulls the pink dress over her head and I quickly type back to Lil.

Marty: *Sure.*

We buy the dresses and drive home in silence.

❧

The lights are on inside of Addison Farm, and I wonder what it feels like to be Lil and her mom, banished to the trailer with a warm home and family only feet away. Maybe it's freeing, like they don't have to worry about what everyone thinks and Lil and her mom can eat dinner in bed while watching a movie. Lately, every time I have to sit around the table with my parents, I feel shackled to the chair, forced to place my napkin in my lap and ask to be excused, like a prisoner. But then I feel bad for not being thankful for having a healthy meal and two parents and a house with all upgraded appliances.

"About time you showed up," Lil says, sticking her head out the door. She has her hair pulled into two buns, which sprout from the top of her head like antennae. "You almost missed her."

"Who?" I say.

"My mom. She wants to apologize to you."

Lil's mom is standing in front of their tiny mirror putting on red lipstick. She's wearing a waitress outfit, the old-fashioned kind with an apron and orthopedic shoes. Definitely not a stripper. The night I met her feels like yesterday and forever ago in the same breath, and I think she's as pretty as I remember.

"Marty," she says, turning to greet me. Her voice is smooth and warm, like velvet, and seems to cover the entire trailer. "I want to apologize. I was rude and you didn't deserve it." She rubs her thumb over Lil's cheek, and Lil lets her. "You saved my daughter."

It's a mirror image, the present and future Lil. I can see it. In this moment, standing in their home, a small space filled with a beat-up mustard couch, its stuffing coming out of the cushions, and two single beds, one with a flowery comforter, the other with tie-dye. A broken mirror on a wall with water damage and the stale smell of cigarettes in the air. My head clears of all the cloudy confusion I've been holding onto for the past week, and all that's left is a bright blue summer sky.

"Thank you, but you don't need to apologize."

"Yes, I do. People don't do that enough in this town. I was wrong, and you need to know that." I nod; I can't think of what else to say. Because she's beautiful and honest and makes me want to wrap myself up in her voice like a baby. She's so Lil and at the same time, so not.

"Now, I have to get to work. I'll see you in the morning," she says to Lil. "I hope I see you more often, Marty."

After she's gone, I say, "Your mom's great." And I mean it. I like her and not just because Lil made me promise, but because she loves Lil. It's in her eyes, like her daughter is the one thing that makes living in a trailer okay.

"Enough of the serious shit. We need some music." Lil walks over to an old record player propped up on an end table in the corner.

"Does that thing actually play? It's, like, a thousand years old." The record player looks like the one my grandma had with her in the nursing home, a wooden box that flips open to reveal a turntable.

"Yes, Pollyanna. It plays better music than the modern stuff you use." Lil pulls a record from a crate of what seems like hundreds. So much music, so many words.

I stand in Lil's trailer, looking around at the walls and beds and blankets. Nothing is new. Even the mirror has a crack down the center. Yet, it seems to sing with life. The bare beige walls hold stories locked somewhere in the insulation. The couch hums with bodies that have spent time wondering why this trailer is their home. Even the air speaks to me.

My house never does this. Its hard granite counters don't

remind me of my grandma and her swollen knuckles and the perfect blueberry cobbler she made every Sunday. Or the way she smelled like lilacs. I never smell lilac in my house anymore. All the walls that held my grandma's smell were torn down when my mom made everything open-concept.

"What band did you choose?" I ask, fidgeting with my hands.

"The Ramones."

I nod. I have no idea who they are. Other than my recent introduction to Bob Marley, my music stylings haven't changed much.

The record cracks when Lil sets the needle down on it. Nerves start to grumble in my stomach. I don't know what I'm supposed to do. Dance? Sit down and listen? Pretend I know the words and sing along? I'm used to choreographed numbers with blocking and a chorus to cover me up if I make a wrong move. But here I'm exposed. What if I do everything wrong? What if all the steps I take lead down a path that leaves me alone? What if screaming and dancing and writing words down on paper that should be kept locked in a dark place makes the world hate me? I can't be hated. I need to be loved. If some days I have to pretend to like someone's terrible outfit or tell Sarah she deserves a boyfriend or look at my mom and quietly think her life of volunteering isn't about helping others, it's about helping herself, I guess that's okay.

I guess...

But then the song snaps on, like it's being born into the room, moving fast like an oncoming train of guitar chords. It's a frenzy, each note pumping into my veins, and all my confusion starts to melt. It's the same way I feel when I know something is going to come out of me that lives in the back part of my brain, the part hidden behind all my nice-ness.

I don't know if I want that coming out here, in Lil's house, for her to see. But I'm pretty sure it comes out because of Lil. Because she won't fall for my choreographed dances and costumes. Taking a deep breath, I close my eyes and listen to the music. And I like it.

I wanna be...

Maybe I was wrong. Maybe Lil didn't plant something inside of me. Maybe she pulled something out. Maybe it's been there all along, but I covered it in dresses and makeup and smile after endless smile.

Hurry, hurry...

Go insane.

But what's wrong with smiling and being nice? What's wrong with wanting to make people happy? I'm happy when others are.

Control... Control... Control...

CAN'T CONTROL.

Or maybe I'm not. Maybe the real me is slowly dying and all the words coming out are my true self's final cry: *save me, before I drown in everyone else's idea of who I am.* Maybe I'm meant to take a path that isn't straight. Where equations don't end in solutions, but in more questions. When I think about that possibility, the music in Lil's trailer shatters me. And I'm transported. Every word, every beat pounds in my heart and my limbs and I'm jumping inside and out. I don't care what I look like. I don't care if Lil laughs at me. I don't care if I'm supposed to step my foot here and kick my leg at this beat. I'm shaking off years of shackles I didn't know I was wearing and pounding my fist in the air and breaking the chains around my chest that tell me I can't be free, that tell me I can't be who and what I want. I'm screaming all over again, this time not with my voice but with my whole body, writhing to the guitar and gruff voices of the song. Why is it so easy to dance freely here in this dingy place and not in my everyday life?

I open my eyes and look for Lil. She's doing the same thing. Falling in on herself and letting the music cover her. The buns on top of her head are loose from shaking; dark strands of hair fall in her face. I fling my head, trying to clear it of everything and just live in the moment. In the music.

As it flows around the trailer, bouncing off the walls and circling through the air, I laugh and scream and shake my hair until it's tangled in knots so gnarled they might never come out. But when the song ends and I'm back in my skin and my brain, I worry that if the tangles get too deep, I might have to cut all my hair off.

Then how would I recognize myself?

∽

"Where does your mom work?" I ask Lil later that night. We're sitting on the roof of her grandpa's barn. The sky is clear.

"At a restaurant about thirty miles away. She works the night shift most days."

"Why doesn't she have a job in town?" Lil doesn't answer, just lights a cigarette and exhales a long stream of smoke that grays the color of the sky. I decide to try another question. "What about your dad?"

"Rolling down some lonesome highway, maybe. Or dead in a ditch. Either way, our relationship would be the same. Nonexistent." Lil takes another drag on her cigarette.

No dad? I don't know what it would feel like to take a million breaths and not know your father for any of them. Even on my worst day, I wouldn't want my parents to leave.

I change the subject. "Are you going to the dance next weekend?"

Lil sits up on her elbows. "The Hot Shot dance? I don't think so."

"Why not? I promise it will be fun."

"I don't do organized school functions."

"Please." I nudge her in the side and she breaks into a smile.

"No. Besides, you'll be busy dancing with Alexander the Great Big Boner."

I roll my eyes and touch Matt's bracelet.

"He's just a friend. I like someone else, anyway," I say.

I really want Lil to come. I think going to a school dance might help her shake some of the black cloud around her.

"Matt Three-Last-Names? Be careful with him," Lil says, flicking her cigarette into the air.

I groan. "Not you, too. What's so wrong with me?"

"It's not you," she says, setting her eyes directly on me. "I just don't trust a guy who carries around a guitar."

CHAPTER 10

Every day leading up the Hot Shot dance, I sit at my desk in my bedroom, doing homework and staring at the bag of decorations tucked under my bed. My mom's decorations. Red and pink and sparkles galore. All things I thought I liked. My eyes move around the room, and I wonder if my walls are pink because I love the color or because my mom does. Do I like scarves and croissants because I want to go to Paris or because my mom wants to go to Paris?

I can't get the Ramones out of my head.

"We'll meet in the gym tomorrow at 5 PM," Ms. Everley says at the end of the final WelCo meeting before the dance. "Marty, you bring the decorations and we'll get started. It's going to be great."

I look down at the paper where I was supposed to be taking notes.

If the Ramones were sedated.
Does that mean they were medicated?
Or just high on life?
Or trying to find what's right?
Or lost on their way to catch a plane?
Or dancing in the dark in the rain.

I stopped there because the poem started to sound like a Dr. Seuss book and *life* and *right* really don't rhyme and the more I thought about the Ramones the more I missed Lil. And I felt guilty for not listening to Ms. Everley, who thinks

I'm as good as Margaret Thatcher.

"Is everything all right, Marty?" Ms. Everley asks as I walk past her desk.

"Ms. Everley, how did you know you wanted to be an English teacher?"

Her eyebrows rise and she sets down her pen. "If it were up to my parents, I would have been a housewife." She pauses. "I knew that wasn't for me."

"How did you know?"

"Let's just say, some people like hot dogs. Some people prefer the bun," Ms. Everley says, shrugging. "My parents didn't get that. They still don't. But teaching always made sense to me."

Ms. Everley waits for me to respond, but I don't know what to say. What do hot dogs and buns have to do with anything?

"What if I'm different? What if who I thought I was isn't who I am?" I finally ask.

"Who do you think you are?"

"I don't know."

"Well, the good news is that you have time to figure it out."

"Do you know who you are now that you're older?" I ask.

"Some days I think I do. Others I don't."

"But you know you like the bun."

She nods and smiles, "Over a hot dog? Any day. Even if other people don't."

"Why wouldn't people like it?"

My phone buzzes as Ms. Everley opens her mouth to respond.

Lil: *Get ur ass out 2 the parking lot.*

I smile. Just seeing her name on the screen settles my

stomach and clears my vision.

"I better go," I say, slinging my backpack over my shoulder.

"I'll see you tomorrow." Ms. Everley smiles at me. Her shirt seems extra low today, cleavage popping out of the royal blue ruffles with extra bounce; as usual, she's got on makeup a drag queen would be proud of. But if Lil can wear combat boots and a skull ring, why can't Ms. Everley dress like a stripper? At least she knows who she is most days. I may dress pretty, but inside I'm a jumbled mess of a thousand colors running together until they turn a mushy stream of brown. Going by what Ms. Everley says, I do know one thing: I like hot dogs.

I mean, who would ever want to eat just a bun?

Lil's car is parked at the back of the lot, stereo blaring music that echoes off the brick walls of the school. She's reclined all the way back in her seat, red sunglasses over her eyes. It's cold today. Winter cold. I think it might snow, but for some reason the closer I get to the car, the warmer I feel. I knock on the windshield. Lil sits up quickly, a bright red lipstick smile on her face.

"Do you think I'm like Ms. Everley?" I ask.

"Do I think you probably get sloppy drunk on the weekends and have a college thong collection you can't seem to get rid of? No. Why?" Lil puts her sunglasses on her head.

"No reason."

"Well, don't stand out there all afternoon. Get in," she says.

I don't hesitate like I did that first day. I don't look for Sarah's approval. I know she won't get it. Instead, opening the door, I slide into the front seat that feels made for me. As I settle into the car, my mind clears.

"Where are we going?" I ask, just like that first day.

"Haven't you already learned that I'm not going to tell you?" Lil revs the engine and peels out of the parking lot.

We drive through town, the windows rolled down, freezing air coursing through the car. I put my hand out the window and let it curve through the breeze like a wave. Lil smokes cigarette after cigarette and pounds her fists on the steering wheel to the beat of the music. Everything lightens inside me, like this moment might be the best of my life. Like this is what living is supposed to be. Free, with music blaring, with the wind whipping my hair in my face and tangling its length into knots I don't want to brush out. I don't care if I like hot dogs or buns or pink or Paris. I like this, right here, right now.

My phone buzzes; a text message.

Sarah: *Come over right now! I hate my dress! Need damage control!*

I want to throw the phone out the window. Instead I turn it off.

Lil drives until we hit the dirt road we took to get to the party at Lake Loraine. She turns down the path and parks in the exact spot where we parked that night.

"Why are we here?" I ask, a knot forming in my stomach. I thought the text message waterfall would go away. I thought people would ease up as time ticked on. But they haven't. Lil has fought through a barrage of words every day. *Whore, slut, trash.* Someone even printed the picture and taped it to her locker.

Why would she want to come back here?

"I need to do something." Lil gets out of the car. I follow, willing to do whatever she needs. We walk until we get to the edge of the lake. The exact spot where I found her with gross-out guy. "Why do men think mustaches are acceptable?" She asks me.

"I don't know," I say.

"Cops and circus ring leaders are the only professions that should allow facial hair."

"What about porn stars?"

Lil smiles at me and turns back to the water. Her eyes squint and turn dark, like she's looking past the surface to something below. "Sometimes I can still feel his stubble on my skin."

"Lil..." I start to say something, anything that might soothe what she's thinking, but she turns around and grabs a large rock off the ground. Running up to the edge of the water, her boots almost going in, she flings the rock high into the air and yells. A deep, throat-breaking yell that echoes back to us from the other side of the lake.

I let her stand there, watching the ripples from the drowning rock until they reach the shore and disappear. She lights a cigarette and exhales the smoke out into the air.

"So are you going to dance with Alexander the Great Big Boner tomorrow night or what?" Lil asks, sitting down in the sand. I sit next to her and shrug.

"I don't know." Picking up a stick, I start to draw on the ground, writing my name and then Lil's. "Can I ask you something?"

"Sure." Lil puts the cigarette out in the sand.

I take a deep breath. "What does it feel like?" Even in the cold my cheeks burn with embarrassment.

"What does what feel like?"

"Sex. What does it feel like?" I ask. I want to know so badly, and Lil is the only person I know who's done it. Maybe if I know, I won't be so anxious.

"It feels like falling on the bar of a bike a thousand times," Lil says, pulling her knees to her chest and resting her chin on them.

"That sounds horrible."

"It is."

Sarah and I have been planning what we want our first time to be like since junior high. We agreed that we want to lose our virginity the summer before college so it would be with someone we know from our hometown. I said I wanted rose petals on the bed and Sarah said she wanted Debussy's "Clair de Lune" playing in the background.

We also agreed that no matter what, whoever it was, we would be in love. Real love. Passionate love. We would stand in front of each other naked and look and I wouldn't be scared of his private parts because I was comfortable.

"Did you love him?" I ask.

"No," Lil says flatly. "I just wanted to do it. Like ripping off a Band-Aid or something."

"Have you done it with a lot of people?"

"A few." Lil looks at me and I wish I could live in her head for a day, to see the world in different colors or know what she does. "You shouldn't settle for anything less than love, Marty. A boy who will take his time and care about you. What it feels like physically doesn't matter. How it changes you in your heart does."

"Have you ever been in love?" I ask.

"Love?" Lil shakes her head. "There are people like you and there are people like me. There's Juliet and then there's Rosaline."

"I think you're a Juliet."

"And that, Pollyanna, is why she ends up dead at the end." Lil stands up and wipes the sand off the back of her black jeans. "Come on, I'll take you home."

"Um, Lil?"

"Please don't ask me about blow jobs." I laugh and squirm at the same time, and then point to her cigarette butt still stuck in the sand. She picks it up and we walk away from Lake Loraine.

∾

When all the decorations are hung and the gym is covered in red and pink bulls-eyes and cupids holding rifles, I step back and look at my work. A banner hangs over my head. "Shot Through the Heart" . I wish Lil was coming tonight, so she could make the pit in my stomach go away. As I walked around directing the WelCo kids about where to hang everything, I couldn't stop thinking that I have no business telling them what to do. I can't get my own brain straight. It's a mess of words and music and sex and the desire to see Matt tonight. Who am I to tell someone else how to decorate?

As I stare at the words I painted on the paper, the theme my mom came up with, all I notice is that I painted outside of the lines. Little bits of red and pink run past the letter shapes I drew, making the banner imperfect. And the girl inside of me, the one that wants to see the world as a bunch of jumbled, curved lines, is happy. But the outward girl, who's wearing a hunter green dress that falls right above the knee and cinches at the waist so my boobs look just the right size, a small C cup, is mad I was so sloppy.

"Let's all give Marty a big round of applause for her great work," Ms. Everley yells to all the WelCo kids. "This place looks great. You should be proud of yourself, Marty!"

"Thanks," I say and force a smile. *Proud of myself.* I don't know what that is anymore. A few weeks ago, proud of myself would have meant making sure everything for this dance was perfect. The kind of perfect people remember and talk about. Now, I'm not sure what to be proud of. Proud I've spent years hiding the person locked inside me? Tonight, she wants to scream at the top of her lungs: *this is a dance that celebrates the killing of innocent animals! I can cover the entire place in glitter, but Bambi still hates us!* Or proud that she's coming out now and I didn't die with her locked inside of me, drowning on unwritten, unsaid words?

In the bathroom, I fix my makeup and reapply pink lip gloss. Matt's black jelly bracelet is still on my wrist. Anxious energy rumbles in my stomach, so I text Lil.

Marty: *Please come 2 the dance.*

I wait for a response, but it doesn't happen. The DJ stars to play music that vibrates the walls of the bathroom. People are shuffling in, girls doing the same thing I am before heading into the gym-turned-meat-market to grind with boys in an acceptable arena.

I walk out and wait for Sarah at our designated meeting spot outside of the gymnasium. *I'm not walking in there alone. I don't care if you're in charge of the dance*, she said to me earlier this week.

She walks through the doors, a red pea coat covering up her pink dress. Makeup is applied expertly to her face, not a brushstroke out of place, and her hair is pulled half back, red curls falling around her shoulders.

"You look great," I say.

"No thanks to you." She takes off her coat and hands it to the freshman coat checker.

"What?" I ask.

"My text message. You never came over." She purses her lips at me, hands on her hips.

Shit. "Sorry, I got carried away with the dance."

"When did you become a liar, Marty? Pippa saw you leave with Lil yesterday. What are you thinking?" Sarah grabs my arm and pulls me into a corner. Her tight fingers hurt my skin. "Are you trying to completely slaughter your reputation?"

"I'm being nice."

Sarah laughs, a condescending sound that comes through her teeth. "Marty. Lil is trash. Pippa told me she lives in a trailer. A trailer! Let alone what her mom did."

"What *did* her mom do?" I ask.

Sarah steps back, arms crossed over her pink dress, a wicked grin on her face. "She didn't tell you? And you're willing to let it all go for a girl you barely know."

I stare at Sarah, at the vacant look in her eyes, at the clutch that matches her dress that matches the clip in her hair.

A sophomore girl walks by and says, "Shot through the heart. What a lame theme."

The air gets tight, like all of a sudden I've been placed on a planet where I can't breathe and everyone is an alien. I want to tear down the decorations and burn them. I look around, trying to find a place to catch my breath, and see Alex walk through the door. I race over to him.

"You look nice tonight. Want to dance?" I don't wait for his answer; I yank on his arm and drag him away from Sarah and the banner hanging over the doorway.

"Sure," he says, shrugging his shoulders.

We walk out onto the dance floor. Flo Rida or Usher or one of those artists who can sing and dance like a robot at the same time beats in the background as people gyrate all over the gym, air-humping each other.

"Do you like this song?" Alex asks swerving his hips back and forth. Sarah stands against the gym wall staring at us, jaw dropped. I turn my back to her.

"Sure," I say and mimic his hips. I don't even know the song, but anything is better than listening to Sarah and her mean words.

"You look nice tonight." Alex puts a hand on my hip.

"Thanks." I take a step closer.

"I like your dress," he yells over the music and puts his other hand on my hip.

"I like your shirt. It matches your eyes." My mom always says if someone gives you a compliment you give one back. And Alex's baby blue button down does look great next to his eyes.

"Thanks. My mom picked it out." I stop, my jaw dropping without me thinking, and Alex smiles. "I'm kidding. Not about your dress. The part about my mom."

I laugh a little, but then wonder if he has a sleeveless undershirt on underneath. My mind pictures armpit hair sticking out in every direction, little beads of sweat dripping off the ends. I cringe. What am I doing? I move to step back from Alex, but the song changes. A slow dance.

He pulls me closer and wraps his arms around my waist. "And you smell good, too. It's my lucky night." He smiles at me and I force a smile in return. I wanted to get away from Sarah, but I didn't want this. Me wrapped in Alex's arms when all I want is Matt. But I'm here and I can't be rude to him. Not when he's been so nice. So I rest my cheek on his chest. Alex is the perfect height for me. The top of my head fits right into the crux of his neck.

I close my eyes and try to find something, anything that will take my mind off his armpit hair and my sloppy banner. I feel his hips swaying with mine, his hands on my back, his heart beating hard through his shirt. Hard ... Hard ... Oh my God!! He's hard!

I pull back, my face on fire. Alex looks at me, his jaw slacked wide, his eyebrows raised above his blue eyes that look like they might pop right out of the socket. I want to tell him it's okay. I'm flattered. But all I keep hearing is Lil's voice in my head, screaming Alexander the Great Big Boner!

"I need to go to the bathroom," I say. I rush out of the other side of the gym to the furthest open hallway, away from Sarah and Alex and Alex's boner. I don't take a breath until I'm alone. Oh my ... Oh my ... I can't wrap my head around what just happened. Or maybe I can and I don't want to. All I'm seeing are scenes from Health class about anatomy and men and sex.

I lean up against the wall, my head in my hands. Pulling out my phone, I check for a text from Lil. Nothing.

"Be still My Hart," a silky voice says behind me.

End Health scene. Enter wild-beating heart and sexy guitar-callused hands. Matt Three-Last-Names.

My hands drop from my face. He's wearing dark jeans that hug his hips and a green and blue flannel shirt rolled up to expose his arm accessories. I throw my rule about flannel shirts out the window.

"Hi," I say, taking a breath.

"Hi." He strolls over to me and the air gets hard-to-breathe tight but I don't seem to care because all thoughts of male genitalia are gone from my head and I'm staring at Matt's kissable, pouty lips.

"When did you get here?" I ask.

"Just a bit ago. Taking a breather already?"

"Something like that," I say. I play with my hair, unsure of what to do with his body so close to mine. "Did you come with a date?" I almost have to choke out the words. I'm not sure I want to know about the other girl he'll wrap his arms around tonight.

"No. You?" he asks.

"No," I smile.

"I like talking to you." He leans against the wall next to me.

My insides jump a thousand times and I say, "I like talking to you, too." Even though we've barely said a word to each other in weeks. Somehow my brain manages to block it all out.

"It's like I can say whatever I want and know you won't judge me, you know?"

It's because your voice is like honey coating my entire skin in sugar and deliciousness, I think to myself.

"I think about singing a lot now," Matt says, his green eyes so magnetic my knees buckle, the kind of buckle where your whole body changes. "Want to dance again?" He extends his hand to me, palm up.

"Right here in the hallway?" I ask.

"It's too crowded in there. Plus, I hate this song."

"Wonderful Tonight" by Eric Clapton wafts into the hallway from the gym.

Matt wiggles his fingers and I giggle a little as I take it. He pulls my body against his. I might die right here and now. A wonderful death, my heart exploding from too much ecstasy. I'm glad Alex got a boner because it led to this.

"Nice bracelet," he says, running his fingers over the one he gave me.

"I thought it went well with my dress." I take another breath.

"You look good," he whispers in my ear.

"Thanks," I say into his shoulder, and hope my knees don't give out.

And then Matt sings, "Many have I loved, many times been bitten, many times I've gazed along the open road."

His voice is off-key and gruff and if I were judging him for an audition I'd demand he be placed in the chorus so we could stare at his face, but not hear him. Yet I don't care. I would swear what he's singing is a lullaby. The most beautiful song I've ever heard.

"That's my favorite," he shrugs.

"It's beautiful."

He puts his hand on my face, cupping my cheek so it fits perfectly into his palm. "You're really pretty," he says. A chorus of angelic voices goes off in my head, booming around us like it's the show-stopping number at the end of Act One of the musical entitled Meet Me in St. Marty's Pants. "You still haven't come to see me play at Vinyl Tap. I'll be there over the holiday break, if you want to come by."

I nod. Actually speaking would ruin the moment; even if I tried, all that would come out would be a squeak.

Matt drops his arms and steps back from me. "Well, we'd better get back in there. I wouldn't want people starting rumors about us." He winks at me and turns his back, walking into the gym.

Why must these moments end? Why can't life be one long slow dance?

I wait until he's disappeared through the doors before I move. Right as I walk back into the blaring music and the smell of sweat that permeates the air, my phone buzzes.

Lil: *I'm here.*

My stomach flips. I look around the gym, trying to find her. I can't wait to tell her what just happened. It's crowded and people are jumping up and down to the heavy beat of the music. My eyes scan the crowd. Sarah is grinding with Tony Pisano, a pimply boy in our grade whose parents own the only pizzeria in town. Alex is sitting on the bleachers alone. My heart pinches when I see him leaning, elbows on his knees, and tapping his foot to the song.

And then I see Lil standing on top of a speaker at the DJ podium. I don't know how she got up there. The skinny, middle-aged DJ is frozen in shock—probably cause on the top of Lil's head is a pair of antlers with red lights twinkling on the ends. And she's wearing a shirt that says in all-capital letters, OPEN SEASON, with an arrow pointing down to her crotch.

Slowly, everyone turns to see her standing there, like a hunting trophy on display for the whole school. I laugh, a deep freeing chuckle from the bottom of my gut, and without thinking about the eyes that might watch me or the words that might be said, I walk over to her.

"Nice shirt," I yell over the music.

"Thanks, Pollyanna." Lil jumps down off the speaker. "Bitchin' decorations. 'Shot through the heart'. Solid."

"Don't say things you don't mean," I smile. "They suck."

"I'm sorry, girls," Ms. Everley comes up to us at the DJ table. "But Lil, I can't have you here in that shirt."

She shrugs. "Want to get out of here? These songs suck."

The eyes of everyone in the gym are on my back. I feel them for the first time as Lil speaks. I look over my shoulder at Sarah, who's standing still and staring at me, her eyes narrowed. At Alex, who's smiling.

And Matt. He winks at me. Again.

"Absolutely."

I walk out of the gym as the music beats louder, hand in hand with Lil, her antlers twinkling above us.

CHAPTER 11

"Led Zeppelin!" Lil yells. "His favorite song is a Led Zeppelin song!" She laughs so hard it shakes the walls of the trailer.

"What's wrong with Led Zeppelin?" I ask.

"Why didn't he just sing you a Rolling Stones song, or better yet, the Beatles? What a guitar-playing dick."

"I can't believe you're focusing on the song and not the fact that he sang to me. It was so romantic," I say.

"Romantic? It's cheesy and so fucking lame."

"I think it sounds very romantic," Lil's mom says as she checks her makeup in the cracked mirror, running her finger along her bottom lip. She doesn't even flinch when Lil says fuck, whereas I'm so uncomfortable, like my insides are squirming in a heap of dirty words. I want to grab Lil's mouth and clamp it shut. You can't say things like that in front of adults. Not until you're in college, anyway. I can't even say "tampon" in front of my mom without her clicking her tongue and pretending to wash the dishes.

"And I never want to see you in that shirt again," Lil's mom adds.

"It was just for effect and it worked." Lil smiles. "Don't encourage her, Mom."

Lil's mom told me to call her Maggie, but it seems wrong. I've never called a grown-up by their first name before. My dad has a strict rule against it, even though I think he just likes having people call him doctor when he's really a dentist.

"What's wrong with a little crush?" Maggie asks.

"Because they crush *you* in the end."

"Don't listen to her, Marty. She's a Grinch this time of year." She kisses Lil on the top of her head, a quick, affectionate peck, and I smile. It's as if every time Maggie touches Lil a light glows brighter in the trailer.

"I'll see you in the morning," Maggie says, putting her pink and blue apron on, and walks out the trailer door.

"Seriously, Marty," Lil says, turning to me, face serious. "This isn't a Disney movie. Matt is not some prince in tight pants with good intentions. He likes sex. Probably raunchy, bend-you-over sex and you are one-hundred percent vanilla. You can't like him."

"Maybe I want to swirl my vanilla with his chocolate."

"Life doesn't work that way, Pollyanna."

"Why can't you be happy for me?"

"Happy that you like a douche with long hair who wants to ride your Lazy Susan two ways from Sunday and leave you? Look, I told you there were two kinds of people in the world. People like you ... and people like me and Matt. Don't be naive."

I hate feeling like I'm not in their club. Like because I haven't had sex and can't say fuck without squirming I'm not allowed in their world.

"Maybe I want to be more like you and Matt," I say. I've been trying to understand all the changes that are happening with the music and the dancing and the writing. Is all this truth telling me becoming more like Lil, or me figuring out I had parts of Lil inside me all along, parts that I never knew existed because they were camouflaged in lip gloss and manners?

"No, you don't," Lil snaps.

"Then why doesn't anyone want to kiss me?"

"It's just a kiss."

"This coming from the girl who said I had virgin stink and told me all *she* wanted to do was get laid." I cross my arms over my chest. Lil couldn't understand. She knows what it feels like to have a boy want her. She knows what it feels like to say whatever she wants. I couldn't say fuck casually like she does. I've tried. I end up saying it with too much emphasis on the F and it comes out sounding like a passionate "yuck" or "luck". When Lil says fuck, she sounds like a rock star.

"Look, do whatever you want. I'm just saying you deserve better."

Better? What does that even mean? Better like Alex? Better like what my parents have? Or is better just a way of saying I'll never fit in? I'll be stuck, lost on a road with no end, and I'll never have sex. I'll die a virgin with a dried-up vagina all because I deserve *better*.

I want to change the subject. My brain is getting tangled in curse words and deep fears I'm not sure I want to face here in Lil's trailer where the world feels brighter, so I ask, "What song is acceptable for a boy to sing?"

Lil shakes her head. "No song."

"Come on. I know you have one," I say.

Because tucked behind all the black is Lil's heart and I know it's big and probably broken.

I'll catch her in English class, staring at Ms. Everley but not really seeing her. She's going past the teacher and the classroom and the blackboard to a place I don't know. It makes her blue eyes murky and sad. When I see Lil like that,

I want to tell her everything is going to be all right. That she can curse at the moon all night long, but it won't bring back the sun. Then she'll snap out of it and make a sharp comment about how Ms. Everley probably bangs frat boys on the weekend, and we're back to normal.

"If you can't tell your friend, then who can you tell?" I say.

"No one. That's the point."

"Just do it." I say the words flat and strong. I want them to sound the way Lil did when she told me to scream. "Sing it to me."

"Sing? Birds die when I sing."

"Sing it."

Lil grumbles, but she can't walk away from me like she did before. If too many people walk away in your life, eventually you start leaving before they do so it won't hurt as bad. But I'm not going anywhere and I won't let Lil turn her back either.

"Pretend it's just you," I say.

"That's impossible. You're standing, like, two feet away."

"I'll close my eyes and I promise not to open them until you're done." I make a cross over my heart.

"I can't believe you're making me do this. If you open your eyes, I'll hold you down and shave your head, Pollyanna. I'm not kidding." Lil sounds tough, but then her shoulders pull back and I know she's going to sing.

"I won't," I say, hoping she can hear the steadiness in my voice.

At this moment, in this dingy old trailer, Lil's pale skin seems to light up and her eyes flare like a deep sapphire blue ocean full of so many possibilities. When we close our eyes, Lil and I are transported. There are no walls around us, no roads leading from one place to another. It's just in an open field with nothing but the sky to close us in.

A beat later, Lil's song grows like a sunrise, blanketing everything between us, inside and out. I can barely concentrate on the lyrics because Lil's voice is so beautiful and tender, and her words don't sound like words but like life.

And then all that's left in the space is the sound of silence. The beautiful birth of nothing and everything at once. No words—and yet all the words that were ever spoken between me and Lil erupt over me like a consuming waterfall. I can't speak because I'm so filled with Lil and her pain. And I know it's a pain I can't heal, that only Lil can do that. Even that first day, I knew I couldn't save her, but I never considered that maybe it isn't about saving someone, but helping them to save themselves. Like Lil's done for me.

Lil grabs my hand and in this moment, right here, she knows I know her. She knows I'm not playing nice.

"What's the name of the song?" I ask.

"'Human'." Lil says. She looks down at our intertwined hands and then yanks me toward the door. "Come on. The Killers sound better with wind in your hair."

❧

We drive around for what feels like eternity, listening to the song and letting the freezing cold winter wind swish through the car. I hear the song so many times I memorize the lyrics. Beside me, Lil sings it at the top of her lungs.

The words circle around us in the darkness and make everything light. As we travel down the straight roads, I imagine a path for Lil, one with flowers in her hair and sunshine on her back. Somewhere warm and bright, so she can forget the darkness and the people who were supposed to love her, like her dad and grandpa, who walked away. She's happy in that place, with eyes that don't get lost.

I'm not the one that deserves better. Lil is.

We end up back on the roof of her grandpa's barn. Lil puffs smoke rings into the sky. They grow bigger the higher they climb. I count the stars and wonder how many different places exist. How, for some reason, Lil and I were placed on the same planet in the same city at the same time.

"Do you think your grandpa minds that we're up here?" I ask.

"No, he's probably passed out after making love to a whiskey bottle."

"Is your grandma dead?"

Lil pulls her black leather coat up around her ears and hugs her chest. "Yeah, she died when my mom was in high school. I never knew her."

"That's so sad," I say, and think about my grandma, her salt and pepper hair and all her crazy words and how my life would be less without her.

"My mom said Grandma never missed seeing her cheer a game even though she hated football."

"Maggie was a cheerleader?"

"Captain of the squad." Lil throws her arms up in a perfect V, then sinks back onto her palms.

"What happened with your mom?" I ask. Sarah's words have stuck in my mind and a part of me hates that she knows something about the people I care for that I don't.

Lil gnaws on her bottom lip and fishes around in her purse for her cigarettes.

"You can tell me. I'm not going to say anything," I say.

She digs deeper in the purse, not making eye contact

with me. "Where the hell is my pack?" Her hand searches the bottom of the black bag before pulling out her Camel Lights, but her grip is sloppy and she drops them. They roll off the roof of the barn into the dirt flowerbed below. "Shit!"

"Come on, I'm your friend."

Lil looks at me, her eyes intense and clear. "What if you tell everyone? What if you can never look at my mom the same way? What if you don't want to be my friend after I tell you?"

"I promised you, didn't I?"

Lil's lungs fall flat, the air she's held in so tightly finally emerging in a rush. "Did you know my mom won't kill a cockroach? We used to have them all over the place in Florida. The flying ones. They're the worst. But Mom never killed one. She used to talk to them, like she was trying to convince them that life outside of our apartment was better. 'Don't you want to fly out this door?' she'd say, and shoo her hands in the air." Lil laughs a little. "I'd wait until she went to bed and then I'd kill 'em all. She'd wake up in the morning and say her pep talk worked."

"I can see your mom doing that," I smile.

"Good. Then maybe you'll believe this next part." Lil looks up into the sky. Her eyes glaze over, and I know she's gone to her dark place. I want to grab her hand and remind her that not every footprint hurts. It's only when people stomp on you that it bleeds. "When she was in high school, she got pregnant. To this day, she's never said who the father was, but I know she knows. I know that she's seen him walking around town with his perfect family, living the perfect Minster life, and not caring that hers turned to shit." Lil sits up straight, her body becoming the statue I've seen before. "She never told anyone. I mean, this town barely accepts Democrats, let alone pregnant teens."

"What happened?" I ask.

"When she was six months along, she went into labor and miscarried. The baby came out dead. She didn't know what to do, so she buried it in the field and never told a soul."

Oh my God. It rings a million times in my head.

"This field?" I look out at the barren land below us. The dried soil, plowed lines dragged through the cold dark ground.

Lil nods. "Her dad found the baby a few weeks later when he was working. And just like that, the woman who was Minster's Homecoming Queen, who got straight A's, who won't kill a cockroach—she was branded a murderer. The whole town turned against her, even her dad. My mom couldn't go anywhere without people yelling at her. The only person who stuck up for her was my grandma. When she died, Maggie couldn't take it anymore, so she bolted and never looked back. She would've choked to death on their hate if she didn't."

"Why did she come back?" I ask.

Lil looks at me, a desperate hard look that makes my heart want to break in two, one piece for Maggie's pain and one piece for Lil's.

"Because when my grandpa said we could live in his trailer as long as we stayed away from the house, as shitty as that sounded? It was better than living in our car."

"Your mom must have been so scared," I say. I can't handle a kiss and Lil's mom survived hell.

"You believe me?"

"Of course I believe you."

Lil eyes brighten and a beautiful big-as-the-moon smile spreads across her face.

"If you tell anyone I sang to you tonight, I'll tattoo the word 'virgin' on your forehead."

"I won't," I say and make an X over my heart. "I promise."

&

I get back to my house, my mind buzzing with lyrics and stars and the truth. It's like Lil was testing me that first day to see if I could handle all her spikes and prickers. And I think most people don't pass her test. She probably likes it that way, so she doesn't have to open her heart. But fighting is exhausting, and I can see her getting tired.

When I walk in the back door, my mom is sitting at the kitchen table, her hands wrapped around a steaming cup of chamomile tea. A rock drops in my gut.

"I'm not late, am I?" I look at the clock on the microwave. It's 11:30.

"No," my mom says, taking a sip of tea. "Sit down with me."

The whole scene is weird. My mom never goes to bed later than 10:30. Ever. The only time she's stayed up late was the night my grandma died. Our kitchen was in the middle of being redone and my dad and she sat on folding chairs in a barren room, with no appliances or counters or walls, passing a wine bottle back and forth until one in the morning. I walked down and saw them because I could hear my dad crying so hard I woke up.

"Who's dead?" I ask, trying to keep the terror out of my voice.

"No one's dead."

"Then what's wrong?"

"Martina, we raised you to be a good person. I thought

that if you saw me volunteering and your father running a successful dental practice, you would know the life you could have and strive for that." Mom takes another sip of tea, slurping the end. "I don't want you spending any more time with Lily Hatfield."

"What?" I bite out.

"Please don't take that tone with me." She sets her cup down on the granite counter and I stare at the stream swirling from the top and dissipating into nothing. My mom is ruining the night and clouding my brain with candy-coated words filled with nothing but weightless air.

In that moment, I want to change everything. I want to tear down the walls and put the kitchen back the way my grandma had it, with cast iron skillets hanging from the ceiling and fresh flowers on the beaten-up wooden counters. I want to scream, *You tore down my grandma's kitchen and replaced it with your calm tone! Where's the life in that!*

But I don't. I breathe. In. Out. In. Out.

"You left the dance with her tonight."

"How do you know that?" I ask.

"Sarah called asking if you were home, and I could tell from her voice that she was upset. She told me you left her alone at the dance."

"Sarah could have called my cell phone if she was that concerned."

My mom shrugs. "That's between you and her." She gets up and dumps her tea down the sink. "People always say the past is in the past, but it never is, Marty. People are defined by their actions and you can *never* escape them."

"You've always told me to help people. That's what I'm doing," I say. I want to say so much more. That Lil has helped me. That it isn't fair to only show your child one road when

141

there are so many others she could take. That my mom's a hypocrite covered in good-smelling lotion and nice clothes and fake goodness. That I don't care what she says, I'm not giving up Lil.

"Yes, honey, I want you to help people. But there's a difference between giving a homeless man money and becoming homeless yourself."

"That doesn't make any sense," I say.

"All I'm saying is if you associate with trash, all of a sudden people start to see you as something to be set out with the morning garbage." My mom walks over to me and grabs my hand. How can she say things without caring what they mean? I stand, frozen in the cold kitchen, and see my mom for maybe the first time ever. Past the brushed hair and polished nails. Past the smooth skin and even voice. Without her exterior, there's nothing.

"I'll see you in the morning, dear." My mom kisses me on the head and walks out of the room.

There are so many words that I want to say, pounding in my head and echoing in my ears, but my mouth won't cooperate. They're locked inside me and I don't know if I'll ever have the courage to let them out. Instead, I take a breath and whisper, "Clear your heart." Cut the cord.

CHAPTER 12

Walking up to my room with my mom's words banging in my head, I want to punch the wall or run out the door or scream at the top of my lungs. I get out my yearbook and look through the pages. Minster High's Nicest Person. Me, all dressed up in costume and stage makeup as Sarah Brown. The smile I plastered on my face day in and day out just in case someone might take a picture. I thought that was me. But I was wrong. Those moments were as deep as the pages they were printed on. Thin, flimsy, and breakable.

I ignore the seven phone calls from Sarah the next day. My room turns into a bomb shelter where I'm protected from the people living downstairs and across the street. Papers are scattered across my bed and on the ground—all the words I've ever written.

Deep and wide,
Shallow and thin,
How to define,
What I'm feeling within,
Truth and lies,
Over and begin,
A breath away from breaking again.

I stare at my grandma's picture and wish she could talk to me. I miss her at least once a week. I'll hear her rough voice in my head and remember the thick calluses on her fingers and wonder if she would be proud of me.

This is you, Marty, she would say, grabbing my arm and pointing to the smallest freckle she could find. *There are lots of freckle people out there, but only one is shaped like you. Just make sure you stay away from moles. They cause cancer and eat you alive.*

My parents blamed dementia for Grandma's crazy words, but to me, they made sense. The whole time I thought I was living amongst freckle people, I was really being eaten by moles.

It takes a few days of me avoiding Sarah and asking my dad for a ride to school instead of taking the bus. A few days of me walking down the hall with Lil and laughing and not caring what everyone thinks.

Just a few days, and the crowd sets its eyes on me and rushes, full speed.

ço

Without my normal routine of meeting Sarah in the bathroom to fix our makeup, I walk straight to my locker. It feels weird not doing what I'm programmed to do, kind of like I forgot to put on underwear or deodorant and I'm worried I might start smelling during the day. But then I remember that robots are programmed and I don't want to be that. I don't want to be my mom and Sarah. If I stood next to Sarah today and watched her paint globs of lip gloss on her lips, I might burst into a million angry bubbles.

I grab my math book—and that's when I feel it on my back. It's kind of hot and itchy, like a wool sweater, and it makes the hair on the back of my neck stand up. But when I turn around, the eyes that were staring at me are gone. Taking the brush from my locker, I run it through my hair, then slyly check my armpits for a weird smell. Nothing.

In Physics, it's back. Hot and itchy. But when I look around the classroom, I don't catch anybody. It doesn't come until Study Hall, when I walk into the library and it hits me like a slow-moving tidal wave. Instead of feeling it on the back of my neck, I see it, one by one. Thirty sets of eyes glaring at me. Laughing.

I plop down behind a computer and breathe. Eliza Moore giggles five seats over. I force myself to concentrate on the homework I want to get done before the end of the day. Math problems. I pull them out of my backpack, but it's no use. Flicking on the computer I go to the one place I know will give me the answer I need. My fingers shake as I type the website into the browser. F.A.C.E.B.O.O.K. *Please*, I beg in my mind. *Please.*

My eyes get big as my homepage pulls up. The news-feed is full of activity; there's a new page everyone in school seems to have "liked". My breath hitches in my throat and prickly tears sting my eyes, threatening to come streaming out at an uncontrollable rate.

Pippa Rogers Likes: *Minster High's Nicest Lesbians.*

John Arthur Likes: *Minster High's Nicest Lesbians.*

Sarah Wellington Likes: *Mister High's Nicest Lesbians.*

Sarah? My hand shakes as I move the mouse over the link and click. In less than a second, I'm staring at myself. Someone has photoshopped my face and Lil's on top of two female bodies and they're kissing.

"Oh my God," I squeak. The body isn't anywhere close to mine. It's tall and skinny and black. Lil's isn't any better. She almost looks like a midget. Why would someone do this? I want to turn off the computer and run away from the library, screaming, but I don't. I do the one thing I shouldn't. I start to read people's comments.

I didn't think nice meant this! I should have tapped her ass a lot sooner. Too bad she plays for the other team.

I don't think we have 2 wonder which 1 plays the man and which 1 plays the woman.

DYKES!!

The screen goes blurry and I clutch my stomach. I think I might throw up. Everything in my body is hot and itchy, eyes and words and so much pain I can't get my dry tongue to swallow anything down. A tear escapes and rolls down my cheek. *Not here. Please.*

But I can't stop it. Soon, my entire face is covered in water. I jump from my seat and run away from the eyes locked on me, hiding in the farthest, most secluded part of the library behind stacks of old books that smell like mothballs.

Pulling my knees to my chest, I bury my face so no one can see me. My shoulders tremble with every tear, and whimpers slip through my lips. My ears burn with all the words written on the page.

"I didn't think anyone came up here." I barely hear the male voice through my sobs.

"Just leave me alone," I say through my knees, my face still hidden.

"See, I can't do that. My brother told me that if a girl is crying, it's probably my best opportunity to get in her pants."

I look up and find Alex squatting in front of me, a bright smile on his face.

"I thought we'd established that your brother's not very smart," I say, practically hiccupping the words.

"He's not, but I got you to look at me, didn't I?" Alex sits down next to me, his back resting against the bookcase, long legs stretched out, red Converse sneakers on his feet.

"Are you sure you want to be seen with me?"

"Why wouldn't I want to be seen with you?"

"Haven't you heard I'm not into guys?" My head falls into my hands and I start crying again.

"I don't believe anything I read on the internet."

"That's not very smart. It's actually a wonderful learning tool," I say through my fingers. Alex leans into me and elbows my side. A tiny laugh escapes my lips.

"You know what else my brother says?" he whispers. I look at him, my head cocked to the side. "No, this one is actually good. He says people are assholes. He's usually referring to me, but in this instance I think it fits."

"Why would people do this?"

"Assholes," he shrugs.

"Do you think I'm a lesbian?"

Alex looks me up and down, starting at my head and scanning my entire body, all the way down to my feet. I get self-conscious imagining what my swollen, red face must look like and rub my cheeks with my palms.

"Well, I'm not sure what a lesbian looks like. My gaydar isn't very good. I mean, my uncle's been gay my whole life and it took me until last year to figure out that his roommate actually shares *his* room." Alex puts his finger to his mouth like he's thinking. "But if I had to guess, my answer would be no. You're not a lesbian."

"I'm not a lesbian," I say, shaking my head.

Alex exhales a long heavy breath. "Oh, thank God. There's a chance for me yet." And then he laughs. The sound makes my heart just a little bit lighter.

"But the rest of the school thinks I am! How can I walk down the halls with everyone staring at me?"

"Do you care what they think?"

Alex looks into my eyes and holds my gaze, like he knows I need him to mentally pick me up so I can get back on my feet. Do I care what people think? Part of me screams YES! But the other part of me, the part that's changed, knows I only care if people know the true me. That if my mom and Sarah and Pippa Rogers want to imagine a person they think I am, it's all a lie anyway. No matter what they say.

"Well, it's almost time to go to English." Alex stands up and holds out his hand. "Can I walk you there?"

I stare at his palm. Guilt pinches in my chest that I can't like Alex the way he wants me to like him. That my so-called lesbian brain is so wrapped around Matt there's no room for Alex. But I push the sensation down and slip my fingers through his.

"You and Lil would have some darn fine babies," Alex says as we walk out of the stacks. I elbow him in the side and he flinches dramatically.

"That's not even physically possible."

"I'm just sayin'." He shrugs his shoulders, and I smile.

Alex holds my hand all the way to English, with no regard for the eyes that follow us the entire time.

Lil is sitting in her seat when we get to class. The other students look from me to her and back again, waiting to see what we do, but Lil doesn't blink. She just spins her nose ring around and around, looking bored.

"So I'll pick you up at six on Friday," Alex says in a tone louder than usual. Our hands are still locked together, and I look at him, brow furrowed. He widens his eyes. "For our date."

I nod, anxious waves hitting my stomach from all the eyes on us, and whisper okay. Then, almost in slow motion, Alex releases my hand but spins my shoulders around to him. My hair whips through the air and hit his chest as I turn. And we're face to face. He leans down and places his lips on mine. They're warm and smooth and before my brain registers that he just kissed me in front of the entire class, it's over.

"I'm looking forward to it," he says loudly and walks to his seat in the back of the classroom. I gasp. Was that my first real kiss? I discount it and put it in the "stage kiss" category. Alex did it for show. For me.

Alex nods at Lil as he passes, but her black-rimmed eyes are on me. Then her mouth turns up into a devilish grin.

I breathe and stare back at everyone as I take my seat, my cheeks on fire, the whole class whispering. With Lil next to me and Alex in the back of the room, I don't seem to care as much. Or maybe it's the kiss. I can't tell; my mind is so fuzzy. My phone buzzes and I take it out of my purse.

Lil: *I can't believe u r cheating on me with Jock Strap.*

I laugh and snap my phone shut, but as the class drags on and the adrenaline of the moment wanes, I sink back into the hole I was in earlier. I've gone from Minster High's Nicest Person to a piece of meat for the school to play with. Out of the corner of my eye, Lil rubs her black pen in the groove she made her first week at school, digging even deeper into the wood. Her black boots tap the metal leg of the desk to a rhythmic beat like she does every day. Would I take back our friendship if it meant erasing the Facebook page? An answer rings from the bottom of my heart, from the place I hid until Lil walked into the classroom her first day. No.

But it still hurts, like a world is pressing on my heart so heavily I might crack in two. If I'm not moving with the crowd, it means I'm bumping against them. And they're stomping hard so I don't slow them down.

∽

"Can I speak with you, Marty?" Ms. Everley asks as I walk out of the classroom.

"You want a ride, Pollyanna?" Lil says from behind me. People are staring and I breathe, pushing down everything that makes me want to jump out of my skin. "I can wait in the parking lot."

I turn and smile at Lil. "Thanks."

"Lesbos," Mike Polanski whispers as he walks past. My stomach drops to the floor.

"This won't take long," Ms. Everley says as she stuffs last night's homework assignments into her bag. She waits until everyone has cleared out of class. I fidget with my hands, wringing my fingers together. I just want out of this school and into Lil's car, where I feel safe.

"That was quite a display," she says finally, sitting behind her desk and folding her hands together.

"Pardon?"

"You and Mr. Austin."

"Oh, that. Um..." My face heats up.

"Is there something you want to talk about?" Ms. Everley smiles. Her hot pink lipstick matches her hot pink scoop neck sweater.

"Why would you say that?"

"Well, for starters, you look like you got beat up your eyes are so swollen."

I dig in my purse for my mirror and check my reflection. I look like hell. Red splotchy bags below my eyes; not a speck of makeup left on my face. I can't believe Alex would even want to come close to me.

"Remember when we were talking about hot dogs last week?" Ms. Everley says, and motions for me to sit down at a desk.

"How some people like hot dogs and some people like the bun?"

"Exactly. If you were a vegetarian, would you eat the hot dog or the bun?"

"The bun," I say, not knowing where this conversation is going and why Ms. Everley has such a deep fascination with summer picnic food.

"Right. To a vegetarian, the hot dog would be gross; they would never even touch it." I nod and wait for her to bring up condiments. "Is there anything wrong with being a vegetarian if deep down inside you know that's who you are?"

"I don't think so," I shrug.

Ms. Everley gets up from her desk and walks over to sit next to me. "I heard some kids talking today, and I want you to know that it's okay to be who you are. Whatever that is."

I cringe and say a little too loudly, "Those are lies!"

"For you, maybe. But there are other kids in this school for whom that might not be a lie and how you react could change how they act."

"But I like boys! One boy in particular."

"I know. You and Mr. Austin made that quite clear." Ms. Everley gets up from the desk to wipe down the chalkboard. My stomach sinks as my mind pictures Matt a thousand times over. "All I'm trying to say is that if you didn't like boys, if you were a vegetarian and only wanted to eat the bun, that would be okay, too. Like I told you, I prefer the bun and I'm not ashamed of it."

I gape at Ms. Everley, at her tight sweater and black pencil skirt. At her shiny pantyhose with a black line up the back and tall stiletto heels.

"Are you saying," I gulp, "that you're a vegetarian?"

She smiles at me. "I tried meat once in high school. It's definitely not for me."

"But I know I like hot dogs," I say.

Ms. Everley nods and puts the eraser down in the tray. A thin line of chalk dust collects on her skirt. "As far as I'm concerned, Marty, you can be whatever you want. And I'm always here if you need to talk."

I stand up and grab my backpack off the ground. "Can I go now?" Ms. Everley nods, but I stop at the door.

"Thank you."

"Rotate ice with a heating pad," she says. "For your eyes. It'll bring down the swelling right away."

"How do you know that?"

"I've cried over a lot of girls in my time." Ms. Everley smiles at me and goes back to picking up the room.

I meet Lil out at her car.

"In trouble for your make out session with Jock Strap?" she asks, lighting a cigarette before we're even off school property.

"If I asked if you prefer a hot dog or the bun, what would you say?"

"Penis. I think I've made that clear." Lil turns up the music and rolls down all the windows. I lean my head back on the seat and let the wind rush through my clouded brain.

If you're shallow and thin,
You can't feel when people step on you,
But when you're deep and wide,
The weight of every person,
Who jumps on your soul?
Becomes a heavy ball,

You have to fight,
To toss off.
I'll take my chances though,
Even if it means I might get crushed some day.

CHAPTER 13

Lil tells me that taking the bus is for fucking douche-bags. She's going to pick me up and take me home every day from now on.

"I'll get you at the corner," she says as I get out of the car.

I barely nod my head I'm so tired. Up in my room, I rotate ice and a heating pad just like Ms. Everley said. The swelling in my eyes goes down almost instantly. At least I won't have to explain to my parents what happened.

And Ms. Everley is a vegetarian? But she doesn't look like one. In my mind, she becomes one big bun with boobs.

When Lil and I walk into school the next day, Sarah, Pippa, and Eliza are just walking out of the bathroom, lip gloss freshly applied. My stomach drops to the floor and an anger I've never felt consumes my mind. It shocks me how much I want to punch Sarah in the face. How could she like that page?

"Well, if it isn't Thing 1 and Thing 2," Pippa says.

Lil stops, her clomping boots becoming silent, and licks her red painted lips. Pippa's brown eyes get wide. "Has anyone ever told you, you look like a Weeble Wobble?" Lil says.

Pippa brushes her dark hair over her shoulder. "Whatever, carpet muncher."

The words sting deep in my heart, but I tap my foot on the ground and force myself not to care. I can't bring myself to look at Sarah. A part of me knew she was capable of doing

154

this, but another part thought we shared enough that she wouldn't dare. Lil doesn't even blink. Compared to "whore," I'm sure "carpet muncher" doesn't seem so bad.

Pulling on her arm, I force her to walk down the hall away from the three powdered and puffed girls. Nausea is slowly consuming my stomach and I don't want to spend another day stuck crying in the library behind a stack of smelly old books.

Lil turns when we're halfway down the hall and yells, "Nice dress, fire crotch!"

"Lil!" I whisper.

"What?"

"You can't yell things like that," I say.

"Isn't Sarah supposed to be your friend?" Lil snaps. "She sucks ass."

"But if you call her names, we're just as bad as them and I don't want to be like that."

Lil looks at me. Tears are so close to the surface they prickle my eyes. "Fine. I won't say anything," she says through clenched teeth.

"Thank you." I squeeze her arm. I'd hug her but I'm afraid someone will snap a picture and things will just get worse.

The Facebook page disappears after Ms. Everley brings it to Principal O'Neill's attention and he threatens to open an investigation. But the words don't go away. People hiss and laugh and whisper when Lil and I walk by, but as the days pass and it starts to snow, I care less. Seeing the ground blanketed in white with frozen solid soil underneath reminds me that life changes seasons, like my grandma said, and soon enough I'll be wrinkled with a day job and not free, driving in Lil's car with the windows down. The thought makes me sad, sadder than if the entire town thinks I like to make out with buns instead of hot dogs.

Each day when I get home from school, my house has changed. It starts with the Christmas lights. My mom insists on white. *Color is tacky and we are anything but*, she always says. Then it's the eight-foot Christmas tree. Then the ten nutcrackers on the mantle. Then the Nativity scene on the dining room table and the red and green towels and the mistletoe and garlands down the front staircase and the Santa toilet seat covers and my mom's endless Christmas sweaters. Soon my house is covered in so much shit, I can't find myself anymore. And it all makes me wonder if any part of my parents' existence is real or if life is just about covering up the truth with knickknacks and ugly Christmas sweaters with actual bells that hang off the front like chiming nipples.

My mom prances around the house with a big, fat smile on her face, totally content with herself, and I wonder if she knows this is all a way of disguising her real self. Like Sarah and her lip gloss. To them it isn't about loving everyone, like Jesus said, but loving the *right* people. That doesn't include homeless people, ugly people, poor people, gay people, or wonderful, bruised, banished-to-a-trailer people. I'm pretty sure Jesus would spit on my house and its plastic representation of love. Wasn't he born in a barn? I bet he'd rather be at Lil's. I bet he'd take one look around her trailer and remember what it felt like to be banished and he'd love her.

❧

I go downstairs Christmas morning to find that my parents got me a car. It's a twenty-year-old silver Honda that belonged to an old guy who died at the retirement home. My dad even put a big red bow on the hood, like in those holiday car commercials, except my car has rust around the base and a half-cracked windshield.

"Sorry, honey, but I couldn't get the entire bumper sticker off," my dad says as we stand in the snow, bulky winter coats thrown over our pajamas. At one point the sticker said *over worked and under laid*. Now, all that's left is *worked* and *lai*.

"Thanks, Dad. At least you got the *d* off. Now, I won't be completely mortified at school," I say.

"We figure you can take it to U of M and come home on the weekends when you're missing us." My mom smiles as she looks at the car, no regard for what I've said, like she didn't even hear me.

I stare at the car, the interior freshly cleaned and shined with Armor All, and all I can smell is death. I should be happy that I finally have a mode of transportation other than the bus, but it feels wrong to me, like this is another way of manipulating my life. I can already hear my mom telling me that she never wants to see my car parked in front of Lil's house again.

After all the presents are opened and my mom's neck is properly gleaming with new jewelry, I decide to take my car for a spin. I drive over to Lil's and knock on the trailer door.

"Pollyanna, what are you doing here? Wait, is that a new car?"

"Merry Christmas!" I say, and hold out a card. "Yeah, my parents bought it from a dead guy."

"What the hell kind of bumper sticker is that?"

"Long story," I say, shaking my head.

"Solid. Want to see what Maggie got me?"

I walk into the trailer, an ease coming over my body that's been missing all day, and take off my black pea coat, putting it on the bed. I was so anxious to get out of the house

I didn't even change out of my pink fleece pajamas and Uggs. "Where is she?"

"The store," Lil says as she rummages around in the closet. "We ran out of popcorn. I have a feeling she'll have to drive to Finley to find a place open today, so she might be gone a while. Tah-dah!" Lil emerges in a long black fur coat that goes all the way down to her ankles. She twists her hips. "Maggie found it at a thrift store in Columbus."

My hand skims over the glossy material. "My parents get me a dead man's car and you get a dead animal's coat. That sounds about right," I say and laugh.

Lil sits down next to me and smiles. Her face is scrubbed clean, no black makeup around her eyes. The white twinkle lights hanging in the trailer make a halo around her head and I think she might be the prettiest person I've ever seen.

"Open the card," I nudge her.

"I thought we agreed not to get each other anything."

"It's not what you think. Just open it." I smile.

She pulls out a white piece of paper with red and green writing in perfect calligraphy. An invitation to the Hart's Annual Post-Christmas Day party.

"A party at your house?" Lil says as she reads the card. "You know I can't come."

"I know. But I wanted you to know that I think you and Maggie should be there."

Lil takes the card and tacks it up on their cork board next to Maggie's waitressing schedule and Lil's school picture, in which she refused to take off her red sunglasses. "Thanks."

"Well, I better go. My mom will send out a search party if I'm not home for dinner."

I walk out to my car, but Lil stops me before I get in. "I

have something for you, too."

In her palm is the skull ring, silver and glinting off the snow.

"I can't take your ring."

She shoves it in my hand. "You already did. Merry Christmas, Pollyanna."

Lil disappears back into the trailer and I slide the ring on my finger. It fits perfectly.

☙

Outfitted in the gold dress my parents gave me for Christmas and Lil's Christmas gift, I stand in the foyer waiting for guests to arrive, twisting the ring around my finger. A stack of red and green house shoes sits next to me. *I don't want people scuffing up our bamboo floors*, my mom said. It's the same every year and in the past, I've loved it. My mom will flash the new necklace or earrings or ring my dad gave her. My dad will drink gin and tonics and tell bad dentist jokes, like *how many dentists does it take to change a light bulb? Three. One to administer the anesthetic, one to extract the light bulb, and one to offer the socket some vile pink mouthwash.* And I'll walk around the house passing out refreshments and getting compliments. *Marty, don't you look pretty. Marty, isn't that nice of you. Marty, will you marry my son, the one who can't get his life together and is high on pot every day?*

Except this year, I'm different and the thought of seeing Sarah and mean old Mrs. Schneider and my mom all painted and pretty for the show makes me want to scream. As I got ready, I decided the only way I'd survive and not end up running around the house screaming or writing poetry on my mom's perfect walls is if I let my mind think what it wants.

Mrs. Schneider is the first to arrive at the party every year. She walks in carrying a blue sweater and hands it to my mom.

"I finished it this morning. I had a bunch of free time since my kids don't visit me anymore and the nursing home won't let me drive outside of Minster," she says. Mrs. Schneider's the kind of mean that only affects old people because they realize they're dying and they want everyone to pay attention before they aren't able to say any more words because they're dead. She likes me, probably because in the past all I've done is nod and smile at her.

"Thank you!" My mom beams and hands me the sweater. The pokey thick material makes me sweat just from looking at it. "What do you say, Marty?"

"Thank you." My teeth are clenched so hard I might chip a tooth.

"Merry Christmas, Mrs. Schneider," my dad yells as he hands her a red pair of slippers.

"I thought I might freeze to death on the way over. The roads were terrible. What are my taxes paying for, anyway? A bunch of poor people who don't want to work for a living, that's what," Mrs. Schneider says. My dad holds her arm as she wiggles out of her shoes.

I smile. In my head I'm writing.
Chanel No. 5 won't cover your smell,
Or the fact that you're old,
And mean as hell,
So enjoy the party,
And did I mention,
Your kids really should,
Have a mothball intervention.
Ah. It's like a piece of the boulder on my chest has

chipped off, and even though I'm locked in my house with a bunch of vapor-filled people, I'm me.

The next to arrive are the Wackers and all four of their kids. Each one is more obnoxious than the last.

"So good to see you," my mom says, and holds out her hand to shake.

The youngest bolts away from the door, leaving a trail of white snow across the floor.

"Jimmy, get back here!" Mrs. Wacker yells before heading after him in her heels.

My mom leans into my dad and whispers, "Why must we invite them every year?"

"They're clients." He smiles and speaks through his teeth. "Big families mean big money."

My mom turns toward Mr. Wacker, who's holding his other three children by the back of their shirts, a smile as big as the moon returning to her face. "It's always so lovely to see you." She hands him their slippers.

"She's the one who insisted on four. I would have stopped at one." Mr. Wacker swipes the shoes from my mom and trudges into the living room.

The oldest is an asshole,
The next two are just brats,
The youngest is a whiner,
And the parents are living doormats.

Another rock chipped away. Soon everyone starts to file in. My chest is getting lighter and lighter.

No one's skin is that color,
When snows on the ground,
You look like an orange,
All wrinkled and round.
Chip.

You can drive a BMW,
All fancy and long,
But it won't change the fact,
You have a gumball-sized dong.
Chip. Chip. Chip.

I think Lil would like that one. I'm not sure I could say the word *dong* out loud, but it sounds like something Lil would do. As I walk around, it's like she's here with me and I smile. I'm sure my mom thinks I'm enjoying myself, when really the party is comparable to what I think going to the gynecologist is like. I've never been, but we saw a video in Health class that made Maxwell Smith pass out. That's kind of how I feel right now. Like my legs are stuck in stirrups.

The doorbell rings, and I answer it. Sarah and her parents stand under the twinkling lights of my front porch.

A bright halo she's wearing,
Around her pretty head,
Like one of the angels,
Who sang 'round Jesus' bed,
Best friend or enemy,
She stomped on my heart,
With one click of a button,
Our friendship fell apart.

CRASH! The boulder is back and heavier than ever.

"Merry Christmas, Mrs. Wellington," I say flatly.

"Marty, it's so good to see you." She wraps her boney arms around me and gives me a light hug, the kind when people pat your back but don't fully embrace. "Is your mother in the kitchen?"

I nod and the Wellingtons make their way into our home like it's their own. All except Sarah, who stays in the foyer, arms crossed, holding a pair of green house slippers.

"These don't match my outfit," she says, holding up the shoes.

"You could always leave," I say, so much animosity flowing through me. It's been weeks since the Facebook page and all she's done is hang out with Pippa and Eliza.

"I can't believe your parents got you a car."

"I think it smells like death." I stare down at my feet and move my weight from one foot to the other, not wanting to make eye contact. I always knew we'd grow apart at some point, like in college when I got a boyfriend or Sarah joined a different sorority. But everything that's happened has made me wonder if I imagined a bond for years because it was easier than walking different paths. Was it easier to be friends than be nothing at all?

"So where's Lil?" Sarah says, emphasizing the *L* with a dash of condescension. Bitchy meets insecure.

"Why do you care?" I bring my eyes off the floor and stare at her hard, so she can see what her actions have caused. Color rises on Sarah's cheeks. She fidgets with the slippers in her hands, pulling off a piece of lint and dropping it on the ground.

"I don't. It's just," she pauses and looks at me. "I miss you."

"You miss me?" I bark a little too loudly. "You liked that page, Sarah! Hell, you could have been the person who started it!"

"I didn't, I swear!"

"But you didn't stop it either." I step closer, a fire so low in my belly I might explode.

"I couldn't believe you were dumping me for *her*."

"You don't get it. No one needed to be dumped. You could've just been nice for once. *Lil* understands me."

"The daughter of a slutty, baby-killing teen mom turned stripper understands you? A person who wears clothes like she's dying and who would scare the devil himself? How can someone like that understand you?" Sarah points to my perfectly ironed gold dress. "Marty, I'm trying to save you before you fall down a hole you can't get out of."

My hands shake as I stand in front of my ex-best friend, words rising in my throat. Words I wanted to say the first time we played Barbies and she told me I had to be Ken. Words I should have said long ago, but couldn't formulate.

"Fuck off." I turn and stomp back to the kitchen, leaving Sarah, jaw slack, holding a pair of green house slippers. My mom's silver punch bowl that I polished for two hours yesterday sits on the corner of the granite island. I dig the ladle in and pour myself a heaping cup of egg nog. And then another. Leaning against the island, I gulp down the drink, trying to clear my head. The lights in my house seem too bright and hurt my eyes. Voices are bouncing around the open space, clogging my ears. At this moment, I hate my house.

"I told Marty I didn't want her spending any more time with that girl," my mom whispers to Mrs. Wellington as she stands by the sink, rinsing a glass. "You and I both know she's trash."

My hands clench so hard the nails dig into my skin, leaving little crescent moon imprints.

"Maggie knows better than to come into town. She's not wanted. And that includes her daughter, Lily." Mrs. Wellington takes the glass from my mom and wipes it with a Santa Claus kitchen towel.

I swig the rest of my drink and slam the cup down on the counter.

"Her name is LIL!" I scream. Both women turn around to

look at me.

"Martina Hart, what has gotten into you?" My mom half whispers, half barks.

"It's not about what's gotten into me, it's about what hasn't gotten into you!"

"Don't take that tone with me?"

"Or what?" I cross my arms over my chest.

My mom stomps over to me, her intense brown eyes becoming darker, and grabs my arm tight. "I will not have my daughter cause a scene at our family's Christmas party. Now, you get yourself together."

I yank my arm away. "Jingle Bells" plays over the surround sound speakers and pumps through the house.

"Fine." I grab my keys off the counter. "This party sucks anyway." I slam the door and run to my car. Pressing the gas pedal as far as it will go, I race down the driveway. It's cold and in my rage I forgot my coat, so I turn up the heat to full blast alternating which hand holds the steering wheel and which one sits in front of the vent. At the end of my street I shake my shoulders out and scream a loud, freeing break-from-my-chest scream. When I'm done, I turn toward the only place I can think of to go that my parents won't suspect.

༄

Vinyl Tap is the only establishment lit up on Main Street. Everything else is shut down for the week, Merry Christmas signs and Nativity scenes filling the windows. Going to Lil's would be too obvious. Plus, the last thing Maggie and Lil need is my mom banging down the trailer door and making a comment about their messy home.

I open the door, incense hitting my nose so strongly that I cough. It's warm inside, though. Just walking to the door chilled my legs so much I thought they might break off. I look down at my feet and realize I still have my red house slippers on. *Great.*

As I move through the store, I scan row after row of records, not sure what I'm looking for. I pull out the Beatles' *Abbey Road.* Lil's voice rings in my ears. *The Beatles, Pollyanna? Would you like some tampons with that?* I giggle to myself and look for a record Lil would approve. My fingers skim the cardboard covers. I can almost feel the lyrics radiating up my arm and into my heart.

Picking through a stack of bands that all begin with the letter N, I find one. The cover shows a baby underwater, swimming toward a dollar bill. It's clearly a boy. Nirvana. Lil would like this. I flip the record over to read the songs on the back.

That's when I hear it. Smooth, sexy guitar music. My heart jumps into my throat and I look in the direction of the noise. A door is propped open with an empty crate. Putting the record back in its proper alphabetical place, I follow the sound through the door and into the back storage room of Vinyl Tap.

The space has been converted into a music studio. Boxes with records and posters are piled in the corners to make room for chairs and instruments. A few people stand around. Some I recognize from school. Seniors, to be exact. A guy and a girl are whispering against the wall, him with his arm around her too-skinny shoulder. Stacked on top of his watch are brightly-colored string bracelets, the kind you make at camp when you're bored. Arm accessories.

Now, I know where I've seen them. They're friends with

Matt. I think his name is Cash or Elvis or Kurt Cobain. He kisses the blonde girl's cheek and then turns his attention to the center of the room. My eyes follow his.

Matt Three-Last-Names looks casual and unaffected, as he sits in a chair playing. His body curves around the guitar like it's an appendage. The sleeves on his black button down are rolled up, arm accessories in their proper places; tight dark jeans cover his legs. My knees get weak just looking at him.

As Matt strums chords on his guitar, I melt against the wall. He closes his eyes and taps his foot, a visible energy rolling through him, like each note surges with an emotion that he can't control. His hips move with the beat and I wonder what he imagines when he plays. Does he see the notes in his head or does a scene of something wonderful accompany the music? Or maybe he's imagining sex, because the way he moves his pelvis looks like humping. He's air humping music and I don't know if I've ever seen anything hotter in my life.

I watch his fingers move, plucking each note and chord. I want to be the guitar; I want his hands to feel me all over and know the curve of my hips and the feel of my hair in his hands. No one says a word while he plays, because it's spiritual and lively and so sexy I can't keep my thoughts under control and I know everyone in the room is thinking about sex. It's an orgy of music.

When it's over, I breathe for maybe the first time since I saw him. Matt looks up from his guitar and smiles at the people watching.

"Fucking brilliant!" Elvis with the colored bracelets yells over the clapping. "I want to bone you!" His girlfriend elbows him and he flinches, laughing. Matt smiles at him and then, like he can sense I'm standing in the room, his green eyes find mine and hold my gaze. I smile while little butterflies attempt to escape my stomach into the sex-filled air.

He puts his instrument down and thanks a few people for coming. I stand against the back wall, trying to hold my body upright. But all Matt does is turn me upside down.

"My Hart, this is quite a surprise," he says as he makes his way over to me.

"Well, I was in the neighborhood."

"I bet you were." He takes a loose strand of my hair and tucks it behind my ear, then looks me up and down. Double gulp. "Nice outfit."

I glance at my feet and wiggle my toes. "Trying to get in the Christmas spirit." I laugh as everything in me dies a thousand mortified deaths.

"I like the look." Matt smiles and I forget my name. All I know is he is the hottest thing I've ever seen.

"Dude, we're going to Carissa's for some refreshments." Elvis lumbers over, his arm still wrapped tightly around his girlfriend, almost like she's holding him up. He looks at me and then my shoes. "What's up with the slippers? Gift from your girlfriend?"

I fumble. Of course, he would know about the Facebook page. He might be a stoner but he's not blind. Heat rises in my cheeks and I struggle with what to say.

"Girlfriend, huh?" Matt says and smiles his crooked grin at me. "I didn't think you could get hotter, but apparently I'm wrong."

"I don't have a girlfriend," I blurt out, and cup both my burning cheeks with my hands. Did he just say I was hot?

Matt winks and then turns to Elvis and Carissa. "I'll pass, but thanks for the invite."

"You could do it with a girl," Elvis says to his girlfriend under his arm. "I'd totally be into that." Carissa shakes her head and drags Elvis-Cash-Kurt-Cobain out of the storage room.

Matt turns to me. "So what did you think of my playing?"

I stammer. "Magical." It's the only word, other than SEX, that comes to mind. A magical tour of all things Matt. I swear I could feel his soul in every note.

"If you're not taking those awesome slippers anywhere else tonight, want to grab a coffee?" he asks.

I nod. I'm speechless, an overwhelming happy feeling flooding my veins. Thank God I left my parents' lame party.

"Let's get out of here," he smiles.

We walk out the back door of Vinyl Tap and into the alley. Cold wind shoots between the buildings, sending my shoulders into instant convulsions.

"Where's your coat?" Matt asks.

"I kind of forgot it."

He smiles and wraps his navy blue fleece around the two of us. His arm hugs my shoulder as he pulls me close into his side. He smells like autumn, fresh leaves and clean air. I take a breath and drink it in. Holy hell. I might faint.

"So did you really like it or are you just being nice?" Matt asks into my ear.

My face turns up toward his, his breath warming my nose. "I really liked it," I say. I want to say so much more. That I'm done being nice just because I'm supposed to. That I feel like I'm standing on the edge of a cliff with wind whipping my hair all over the place and I'm ready to jump into the abyss no matter what's down there. "You looked amazing. I mean, sounded amazing."

Damn it. Freudian word flub. I'm losing it.

"You look amazing, too." Matt smiles and I melt clear to the cold, snowy pavement. Every time I wear this gold dress, I'll remember tonight. Not the bad Christmas party and Sarah's mean words, but Matt and the way he played the guitar and how I wanted to know his hands inside and out and have them know me.

We walk for a few more seconds in silence, the crunch of our footsteps the only noise, before he turns to me. "Are you sure you don't have a girlfriend? Because I don't want to piss anybody off."

"No girlfriend." I make an X over my heart and smile at him.

A weird expression crosses his face, like two things in his head are battling each other and he can't decide which one wins.

"Can I be honest with you?" Matt asks. I stare into his eyes, mine getting wide at the thought of what he wants to confess. "You make me feel good, but I'm not good at being careful."

"You make me feel good, too." I lean into his side more. My mind somersaults in euphoria just saying the words.

"But maybe this is a bad idea."

"What's a bad idea?" I ask.

"Remember last year when you told me that sometimes it isn't about solving the math problem, it's about the process? That even if the answer is wrong, at least I attempted to work it out and it just went all screwy at some point."

"Sure," I say, totally thrown.

"I'm confused," he says.

"Okay." I shrug my shoulders. *Me too.* I'm lost in the land of math and I want to be lost in the land of Matt.

"I like you, Marty," he says, wiping a few strands of hair from my forehead. Shivers climb up and down my spine in crazy, sexy waves. He reaches for my wrist, his fingers thumbing the black bracelet. "You still have it."

I nod, unable to speak.

"Maybe if I..." He takes hold of my hand and presses it to his lips. My breath catches in my throat. *Oh God. Oh God!* My insides scream. "Maybe we could ..."

His face leans down toward mine and I close my eyes. This is it. This. Is. It. It's like waiting for the first firework to go off. I'm scared of the noise, but I can't wait to see the colors. And then his lips fall on mine. YYYEEEELLLLLPPPPP!!!!! A thousand times over and over and over. They're soft and sweet as they move with mine. I try to keep my hands from shaking, but when he wraps his arms around my back like he did when we danced, and his coat falls to the ground, my knees rattle together. It's like the sun that lives in my soul is exploding into a million pieces of light and I'm on fire. And it's better than any thought I've ever had, better than any movie scene I've ever watched, better than any moment of my living and breathing seventeen years on this planet.

His hands travel up my back to my neck and tangle in my hair. But the second I think he might go a step further, he pulls back, his lips inches from mine. "Shit," he whispers. Pause. I want his lips back on mine. Pause. I want to do it again. Pause. I can't wait to tell Lil. "This is trouble."

"What's wrong?" I ask, my voice coming out breathless.

"You make me do and say things I shouldn't."

DOUBLE YELP! I go back at him, running my fingers through his hair and groping his chest and back. I taste his tongue and lips until our mouths are so mixed up, I don't know who is leading and who's following. I don't even know my name anymore. It's all been replaced by his lips on mine and our tongues touching and his fingertips on my cheeks and then my collarbone and then back into my hair. I'm on the verge of letting it all go. It's like the caged animal inside of me has been set free and now I can't control it. I want every single piece of him.

"Look, Marty, I like you," Matt says, out of breath.

"I like you, too." I pull down on his neck and kiss him again.

"I better go." He drops his arms from around my body and grabs his coat off the ground. "Keep the slippers. They're sexy." He looks at me, his green eyes wicked and sweet at the same time. My arms want to reach out and grab him, to never let go, but I hold them down tight at my side. Matt leaves me alone outside of the record store, his breath still in the cold night air that travels up my legs and around my dress, chilling my bones to the core.

Everything moments ago was hot and sweaty and delicious.

Another gust of arctic wind blows down the alley, scorching my burning cheeks like ice on fire. My phone buzzes with a text message and I jump.

Mom: *Get home right now young lady.*

I stare at the phone. My mind spins with thoughts of Matt pressed against me, his tongue on my lips and neck and ears. And his body, disappearing into the blackness of the night.

જ

All the guests have left when I pull into the driveway, but every light is on. I park behind my dad's Audi and cut the ignition. *Let's get this over with*, I say to myself.

My parents are cleaning the kitchen when I walk in. My mom is rinsing dishes and handing them to my dad to load the dishwasher, their movements synched like a well-oiled machine. I hang my keys on the key hook and they turn around.

"Well, that was quite a display," my mom says, smacking the Santa towel over her shoulder.

"It wasn't a display," I say.

My mom shakes her head and grabs the edge of the sink. "Where did you go?"

I stare at them, tight-lipped, the smell of Matt still on my dress.

"Did you go to Lil's?" my dad asks as he pours detergent into the dishwasher and starts it. At least he used the right name. I still don't answer.

"Are you a lesbian, Marty?" my mom finally asks when too much silence has passed between us.

"What?" I bark.

"I just can't wrap my head around a daughter of mine defying my very explicit rules."

I run my hands over my lips, lips that were just kissing the hottest guy in school. Lips that want to do it again and again and again.

"I'm going to bed." I turn and head for the stairs.

"You're grounded for a month," my mom says as she turns back to the sink. "Leave your phone on the counter."

I stop in my tracks, my fists clenching around the one thing I don't want to give up. Taking a deep breath, I smack the phone down and step my way up the stairs as lightly as I can.

Once in my room, I slam my bedroom door so hard

specks of pink paint chip off the wall and land on my white carpet.

&

When I was younger
I wanted a boy to kiss me
So I knew I was pretty.
When I was older
I wanted a boy to kiss me
Because my body begged
To know the life caught
In another person's soul.
After I was kissed,
I wanted to go back
To before
When I wondered
What it would feel like
To be kissed.

CHAPTER 14

To: <u>RPMcMurphy@o-mail.com</u>
From: <u>marty.hart@o-mail.com</u>
I'm grounded for a month. A month! No phone unless I'm at school. Don't text me.

To: <u>marty.hart@o-mail.com</u>
From: <u>RPMcMurphy@o-mail.com</u>
Grounded? What'd you do? Get sloppy drunk at the X-Mas party and take ur bra off?

To: <u>RPMcMurphy@o-mail.com</u>
From: <u>marty.hart@o-mail.com</u>
Yelled at my mom and left the stupid party. Told Sarah to fuck off. Went to Vinyl Tap and made out with Matt. :)

To: <u>marty.hart@o-mail.com</u>
From: <u>RPMcMurphy@o-mail.com</u>
Shit, Polly. Maybe I should've come to the party. I would've liked 2 c that. Not the making out w/ Matt part. No offense. :) U didn't let him... strum ur guitar, did u?

To: <u>RPMcMurphy@o-mail.com</u>
From: <u>marty.hart@o-mail.com</u>

LOL!! NO! I did NOT let him strum my guitar... but I might. :)

To: marty.hart@o-mail.com
From: RPMcMurphy@o-mail.com
With u in the slammer, there go my New Year's Eve plans. Maggie will be bummed. I'll c u next year, Pollyanna.
PS- Matt doesn't deserve ur guitar strings.

To: RPMcMurphy@o-mail.com
From: marty.hart@o-mail.com
HAPPY NEW YEAR! *throws confetti* I'll c u at school.
PS- U R a Juliet, whether u like it or not. :)

To: matt.3.names@o-mail.com
From: marty.hart@o-mail.com
Hi Matt!
I wanted to wish you a Happy New Year! It was great 2 c u the other night. I'm grounded for a month, but it was worth it. :) Maybe when I'm released we can hang out again?
-Marty

To: marty.hart@o-mail.com
From: matt.3.names@o-mail.com
Have I told u I think it's cute u use email? Very vintage, just how I like it. Sorry to hear ur locked up for the month. I was thinking about you 2day. I miss ur slippers.
-Matt

From: marty.hart@o-mail.com
To: matt.3.names@o-mail.com
It's OK. What were you thinking about?
PS- I'm wearing the slippers right now.

To: marty.hart@o-mail.com
From: matt.3.names@o-mail.com
How I want to marry someone just like u 1 day.

To: matt.3.names@o-mail.com
From: marty.hart@o-mail.com
Did u just ask me to marry u over email?

To: marty.hart@o-mail.com
From: matt.3.names@o-mail.com
Maybe I did. In 10 yrs will u marry me?

To: matt.3.names@o-mail.com
From: marty.hart@o-mail.com
I don't know if I can wait 10 yrs.

To: marty.hart@o-mail.com
From: matt.3.names@o-mail.com
Don't wait. I'm a mess.

To: matt.3.names@o-mail.com
From: marty.hart@o-mail.com
I like ur mess.

To: marty.hart@o-mail.com
From: matt.3.names@o-mail.com
Hey, I saw u down the hall earlier and wanted to say

hi. Hi. I'm still thinking about u. R u thinking about me? Maybe we could run away together and I'll play my guitar and u can sing and we'll make money street performing.

To: matt.3.names@o-mail.com
From: marty.hart@o-mail.com
Where would we go?

To: marty.hart@o-mail.com
From: matt.3.names@o-mail.com
New York? LA? Paris? U pick.

To: matt.3.names@o-mail.com
From: marty.hart@o-mail.com
Tokyo.

To: marty.hart@o-mail.com
From: matt.3.names@o-mail.com
When u get married, I'm going to watch from the back of the church and think it could've been me. U'd look nice in a white dress. As long as u wear ur slippers. :)

To: matt.3.names@o-mail.com
From: marty.hart@o-mail.com
I thought we were getting married in 10 years? :)

Matt never responds.
So I write this:
Rapture captured,
A black music note,

Disguised in blonde hair,
And caked in love,
But words filled with air,
Float in the sky,
Only to be popped,
By thorns of substance.

I live out my sentence tucked away in my room, writing for hours and hours. I grumble when I go downstairs for dinner so my parents think their master plan has worked, but really I feel freer than ever. I spend time with Lil at school and email with Matt and nobody seems to care. The people around us become quiet, like the new year has brought a new beginning and even though I'm banished to my pink room, I'm calm.

On my last day of grounding, I decide to go into our basement storage room and clean out my bin of spring clothes to give to charity. Something inside tells me that by the time the weather gets warm, I won't have any use for the clothes I wore last year. I pull out dress after dress and stack them in the giveaway pile. The one I wore for my yearbook photo. The Spring Fling knee-length lavender frock I bought with Sarah. Pink and purple and red and green. So many colors and yet the girl who wore them didn't see the world that way. Now, everything's a rainbow. When I'm done, all that's left of my old clothes are a few of my favorite mod-style dresses and the show t-shirt I got for *Guys and Dolls*. I stuff the giveaway clothes into a black garbage bag and smile at the bonus points I'll get for doing something my mom usually has to nag me about for weeks every spring.

When I place the near-empty bin back on the stack, my eye catches a brown box pushed into the farthest corner of the storage closet. The handwriting on the top is a thousand memories rolled into perfect cursive; it makes my stomach drop to my knees. My grandma. "Robert's Memory Box". Anxious, like a piece of her might be locked in this musty dark corner of our storage room, I push aside the bins in my way and tear it open. Inside is every school photograph of my dad from high school, a jersey from his basketball days, his Minster High School diploma. Even a spelling bee trophy. My grandma kept it all.

I rummage around, putting together the pieces of my dad's younger life. A life I wasn't part of, a life in which he played sports and went to dances and sat in a desk day in and day out. When he was like me, maybe, lost or confused. Before fixing braces and cavities became his passion.

At the bottom of the box, I find a stack of black and white photos. Each one is a different scenic shot. A cornfield in the middle of summer. A barren tree. An empty railroad track that trails into the distance until it meshes together with the sky. I flip over the photo and see my grandma's handwriting on the back. "Robert's Senior Photography Class". The railroad photo even has a note from my grandma: *this one's my favorite.*

"My dad was into photography?" I say out loud, looking at the photo like my grandma might answer back.

As I'm about to dig deeper into the box, my mom's car pulls up the driveway. I stuff everything back in its place as quickly as possible and shove the box in the corner again. I make it upstairs with my bag of old clothes just as my mom walks in the back door.

"Here," I say, and drop the bag on the floor, a plastic smile on my face. "I thought I'd clean out my bin in the basement."

My mom nods approvingly at the black bag and slips into her house slippers.

"I'll drop these off at the Salvation Army tomorrow."

I nod and go up to my room to finish out my grounding in silence. But as I sit at dinner that night, I stare at my parents, at my mom's eyes, almond-shaped just like a cartoon character's, and my dad's hands, thin and strong. So many wonderful physical features. Whether I've paid attention before or not, I know them because they're mine.

"Dad, did you always want to be a dentist?" I ask, his beautiful photos still on my mind.

He looks at me, mouth full of potatoes. "I don't know. I guess I just knew I didn't want to be a farmer."

"Why not?"

"Because farming is hard work and not a lot of money," he says.

"So you became a dentist for the money."

"Marty, you know we don't talk about money," my mom says, patting the side of her mouth with a cloth napkin. She's still dressed in her white Shady Willows Retirement Community and Nursing Home collared shirt.

"Why not?"

"Because it's rude." My mom cuts her meat with precision, the fork in her left hand and a knife in her right, sawing with just enough pressure on the pork. She takes the newly-cut piece and places it in her mouth, chewing quietly for at least ten seconds before swallowing.

I look back at my dad. "Did you ever want to be something else? Like an artist maybe?"

"Marty, where is this coming from?"

I keep wondering if my dad thinks about taking pictures. If he remembers that specific time in his life and wishes he'd held strong to what he loved. Maybe all this wanting and desire and need for life *is* from my parents, but they've spent so many years fixing people's gnarly teeth and decorating a house with meaningless shit that it's been suppressed too far below the surface, and they don't know how to let it out anymore.

"I want to know you guys better," I say.

"Honey, you've known me your entire life." My dad gets up from the table, his plate in hand, and walks into the kitchen. The only thing I hear is the sound of his slippers swishing against our bamboo floors.

I look back at my mom, hoping that for once she'll open the door to what's really under her perfect nails and skin, but she doesn't even look at me. Just takes a sip of her Chardonnay, licks her lips, and then clears her plate.

As I go to sleep, I wish I could know my parents before they had me, before life got so real they lost themselves. They lived so many years without me and had so many experiences and I'll never know those people. In fact, I'm not even sure they remember who they were. Just thinking about it makes me want to cry because someday when I have a baby, she won't know me either. She won't know about the boy with the guitar and my best friend with eyes the color of the sky, because it's all happening right now. Tomorrow it will be gone.

಄

I sit in the parking lot the next morning, waiting for Lil to pull in. As I turn up the heat in my ancient car and rub my hands together, excitement bubbles over me. I can do anything today. Run through the fields behind my house, go pick up that Nirvana record at Vinyl Tap, drive with Lil at lightning speed down Forest Street and hang our heads out the window, screaming. And my parents can't stop me. I laugh to myself; I've changed my mind. Grounding sucks.

At 8:15, Lil still hasn't arrived. The bell will ring in five minutes and while she might not care about school as much as I do, she's always on time. I spin the skull ring around my finger and cut the engine. I can't be late, not on my first day out of seclusion.

But Lil isn't in English, either. I stare at her desk, waiting to hear her boots on the linoleum floor, but they never appear. A lump rises in my throat, and I send her a text.

Marty: *I HAVE MY PHONE BACK!! Where R U? Sick?*

I stare at the screen and tap my pen on the desk in an even rhythm. The bell rings for the end of the day. I haven't taken a single note. Lil must be sick. People get sick. Stuffing my phone in my purse, I pack up my empty notebook.

"Are you thinking about your audition?" Alex comes up next me in the hall.

"What?" I ask.

"The look on your face. Are you worried about your audition for *Grease*? Because I'm sure you'll be great." He nudges my side and smiles.

"Yeah," I nod.

"You're a shoe-in for Sandy. I can't imagine Mr. Spector casting someone else," he says as we reach my locker.

"I was actually thinking about trying out for Rizzo," I mumble.

"What's that?"

"Nothing. Sandy. Thanks." I pull out my phone. Still no text. My fingernails strum on the metal locker. I'm overreacting. Lil probably has her head in the toilet. The flu is going around.

Alex leans his shoulder against the wall, towering over me as I grab my homework. "So I know you were grounded for what happened at your parents' Christmas party."

"You heard about that?"

Alex shrugs. "Small town. Anyway, I've been counting down the days and since today marks the beginning of your free-from-lockdown life, I was wondering if maybe…"

My Math notebook slips from my hands. I try to shove it into my backpack and worksheets spill all over the floor.

"Shit!" I cut Alex off and bend to collect the mess around my feet.

"Let me help you." He leans down at the same time and our heads bang together.

"Double shit." Falling back on my butt, I grab my forehead.

"I'm such an ass," Alex says and shakes his head. "Are you okay?" He reaches out to touch me, but I slink back.

"I'm fine." Crawling on my hands and knees, I start to collect the scattered papers before people step on them. I'm beginning to hate today. Why isn't Lil texting me? Why isn't she here? Rubbing my sore head, I'm blaming everything on her even though I know it's irrational.

As I grab the last piece of paper, Matt Three-Last-Names rounds the corner of the hallway. My breath catches in my throat. He hasn't emailed me in over a week. I want to look away, but I can't. My eyes are stuck on him and the sexy bright yellow vintage Cheerios T-shirt he's wearing.

"Nice to see you, My Hart," Matt says as he passes. He winks and I sit back on my heels, melting clear to the floor. His hair shines in the fluorescent lights of the school and his tight jeans hug his butt in perfect round form. *Breathe, Marty.*

A brunette girl joins him at the door. I recognize her. Senior, cheerleader, name Meghan Whitlock. He touches her arm. A bowling ball-size stone falls in my stomach, but I tell myself she's just a friend. We kissed, after all. His lips touched mine. Who cares about an arm? And Matt e-mails me. That means something.

Remembering his hands in my hair sends tingles down my arms and relieves the gaping hole in my gut. Sort of.

"Here," Alex says. He hands me a stack of papers and stands up.

"Thanks." I look over my shoulder one last time as Matt goes out of view. When I turn back to Alex, he's staring past me in the same direction.

"Well, I can tell you're distracted." He pauses, a tension in his jaw I've never seen before. And then he smiles. "About your audition, of course."

"I am. I'm sorry." The lie falls out of me like water.

"I'll see you tomorrow." Alex walks away, shaking out his arms, his broad athletic figure growing even wider as it shifts into a silhouette.

With no text from Lil, I drive home and spend the afternoon the same way I have the past month. Alone in my room.

❧

Two more days pass. No Lil. No texts. No emails. Nothing. As I pull into the parking lot, nerves zing through my entire body. I tell myself she has the flu or maybe mono, but even in a drugged-out stupor Lil speaks. Last night I sent her a text that said I was going to become a Rolling Stones fan if she didn't respond. And she didn't respond. To be silent isn't in her nature. I stare at the clock as it ticks on. 8:15. 8:17. 8:20. The bell rings; no Lil.

I bang my hand on the steering wheel. That's it. I speed out of the parking lot, not caring how mad my parents will be at me for skipping school, how I'll probably be grounded for life all over again, and drive straight to Lil's house.

I see the silver trailer reflecting in the sunlight half a mile down the road, but it's different today. Colors are painted on the outside in a design that's hard to make out. Did Maggie get creative or something? I know it can't be Lil. She's in Shop at school, not Art.

As I get closer, my stomach rolls with nausea and I almost pull over to the side of the road and throw up the granola I ate for breakfast. The trailer is painted, but not in the way I thought. Colorful words become visible from the road, red and blue and black and green all smeared together. *Whore. Slut. Dyke. Baby killer. Trash.* I blink and pray they'll disappear, but they don't. Tears stream down my cheeks as I pull into the Addison Farm driveway.

I bang on the door, my fist clenched so tight my fingers feel like they'll break.

"Lil, open up!" I scream. Nothing. "Come on, I know you're in there!"

I step back and stare at the external damage done to Lil's home. Somehow I know the internal scars will never fade. *Sticks and stones may break my bones but words can make me bleed to death.* Who would do something like this?

"Please," I say. "Please open the door. Or I'm going straight to Vinyl Tap to buy a Justin Bieber record."

The door flies open. Lil stands in the doorway, her blue eyes bloodshot and swollen, clutching a copy of *One Flew Over the Cuckoo's Nest.*

"Don't even joke about something like that." She points the book at me.

I inhale a deep breath far into my lungs, relief washing over me. "Got you to open the door," I smile.

She shakes her head and motions me inside.

Even with awful words etched into the trailer on the outside, it's the same when I walk through the door, like my chest has opened up to the sunlight and it's warming me. Lil walks over to the record player and turns down the music.

"Reading?" I ask.

She nods, then dog ears her page and closes the book.

"*Anne of Green Gables*," I say and point to Lil's book. "It's my go-to. I read it at least once a year."

She nods, picking up a basket of laundry, and starts to fold. I'm surprised how colorful the clothes are. Purple and red and orange. They must be her mom's.

"Where's Maggie?" I ask.

"At an interview." Lil folds a shirt and adds it to the pile, not looking at me. "Apparently, she doesn't want to be a waitress forever."

I sit down on her bed and wring my hands together. The pressure of what's written outside on the trailer is squashing my breath. I know I need to ask, but what to say? Too many things have been said, said all over in bright violent words. Unclenching my hands, I run them down the cotton material of my dress, pressing it straight, and notice a red string hanging down from the bottom hem. Thinking I can pull it off, I try to snip it with one clean yank, but it unravels even more. Damn it. Wrapping the string around my finger, I give it one more pull and it snaps. No one would know a little section has fallen loose from the rest of the fabric. It's like it never happened. Why can't I do that to the words?

"What happened?" I finally ask.

Lil waves her hand through the air, a red bra clenched tight in her fist. "You know, we thought we'd liven up the place with some spray paint."

"Don't do that."

"Do what?" Lil smacks the bra down and looks into my eyes, her blue gaze so intense it takes up the entire space, like water is slowly filling her insides and she might over-flow.

"Don't be funny. This is serious."

"You don't think I know that?" Lil shoves her hands across the bed, blowing the neatly folded clothes to smith-ereens.

"Just talk to me," I say, and walk over to her. She backs away.

"What is there to talk about? You can see it. Do you want me to tell you that they came in the middle of the night? That they were such cowards that they couldn't even do it in broad daylight? Or that my mom came home from her shift and cried? Or that my grandpa told her it's what she deserves."

"Lil ..."

"Don't! Don't feel bad for me. I don't want your pity. Pity is for pussies." She sucks in a breath, running her hands through her hair.

"I don't pity you," I say and try to grab her hand. She pulls her arm away and runs out of the trailer. I rush after her, the cold of the day chilling me to my core.

"I just want to help," I yell after her.

"Help?" she screams. "Do you want to scrub this piece of shit until the words are gone?" Lil kicks the base of the trailer; rust falls from the bottom. "Because they'll never be gone. Maggie lives with the words people say about her every damn day."

"But they're not true!"

Lil fixes her eyes on me, a burning fire behind the blue that I've never seen before. She grabs a rock from the ground and shoves it in my face. "Truth is subjective. If I told you this was a bird every single day for the next ten years, eventually you'd start calling it that."

"But I'd know it was a rock even if I called it a bird," I say.

She throws the rock into her grandpa's barren field, hurling it hard and high in the air. It disappears into the sunlight and then falls back to the earth with a thud. Lil kicks the ground with her boot, sending up a spray of sludgy snow and dirt.

"You're only one person and you're different, Marty. Most people would call it a bird and move on." She points at the trailer. "This is the truth to everyone. Everyone! We can never just be. Why can't we just be!" she yells into the air, falling back on her heels and dropping her arms to her side like they're two-ton boulders. Tears stream down Lil's face, the blue in her eyes matching the clear winter sky behind her, and she looks at me. "Why won't they leave us alone?"

I run to her and wrap my arms around her tough figure. She stiffens and falls into my embrace like holding up the world has become too hard. And I want to support her. To let her crumble, like I've crumbled so many times with her.

"Someone told me once that people are assholes," I say into her hair.

Lil snuffs a laugh into my shoulder. "Did you seriously threaten me with Justin Bieber?"

I pull back and smooth the dark hair that's caught in her

tears on her face. "I did."

We laugh, a deep belly-shaking laugh in the middle of the field where Maggie's baby was found, next to a trailer with lies painted on the side.

A rock is a rock no matter how badly it wants to fly.

"I want to show you something," I say, walking arm and arm with Lil back to the trailer.

She takes a deep breath, running her hand along one of the words, her finger following the letters. TRASH. "Let me get my coat."

❧

We drive over to my house in my car. It's weird to be on the streets in the middle of the day when I should be in school. I roll down the windows and let the cool wind clear Lil's face of any remaining tears.

Up in my room, she sits on my bed, hugging a pink pillow against her black fur coat. The space looks weird with such a black figure surrounded by all the light, but I like it.

"I can't believe I've never been in your house," she says, shifting back on my bed until she's almost lying down. "It's pink. I like the stars, though. I had some in my room in Florida."

I walk over to my desk and open the bottom drawer. My hand practically shakes as I open the box with all my poems. A thousand questions and worries circulate through my brain, but I swallow them down.

"Here," I say, holding out the box.

"What is it?" Lil sits up on her elbows.

I set the box down on the bed and Lil pulls back the lid. She leafs through the pages, her fingers skimming over all the words I've locked away.

"If I stretched my veins around the entire world,
Would my heart beat with it?
Or would I squeeze the life out of everything,
Would red run over the water and turn it to poison,
Or would my blood mix with life
And we would all know what it felt like to be alive." Lil reads off one of the sheets.

"You wrote that?"

I nod, a nervous bubble squeezing my throat. I've never heard someone read my words out loud and I don't know if it's good or bad or nonsense. Lil's face doesn't reveal anything.

"It's beautiful, Pollyanna," she says. "Like you're screaming all over the page."

An exhale pushes out of my chest, coming from my words and from the box that's kept so much locked up for so long. For the first time, everything in me breathes.

"Not all words are bad," I say as I sit down next to her.

Lil looks at me, and then grabs my hand in hers. "You're my best friend."

We lie on my bed and she reads through more of my poetry with no regard for the time or the fact that we both should be in school or that Lil's home has been ruined.

"You should be a writer, Marty," Lil says.

I shake my head. "I'm not that good." I pause for a second and think the words in my head before saying them into the universe. "You're not your mom."

Lil turns to look at me, her dark hair falling to the side of her face. "What if everyone leaves me like they did her?"

"I won't." I say, grabbing her hand and holding her black polished fingers between mine.

I don't know where I was before this year. Lost in some floating atmosphere, maybe, filled with smiles and politeness and absolute nothing. Lil brought me back from the dead.

We lie, heads touching and hair mixing together, strand after strand overlapping. A meshing of two people, each with her own distinct color and texture, but so beautiful when chaotically woven together.

"I have an idea," I say, sitting up.

"Does it involve little Cupids holding shotguns?"

I roll my eyes, "No."

"Shot through the heart and you're to blame," Lil sings.

"Shut up!" I elbow her and she laughs. "But we have to go back to your place."

"That's fine. This pink is making me want to vomit." Lil gets up off the bed as I stuff all the poetry back in my box. "Seriously, Marty, your poems are beautiful."

I smile as I close the desk drawer. "Let's get the hell out of here."

&

"Do it," I say.

Lil's trailer is silent. Not even she has snappy words for this moment.

"Are you sure, Pollyanna?"

I nod and say, "I trust you."

Lil smiles at me with deep, crystal blue eyes. "Okay. Maybe you shouldn't look."

I close my eyes and breathe. The only sound that echoes in the trailer is the splitting of scissors. *God's blessing.* They touch the hair falling at my shoulders, the cool metal pressing against my skin for just a second. *It's a thing of beauty.* Lil touches my arm and I know I'm safe. *Never cut it.*

Then I hear it. Snip. Mahogany hair rains down from my head and onto the floor. With each strand a weight is lessened in my heart. By the time Lil is done cutting, I'm so free I might float.

CHAPTER 15

My dad is sitting at the table when I walk through the back door, still dressed in his doctor costume of baby blue scrubs and ugly brown clogs, the *Columbus Dispatch* laid out in front of him. I jump at the sound of his voice.

"You're home," he says. "And your hair? I'll leave that one for your mother. How was school?"

I choke a little and set my backpack on a hook by the back door, trying to act calm. "Fine." Shit. Shit. Shit.

"Sit down for a second, Marty." He pats the seat next to him. I spin the skull ring around my finger to keep my hands from shaking. I'm dead. D.E.A.D.

He walks over to the stove and sets the water in the tea-pot to boil. "Hot chocolate?" he asks. I nod, not wanting to say anything for fear the truth will come spilling out of me at a million miles a minute.

I was doing something good today! Helping a friend like you taught me!

My dad empties two packets of hot chocolate powder into mugs, and then sits back down next to me. He smells like mint mouthwash. "You know, I remember painting your room before you were even born. Your mom was so sure you were a girl. She insisted on pale pink." His lips turn up in a smile. "I know most men are supposed to want boys, but I prayed she was right. Not to talk badly about my gender, but teenage boys kind of gross me out."

I want to say to him that mom's always right in her mind. That she just got lucky that what she thought was actually true. Instead, I nod and wait for the last domino to fall.

"It was your grandma's room before that," Dad says.

I sit up straighter. "It was?"

The teapot whistles. My dad nods, getting up to pour water in our mugs. "She liked to see the sunrise through the window in the morning. Said if she was going to lose her mind she better have a good view." He plops three marshmallows on top of each cup and places one in front of me. I blow across the top, steam swirling up my nose.

"She always made sense to me," I say.

"You have her eyes," Dad says.

"I do?" A grin widens on my face behind my mug, but in the next beat it falls. "Some days I have a hard time remembering her."

"Me too."

We sit, our hands wrapped around steaming cups of hot chocolate, taking sips every few seconds. Just like when I was younger and came in from sledding or making a snowman with Sarah. Three marshmallows. Not too many. Not too few.

"Why did you let mom tear up Grandma's kitchen?" I finally ask.

My dad gulps down the last bit of his drink, gets up, and walks over to the sink. "Keeping it the same wouldn't have brought her back," he says as he rinses the cup and puts it in the dishwasher.

"But it would remind us of her."

My dad turns to look at me, resting his back on the sink. "Do you think your grandma would want this, us just sitting around in her kitchen remembering her?"

I chuckle, hearing her rough voice in my head. *Get your ass out of this nursing home and don't come back unless it's to break me out. And bring whiskey. They don't allow me any of that. You'd figure if I'm going to die here, at least I could be drunk.*

He walks over to me and rubs his thumb across my cheek. "I don't need a kitchen to remember her, Martina. I have you."

"You really think I look like her?"

"You bet. A Hart with a heart." He takes my empty glass and loads it in the dishwasher beside his. I smile. I can almost see my grandma in the kitchen with us.

"Oh, and Marty, I won't tell your mother that you skipped school today."

CHOKE. My heart rate spikes. My dad sits back down in front of his newspaper. "As long as you promise me that it will never happen again."

"I promise," I blurt out, adrenaline rushing through my veins.

He nods and turns to the Sports section. "Nice haircut, by the way," he says out of the corner of his mouth, his eyes never straying from the page.

I run my fingers through the shortened strands, my hand almost looking for what isn't there. "Thanks."

In my room, I lie on my bed and stare at my grandma's picture. I imagine her here, sitting at my desk and watching the sun come up over the empty fields. Before the walls were covered in pink, they were covered in her. I close my eyes and still my body, trying to breathe past the paint to the soul below the surface. I think,

If you're crazy,
Then crazy's how I want to be,
You saw colors,
And characters,
Not paint,

And people,
But you knew it would go,
Like the wind through the window,
A breeze on a summer day,
Before the fall clouded the sky,
And death rolled over the fields.
It's not my room anymore,
It's ours.

And I swear, at that exact moment, the air fills with the scent of lilacs.

❧

All my mom does when I come down to dinner is say, "Next time you want to cut your hair, please tell me and I'll take you to an actual salon," while she sips her Chardonnay.

I smile at my dad. He places his pointer finger over his mouth and shushes me.

I drive over to Lil's early the next day and bang on the door. The words are still there in bright color, but I'm determined to fight against them.

"What the hell is it, Pollyanna?" Lil asks, squinting and rubbing her eyes in the morning sunlight.

"You're not missing anymore school," I say. "I don't care if I have to drag you there kicking and screaming. Plus, English is super boring without you."

"So, this isn't about my precious education. It's about your entertainment?" Lil runs her fingers through her hair and yawns.

"Exactly." I go over to her drawers and leaf through her clothes. Settling on a black T-shirt and red skinny jeans, I toss them on the bed. "Now get dressed," I say, hands on my hips.

Lil's eyes flicker, a mix of sadness and anxiety, and I know she's worried she'll break open for everyone to see. That one person will swing one more time and Lil's statue will come crumbling down.

"If you hide, then they win," I say.

Lil shakes her head like she's clearing it and turns on the record player. "I can't get ready without music." She pulls out a record and puts it on the turntable, placing the needle down gently, like it's the most precious thing in her life.

A guitar springs to life and fills the trailer with raucous music. Lil bops over to the clothes I laid out; I nod my head to the beat as she disappears behind a makeshift sheet-turned-wall hung up at the back of the trailer.

I could stay here all day, living away from the world with Lil and Maggie, but if there's one thing I've learned this year, it's that living actually entails doing. I won't let Lil fade away in a trailer covered in lies.

She comes out two minutes later dressed, the red jeans tucked into her black combat boots. Inhaling a deep breath, she shakes her arms at her sides, then pushes them out forcefully. "Okay, I'm ready," she yells over the music.

"Aren't you forgetting something?" I point to her face, indicating a lack of black eyeliner.

"I think I'll give my eyes a break for the day." My mouth curls up into a smile as big as the moon as Lil turns off the record player.

"You look beautiful," I say.

"You look," Lil's eyes travel down my outfit. "Weird. Are you wearing jeans on a Thursday?"

I spin in a circle, my legs relaxed in a pair of dark jeans and pink ballet flats. I open my jacket and reveal a black turtleneck. "I'm trying to tap into Rizzo."

Lil's smile actually reaches her eyes. "Rizzo? Is that some sort of hair treatment? Because I'm here to tell you, Polly-anna, with that new hair cut you'd look like a pube lollypop with a perm."

"The character from *Grease*," I giggle. "My audition is coming up."

Lil raises her eyebrows at me. Rizzo isn't just any char-acter. She's a bad girl. The misunderstood hard ass with a soft center. Everyone will expect me to try out for Sandy, but in my heart, I want to be Rizzo. I want Lil to come see the performance and know that part of her lives in me. And if part of me is Rizzo, part of Lil is Sandy and Juliet and any other character with sunlight inside of them.

"Well, I say if you want to be the girl named after a walking pube stick, go for it. No one could play the part better." Digging through her purse, Lil takes out a cigarette and holds it between her fingers, unlit. "I have something for you."

She walks over to her nightstand, which is a cardboard box covered with a crocheted blanket, and picks up a green notebook.

"What's this for?" I ask.

"For you to write in, so the pages don't get lost." Lil hands it to me, a half-smile tugging at her lips. I stare at the plastic cover. It's a cheap notebook, one I would write in at school, but it fills my heart with so much love I might burst.

"Thank you." I wrap my arms around Lil's neck and hold tight to her.

"It's just a notebook, Pollyanna," she squeaks out.

I pull back, my eyes focused on hers. "It's more than that and you know it."

"So Rizzo? Is she cool?" Lil asks as we walk out of the trailer. The air's changing, becoming warmer. I think spring isn't too far off. It might even come early this year.

"Yeah, she's the head of the Pink Ladies," I say.

"Pink Ladies? Is that some sort of lesbian club? Maybe we should join."

I giggle. "If I'm forced to listen to your music, I think it's time you listen to some musicals." I nudge her in the side. "They're cool. Green Day actually wrote a musical."

"Are you tempting me with Green Day? Did we time travel back to the 90s? Because that's the only time people have ever cared about Green Day."

"You are such a snob," I say.

She smiles. "We can't all be nice."

☙

Lil and I walk into school holding hands. Tension radiates up her arm; her elbow is stiff as a board. Her eyes, two hard aquamarines, stay fixed on the path ahead of us. A few people stare; others whisper under their breath. At one point someone coughs, *dykes*. I squeeze Lil's hand and refuse to let go.

"A rock is a rock no matter what people say," I whisper. I'm not leaving her. I'm not her dad and grandpa.

She peels off at my locker, her shoulders back, chest out. I don't know the strength it takes to be Lil, what it feels like to protect yourself with a layer of toughness because the alternative is opening yourself up to being crushed. Crushed by words.

I put my coat in my locker. Everything inside has changed. The collage Sarah made me disappeared after the

Facebook page. I replaced it with a picture of a sunrise I found in a *National Geographic* at my dad's office. The A+ paper I wrote on *The Catcher in the Rye* is taped to the door next to a note Lil passed me in English that says, "Your music cherry has officially been popped". Inside the paper was a Ramones bumper sticker. It's tacked next to the note. I stare at my little private sanctuary and know, inside and out, the girl who lives here. Even if knowing her means life is more confusing than ever.

As I grab my Math book, a person comes up behind me.

"Holy bangs. You cut your hair?" Sarah asks over my shoulder.

I slam the door shut and swing around, ready to pounce. "Real observant."

"Can I talk to you?" she asks, pulling on my arm and dragging me to a corner of the hallway away from the throngs of people entering the building.

"Afraid I might ruin your reputation if people see us talking?" I ask.

She shakes her head. "No, and I get it. I deserve it." She shifts her backpack from one arm to the other. "I heard about what happened to Lil's trailer and I want to say I'm sorry." She pauses and looks down at her knee-high brown boots. "For all of it."

I sink back against the wall and cross my arms over my chest. "Why now?"

Sarah runs a hand over her forehead and presses on her temples, "Because Pippa and Eliza ... kind of, like, suck."

"So you want to be my friend again because your new ones blow?" I huff and start to walk away.

"That's not it!" Sarah yells after me. "I should have never liked that page. I was angry and I saw you slipping away and

I choked. And I'm jealous of Lil, okay? Happy? I miss you. I hate riding the bus alone."

I stop in my tracks. Jealous of Lil? "Why didn't you just say that?"

Sarah twists a red curl around her finger and looks at her feet. "I don't know. I'm not good with words like you. Anyway, I'm saying it now for the entire school to hear."

I don't know if I can forgive her, or if we'll ever be friends again. How do you change the flow of a river and make it run backwards? But Sarah's stuck in my heart whether I like it or not. We have too many years, too much history.

"It can never be like it was," I say. "You hurt me."

Sarah shakes her head, squeezing her eyes shut. "I know, but maybe we could start again."

I want to say no, to walk away and desert Sarah like she deserted me, but that's not who I am.

"Maybe."

A smile shivers on Sarah's face, her big brown eyes glimmering, as the first bell rings.

"By the way, you don't pull off black like Lil does," Sarah points at my turtleneck. "I'd stick to warmer tones." She walks toward the orchestra room, heading in the opposite direction. "I'll see you later," she says over her shoulder, a hopeful grin on her face.

∽

On my way out of school, I stop at the spring musical audition sign-up sheet and pick up the pen.

Name: Marty Hart

Part:

I stare at the word. Part. Who do I want to play? Part

of me is Sandy, the nice girl who falls in love with the bad boy, but another part of me is Rizzo. Lost and confused and broken.

I take a deep breath and write.

"Rizzo?" Alex says over my shoulder. I didn't even know he was standing there. "I would have thought Sandy."

"Me too," I say, almost to myself. "How do you know so much about musicals, by the way? Another brilliant tip from your brother?"

"No, he's way too much of a meathead to be into musicals." Alex pauses, then lifts his hand, and runs his thumb over my cheek. "There's a lot about me you don't know, Marty." He smiles, his blue eyes sparkling.

My jaw hangs open; my cheek turning hot. I can't help but think that there's a lot about everyone I don't know. Including myself.

"By the way," Alex says over his shoulder as he walks away. "I like the new look."

CHAPTER 16

I don't care.
I don't care,
I don't care,
Okay,
Maybe I care,
Maybe I've never cared,
About anything more,
Than this.

> To: <u>matt.3.names@o-mail.com</u>
> From: <u>marty.hart@o-mail.com</u>
> Hi! How R U? I miss ur emails. :)

I stare at my computer, waiting, hoping for the ding of a new email. My mind circles around Matt. *It's no big deal he isn't writing back. He's busy. He said he liked me. But he's confused. I can wait out confusion. Heck, I understand it. I've been confused all year.* I fall back on my bed, hugging my no-name rabbit. *And he kissed me.*

With the days getting longer, the air is changing around me. My grandma would say life is returning to the earth for another go 'round. *It always comes back, Marty,* she'd say. *Death doesn't last.* I wish Grandma was here to meet Lil and see how I've changed. I bet she'd be into the Ramones and want to dance around with me. She'd want to grab hold of the life oozing out of us because she understood that seasons change, that soon enough I'll be in an adult diaper with strangers wiping my ass.

I get up and check my email. Nothing. Grabbing my cell from my purse, I look at it, willing a text to appear even though I'm not sure Matt has my number. Blank. I close my eyes and try to see myself, to see Matt on my skin, to know in the depths of my being that I made the right decision.

I refresh my computer. Inbox empty. Maybe it's not working. I toss no-name rabbit back on my bed and grab my beat-up copy of *Anne of Green Gables*. I walk out to our backyard, into No-Nana Land, and climb to the top of the hunting platform. Turning my face to the sun, I take a deep breath, inhaling the fresh almost-spring air. The earth smells like life, like water running over the ground and making things green. Clean.

Lying back on the hard wood, I close my eyes, an empty hole in my heart like someone punched me clear through my skin and out my back. I've spent days trying not to care about Matt. But then I realized that I do care. That usually when people say they don't, they care about that one thing, that small, pinprick thing, the most. And it keeps pricking you until what was a small drop of blood becomes a gash the size of your heart.

Why isn't he emailing? What did I do wrong? My chest rises in short tight breaths and tears roll down my cheeks. By the time my mom calls me in for dinner, the pages inside my book are covered in water marks.

∼

Lil comes up to my locker the next morning, her shoulder leaning against the wall, red sunglasses propped on her head. She hasn't worn any eyeliner since the first day she went without it. It's as if some of the clouds parted and sun was able to hit Lil's heart.

Maggie called a cleaning crew and had the words power-washed off the trailer. Little bits of red and blue still cling to the outside, but at least the words are gone. All that's left is color.

"Do you think I should find my dad?" Lil asks.

I look at her, surprised. She's only ever brought him up that one time. "Do you want to?"

"I don't know. He's probably a total dick. I mean, he did bail on us. I just wonder if I'm like him. Like, maybe he grinds his teeth at night or can't stand the taste of asparagus like me." Lil spins her nose ring around. "I just ... I don't even know where I'd start."

"Here," I tear a piece of paper out of my notebook. "Write down what you'd say to him."

Writing it down is almost as good as saying it. The simple act unlocks the words in your head and pours them into the universe.

Nodding, Lil takes my pen and writes. I don't look at the page. I don't need to know what Lil wants to say. It's her truth, not mine.

When she's done, she folds the paper up and puts it in her back pocket. Maybe someday she'll be able to hand deliver it. Or maybe it will stay in her pocket and get washed over and over until it disintegrates into a ball of wrinkled paper she finds months down the road. Whatever. At least she did it.

"Want to come over after school?" she asks as we walk down the hall.

I'm about to respond when Matt Three-Last-Names comes into view. His blonde hair bobs amongst the heads of the crowd and my stomach sinks to my toes. Emotions rush over me, tingling my veins and twisting my insides. My feet beg to move forward and grab him and ask why he isn't emailing me, but I lock my knees still, swallowing the tightness in my throat.

His arm reaches in the air, black jelly bracelets lining his wrist, and lands around a petite brunette. Meghan Whitlock. I trip over my own feet. I didn't think that was even possible.

"Whoa there, Pollyanna. You okay?" Lil asks, grabbing my arm and saving me the embarrassment of falling on my face.

"Yeah," I say, and shake my head. Matt and the brunette are gone when I look back down the hall. "I'm fine."

"You sure?"

I nod and swallow the lump in my throat.

Fine. The world's worst word.

&

By the end of the day, I can't take it any longer. My heart keeps swelling and breaking. Then I remind myself that Matt and Meghan could just be friends. Guys and girls can like each other without ripping one another's clothes off. It happens all the time. And Matt is friendly to everyone. If there's something I've learned this year it's that not everything is as it seems.

I trudge out to my car, misty rain covering my face. I slam my backpack down on the front seat and run my fingers through my hair. My brain hurts with all the thoughts swarming around it. Meghan in her short cheerleader skirt with no spanks underneath. Matt's hands. My tight thighs. Maybe I should've been more aggressive? Should've pinned him down and let him ride my Lazy Susan or strum my guitar strings or at least touch my boobs.

Clenching my fingers around the steering wheel, I know where I need to go. I'm sick of being Saint Martina Hart, the girl with the rotten, unused tight vagina. I pull out of the parking lot and head toward Main Street.

A few people walk around Vinyl Tap, picking up records and CDs and smiling like they're walking down memory lane. The Bob Marley poster still hangs on the wall and I draw in my breath sharply. That night at Lake Loraine, locked forever in a song.

I walk back to the storage room door and lean my ear against it. Smooth guitar chords resonate through the wood. Matt is on the other side. This is it. The moment I open myself up to whatever he wants to do. Seventeen years in one body and now I want to be transported into another one. One like Meghan Whitlock's and Lil's and half the other girls in my school.

Everything looks the same as it did the night of my parents' party. Boxes and posters still line the walls. The air is filled with sex, sweaty and thick.

Matt sits in a chair in the center of the room, playing like life is oozing out of his fingers. I peek past the door and just listen, letting the music work its magic on me. Hearing it wipes the ache away from my heart, and I know I want to kiss him again. Even my lady parts seem to jump, finally ready for a change.

I touch my black jelly bracelet. I was overreacting about Meghan. Matt's busy with guitar and school. His pothead mom probably doesn't even have a computer, and he's stuck using the school's computer lab. I smile as Matt plugs the last chord of the song; knowing all is forgiven, I step toward him, releasing the tension I've kept locked in my thighs for seventeen years.

Clapping echoes in the space, but my hands aren't moving.

"That was *so* good!" a female voice yells. It's a little too peppy. A cheerleader. Tension zings back up my legs and snaps anything that was open shut, throwing away the key.

"Did you really think it was good, or are you just being nice?" Matt asks, placing his guitar on the ground. I've heard that before.

"It was good ... and I plan on being nice." Meghan Whitlock walks into view, a short denim skirt and tight pink top barely covering her skin. She might catch a cold in that outfit. I know I should shut the door and leave, but I can't. My eyes are fixed on them, like I'm waiting for a car crash, unable to turn away.

Meghan straddles Matt on the seat. That was a move I was going to make, but I'm not sure I would have done it so smoothly. "Very nice," she says.

He smiles at her, a devilish grin. "I was hoping you'd say that."

Vomit rises in my throat when I see his hand travel up her thigh and under her skirt. I close the storage room door as quietly as I can and step back, clapping my hand over my mouth. I might throw up. I thought stuff like that only happened in movies. His hand. His words.

I run out of Vinyl Tap, knocking my shoulder into a long-haired man inhaling incense smoke by the counter. Air. I need air.

Tripping out the front door, I take a deep breath, swallowing down the bile in my throat. I want to cry. Crying would make me feel better. But I can't. I'm frozen.

The entire way to Lil's, my mind can't shake the image. I turn off the car and get out, staggering up to the trailer like a zombie. *Meghan Whitlock?*

"Where the hell have you been? I thought you were coming over after school?" Lil's head pokes out of the trailer door.

"Sorry, I got caught up," I say weakly.

"I want to show you something." Lil ushers me into the trailer and holds up a T-shirt. GO BUCK YOURSELF is written in all-caps on the front; on the back is a deer holding its middle hoof up. "I found it in a magazine and thought it was perfect. What do you think?"

I stare at the shirt, but all I can see is Meghan on Matt's lap. His hand up her skirt. That should have been me. Could have been me.

"Seriously, what the hell is wrong with you?" Lil asks.

What *is* wrong with me? Why doesn't Matt like me? Why didn't he want to do that with *me*? Why is it when something hits your brain it also hits your lungs and takes your breath away? I walk over to the bin of records and start searching through them. I don't know what I'm looking for. Maybe a song to drown out my thoughts. Maybe the Led Zeppelin record I know Lil doesn't own. Maybe my sanity.

"Take it easy with those," Lil says, picking up the records I've strewn on the ground.

"I need music. Maybe the Ramones or the Pixies or what was that other one you played last week?"

"Sonic Youth?"

"That one." I dig even further into the batch.

"I don't think abusing my record collection is going to

help you, Pollyanna."

I turn and look at Lil, tears welling up in my eyes. "Why not? You do it." The words come out all wrong, with venom on the tips, but I can't stop myself. Everything inside of me feels pointed.

"What's that supposed to mean?" Lil tosses her new shirt on the bed.

"Nothing." I go back to searching through the sea of songs, biting the side of my tongue so I don't cry.

"No, seriously. What did you mean by that?"

I whip around and the words come out before I can think about what they'll do to my best friend. "You hide behind music so you don't actually have to feel. But me? I've done everything right! I'm a nice person! I ruined my reputation. Lost my friend. And for what?! I'm in the same place I was months ago! Sitting in your trailer listening to the same damn songs!"

"What?" Lil bites.

I stop, realizing what I've said. It all sounds wrong. "Wait. That's not what I meant."

"You ruined your reputation? Lost a friend?" Lil bites out each of the words, sharp and hard. "I'm sorry if I've been a burden on your precious perfect life."

"That's not it," I say again, tears pricking my eyes. Why is the world caving in on me?

"I think you better go," Lil says, and walks toward the door.

"You're kicking me out?"

"No, I'm avoiding the instinct to punch you in the face." She swings the trailer door open. I don't want to leave. I don't want Lil to throw me back out to the lions of life. Doesn't she understand that I need her right now?

"But ..." I want to talk, to explain the situation with Matt and Meghan and his hands. "I need to tell you about Matt."

"Matt?" Lil barks. "When are you going to wake up? I told you to stay away from him. He's stringing you along so that maybe one day he can take a ride in that unused body part you're carting around two and a half feet above the ground. That's *it*. Stop being naive and move on."

"You think you're so superior just because you've had sex," I say, wiping tears from my cheeks.

"If the smell fits," Lil crosses her arms over her chest.

"You're just jealous."

I see the words catch Lil in the stomach like a wrecking ball. All the blackness comes screaming back to her eyes, and she looks at me with nothing but vacant darkness.

"Get out."

I want to take it all back. I didn't come here to fight. I came here to be with my best friend, to find some sort of calm in my sea of crazy, and all I've done is smash everything to pieces.

But I don't say that. I run out of the trailer, tears streaming down my face, and drive away from the only place in the world that feels real.

❧

Ice and then a heating pad. Ice and then a heating pad. Just like Ms. Everley said. It works. Kind of. When I wake up in the morning, small red puffy circles rim my eyes. I look tired. *You're just jealous.* It rings in my ears. I shake my head to get the noise out, but it doesn't work. My mind's filled with sweet guitar chords and angry words and Meghan Whitlock's peppy voice. I choke back vomit.

Lil said sex isn't really about the physical. It's about the change on the inside, the part of your soul where you know your true self. I was going to give myself to Matt. And deep down I know I still want to give that to him. So why won't he have me?

As I sit in English the next day, I'm afraid to look in Lil's direction. She's sitting next to me in the seat she stole from Alex on her first day of school. It's hers now. Most days I look forward to this time when we get to be in the same space. But today it's different. I'm ashamed and mad and still confused as hell. Her words about Matt get my skin all prickly and make me want to yell at her again. But then I remember what I said, all the things I didn't mean, and I fall into a gaping black hole of shame.

"Marty? Are you going to answer the question?" Ms. Everley says.

I'm staring at the word FUCK, carved so deeply into the top of my desk. "What?" I say, snapping back to the present. "I didn't hear you."

"Mr. Darcy's proposal to Elizabeth. What did you think about it?"

I blink. *Pride and Prejudice*. "Well," my mind stumbles over last night's reading. Out of the corner of my eye, I see Lil yawn and roll her eyes. "I think Elizabeth and Darcy are both kind of assholes. I mean, he wasn't lying when he said that marrying her would be below him. But she wasn't lying when she said his proposal sucked. So I guess they're both screwed, right?"

Ms. Everley stares at me the same way she looked at Lil that first day, like a ball she never saw coming just smacked her right in the face. "I guess to some extent that's right." She pauses. "I'm not sure Jane Austen would've put it so eloquently."

"Sorry," I mumble, and scoot lower in my desk.

I try to look at Lil without actually turning my head in her direction. I know my response wasn't an apology, but if the world is filled with a bunch of assholes, I'd rather be friends with her than anyone else.

I walk out of the classroom in a daze, thinking about Mr. Darcy and Elizabeth and how life was so much easier when no one kissed until they got married.

Alex falls into stride next to me, matching his pace to mine.

"Interesting response," he says.

"Is that good or bad?" I ask.

"I just mean that you're filled with new developments. I like it."

New developments. That's how I feel, kind of. Like the earth keeps shifting under my feet. Some days I take so many great steps forward and others I take the wrong steps backward and end up with shit all over my shoes.

"Do you want to go to the Carpenter party with me this weekend?" he asks.

I stare at him, not sure what to say. He looks cute in his red Minster High Baseball T-shirt and jeans. He runs his hand through the mop of brown hair on his head. No arm accessories. My stomach rolls.

"Um," I say. It's the annual 'Minster High School Passing of the Torch' party. Every senior and junior is invited. The seniors get drunk and cry about how high school is over while the juniors laugh and say they'll never be like that when they're seniors because who would want to stay another year in this dump of a school? It's held on the Carpenter Farm. Mrs. Carpenter had eleven boys. The rumor is that she kept trying for a girl, but it never happened. One of the boys is almost always a senior or junior.

"I ..." I don't know what to say to Alex. The truth is, I wasn't planning to go since Lil and I aren't the most popular people in the school. But then it hits me like a light turning on in my head: Matt will be there. It's a party after all, with beer and probably pot.

Lil walks out of the classroom door as Alex stands, big gorgeous smile on his face, waiting for my response.

"I'd love to go to the party with you," I say loudly enough for Lil to hear.

"Great!" Alex almost jumps out of his red Converse. "I'll pick you up at seven."

The satisfaction of showing Lil I'm moving on, even though I'm only fake moving on, pops in my heart when I see Alex get so giddy. It's replaced with guilt, heavy enough to pull my arms and chest clear to the floor.

"Great!" I repeat. I say the word the way I used to say all my words, with a forced emphasis on every letter in hopes I might believe in my soul that it's what I mean.

Except, unlike before, I know now that it's untrue. That behind the word is vapor and behind the vapor is a picture of Matt and I'm playing nice so Lil thinks I'm stronger than I really am and so Alex doesn't hate me.

CHAPTER 17

I stand in my closet, picking through things to wear for the party, and see the red scarf I wore the night Lil and I went to Lake Loraine. Lifting it off the hanger, I press it to my nose. The dried leaf smell of that night is still locked in the fibers. I can practically feel Matt's sexy arms around me and hear Bob Marley's pot-filled voice in my ears. My stomach is a ball of nerves the way it was that night, except this time I know what Matt Three-Last-Names' lips taste like and I'm determined to have it again. Screw Meghan Whitlock and her short, panty-showing skirt.

I pick up my phone and call Lil. It rings five times and goes to voicemail.

"Wait for the beep."

Beep.

"Lil, it's Marty. I'm sorry I was an ass, but you were an ass, too. Please come tonight. Okay, bye." I hang up the phone and stand in my closet. I know Lil doesn't like school functions, but this technically isn't one since there will be beer and pot and probably a lot of people making bad decisions.

I grab the gold dress I wore that night at Vinyl Tap and put it on. I know I should be getting dressed thinking about what Alex would like, but my mind can only think about Matt. Matt and Lil. Without them this year would be nothing. The days would have passed as the seasons changed and all I would have to show for it would be a yearbook. Glossy pictures instead of a real living breathing life.

Alex knocks on the front door at exactly seven. I bound down the stairs, too much bounce in my step, and fling open the door.

"Wow. You look great," he says.

"Let's get out of here," I say as I grab my purse off the hook.

"Wait, Marty! We want to meet your date," my mom yells from the kitchen.

I roll my eyes and take a step back as my parents come barreling into the room.

"So this is the famous football player we've heard so much about," my mom says, her glass of wine swaying back and forth in her hand as she talks. She's lying, probably to make it sound like I'm closer to my parents than I really am. I'm sure she wants Alex to think we're a family who sits around the dinner table like a bad show on the CW, one where the mom and daughter are best friends and talk about sex and their periods and penises. They eat candy and French fries night after night and never get fat. Too bad my mom made me eat asparagus tonight, even though I told her I hate how it makes my pee smell.

I'm going to pretend you didn't just say pee at the table, she said into her napkin as she dabbed the corners of her mouth. I didn't say a word the rest of the dinner.

"I wasn't sure you existed," Mom says brightly.

"It's nice to meet you, Mrs. Hart." Alex holds out a hand for her to shake. My mom smiles and gives me the eye. Alex already has the high-school-boyfriend-I-probably-won't-sleep-with-your-daughter-just-heavy-petting stamp of approval.

"We need to go," I say, grabbing Alex's arm and yanking him toward the door.

"You two have fun!" Mom sings. Either she's drunk off her Chardonnay or bubbling with pride that her daughter, the one she thought was a lesbian just months ago, is going on a date with a respectable boy.

We get into Alex's red truck and he says, "Your mom seems nice."

I try not to roll my eyes. "'Seems' being the operative word."

"You guys don't get along?"

"Does anybody get along with their parents?" I ask. But then I think about Maggie and Lil and how much they love each other, how Maggie breathes because Lil does. How she doesn't care if Lil says fuck or shit or boner. My mom breathes because it would be rude to die.

Alex shrugs and starts the car. "Another new development, I guess."

I look at him, guilt pulling down on me once more. "I'm sorry," I say, and change the subject. "Do you have any music in this thing?"

Alex smiles and flips on the stereo. It's tuned to a station that matches our town. A bunch of white people singing about tractors and drinking and guns.

"Country?" I ask, trying to keep the scowl off my face.

"You don't like country?"

I take a moment. A few short months ago, I would have said, *Of course I like country! Garth Brooks is my favorite*, even though I think he's a fat old man with a voice like a horse. But now ...

"Honestly?" I hesitate. "I think it's awful. I mean, a four-year-old could write these lyrics. All they'd have to do is think of all the words that rhyme with beers and rednecks and Jesus."

"Don't forget the pick-up truck," Alex says.

I stare at him, at his red and green flannel shirt tucked into jeans, driving his beat-up truck that has a hint of cow poop coming out of its fibers, and say, "You're, like, a walking country song."

"Riding in my red pick-up with a six-pack of beer," Alex sings in a terrible country twang. "We'll head off to church before I'm so drunk I can't steer."

I giggle. "You're terrible."

"We can't all be beautiful," he says, his cheeks peppering ever so slightly with pink.

I slump a little lower in my seat and play with the black bracelet around my wrist. If Alex really knew me, he'd know I don't deserve the compliment.

We pull up in front of the Carpenter farm. A bonfire is already roaring on the side of the property and music is blaring out into the fields from one of the second-story bedrooms.

"Thanks for coming with me tonight," Alex says as we get out of the car.

I smile and adjust my dress, flattening out the wrinkles. Pulling my phone out of my purse, I check it, hoping to see a text or voicemail from Lil. Nothing. I don't want to be mad at her anymore. I want to be back in her car, hanging out the window, and screaming into the wind.

The house is filled with loud, mostly drunk people. As we walk in, a pack of girls is hugging and crying in the corner, black mascara streaking their faces. Each one is spilling beer out of their red plastic cups onto Mrs. Carpenter's carpet. My mom would kill me if I had a party and ruined her floor. I spilled milk onto the rug in our family room once and she freaked, like Exorcist head-spinning freaked. *That rug costs more than your life!* she yelled before running over with a bucket of soapy water and yellow rubber gloves to cover her manicure. She scrubbed the spot until the entire house smelled like lemons.

"Do you want anything?" Alex asks, bending down to my ear to talk over the music.

"I'm okay," I yell. "I'm going to find the bathroom."

The house is packed. I check down all the halls for Matt. My eyes are on high alert for blonde hair and the smell of sex and my bones feel like they want to jump free from my skin just hoping I'll see him. I peek around a few corners, checking the rooms on the first floor, and then I head upstairs. Along the staircase are school pictures of all the Carpenter boys. I can't imagine giving birth over and over and hoping each baby was a girl, only to be disappointed by a penis.

I open a few bedroom doors and walk in on a couple with their shirts off. Everything smells like stale beer. And I can't find Matt anywhere.

I take out my phone and check it again. Nothing, so I text Lil.

Marty: *Get ur ass to this party, Juliet. Pronto.*

When I start to head back downstairs, I smell it. Sex and a guitar. Like a cherry-wood fire. *Matt.* I gulp and everything in my body drops to the floor. Tonight, we're locked in the same house with hidden corners we could disappear into at any moment. I push the memory of Meghan Whitlock to the farthest part of my mind. Matt's a free spirit. I can't hold that against him. But I can join in. I can finally be a part of Lil and his club. Being better is for suckers and saints.

With each step I take down the stairs and as Matt comes

into full view, my knees rattle more and more. Even my eyes get splotchy. I shouldn't be this nervous. We've made out. But everything since has been a maze of words. Not flesh on flesh.

I keep my eyes on him, on the black T-shirt he's wearing, on the way it contrasts his blonde hair and makes me want to touch him even more. He's like a sexy teenage Johnny Cash. And I'm his June Carter. The good girl who can get him off drugs and help him find God. Even she wasn't perfect. They had an affair, after all.

Our eyes connect at the same moment. My heart beats heavy in my chest. It isn't pumping blood; it's pumping an ocean filled with so many locked away words and warm feelings—but there's a chill at the same time. All the fears and doubts that won't leave me alone. My hot and cold internal faucets are turned on and my skin keeps changing temperature.

Matt looks at me, a crooked smile on his face. Our eyes haven't met in weeks, not since he passed me in the hallway with Alex. There's no way seeing me now doesn't spark something in his system. Our kisses were too good. Too memorable. I'm burning hot everywhere. I return the look and wait for him to walk over. This is it.

And I wait.

And I wait.

The room was too crowded to pass,

He stood there, like his feet might have roots in the ground.

I smile even more widely, hoping my eyes sparkle the way they did the night he told me he liked me. So he might remember what it felt like for us to hold each other. So he'll forget Meghan Whitlock and all the other girls.

She waited as he sang a silent song with his body.

The melody lost somewhere in the air between them.
And before she could hear the beautiful tune,
He was gone.

Matt turns his back to me and walks out of the room. My breath gets short. *What is he doing?* The music vibrating the walls is so loud I can't think straight. It's some emo-wannabe-rocker-white-boy band like Linkin Park or Nickelback and I hate their voices. Every note is like a nail scratching my heart. This moment isn't supposed to be filled with bad music. Bob Marley should be playing.

I slump back against the wall, my chest so heavy I might faint right here next to all the Carpenter boys' pictures. The last thing I'll think about is Mrs. Carpenter's stretched-out coochie. *Why did he walk away?*

"Did you find the bathroom?"

I blink. *Who's talking?*

"Marty, are you okay?" Alex asks.

I snap out of it. "I'm fine."

"The bathroom is just down the hall that way." He points in the direction opposite where Matt walked. I must have made a mistake. He didn't see me. He couldn't have. I mean, we've danced and kissed and he's said things to me he's never said to anyone else. Okay, except for the line he also used on Meghan. It's impossible for him to walk away.

"I think I need a beer," I say.

Alex's eyes widen. "If you say so." We walk into the kitchen and he fills a cup for me, the foam pouring over the edge. "Sorry. I'm new at this."

I take it out of his hand and gulp half. "Me, too," I say, spilling some down the side of my mouth.

"You look like a pro." Alex wipes the beer away with his shirt.

I hand my cup back to him and he fills it again. Gulp. Gulp. Gulp. And it's gone. "Are you sure you don't want any? It's pretty good," I say, wondering if the slur I hear is real or just my brain moving more slowly because it's consumed with Matt.

"My coach would kill me if he found out I'd been drinking."

I swig another half glass. "Does he make you wear sleeveless undershirts? Because I might need to talk to him about that."

"What?" Alex asks with a smile.

I swallow more foamy beer. With each gulp, what just happened moves further away from the surface. I'm determined to drown myself.

I grab Alex's bicep and squeeze. "You have nice arms," I say. "If only you didn't sweat."

"Doesn't everyone sweat?"

I stare at him. A hiccup or burp or maybe a mixture of both escapes my lips.

"Why do guys say one thing and then do the opposite?" I ask.

"Wait, are we still talking about sweating?"

"I mean, you tell a girl she'd look good in a white dress and then you never call. What the fuck?" I say fuck the way Lil would, like a rock star. I even fling my head forward, but it makes me lose my balance and I wobble sideways.

"Maybe you should slow down," Alex says, grabbing my arm to steady me.

"I've been slow my whole life," I say. Breaking from his grip, I refill my cup again.

Drinking and walking at the same time, I make my way outside. Even the ground seems unstable, like it might swallow me whole or thrust up to trip me; I stumble, trying not to spill my beer. But all the bad energy that clogged my veins is dissipating. I think I might love beer. I love the foam and the bubbly way it pops going down my throat and the numbness tingling my arms. It's different than the vodka Sarah and I drank, smooth, like I'm swimming through a container of goo. Warm, happy goo. Maybe I was wrong. Maybe feeling life is overrated. Because it hurts. I don't think anything could hurt beer. Right now, I want to be beer. I want to swim in it and coat myself in it and never come out.

I trip and spill on my dress. *Oops.* I try to wipe it away, but the stain stays.

Outside, the music doesn't get any better, but I don't care. I flap my arms and twirl around in a circle, feeling the loud bass in my bones.

"This song sucks," I say as I twirl around, my arms held out to my sides so I don't fall.

"Maybe I should request some country," Alex yells over the music.

I stop spinning and smile, or at least I feel like I'm smiling. My cheeks have gone numb. "You're funny." I poke him in the chest. "And your pecs are so hard." I rub my hands up and down his flannel shirt, but he backs away. It doesn't bother me.

"Are you sure you don't want to put that drink down?"

I'm about to tell him that I'm in love with beer and why would I ever leave something that makes me feel so good, when Sarah arrives at the party.

"Sarah!" I yell across the lawn. I'm not sure how loud I'm being because everything in my head is muffled, like I'm wearing headphones.

"Hey," she says with a furrowed brow.

"I love you, Sarah." I wrap my arm around her neck and squeeze her to me.

"Um, Athlete," Sarah motions to Alex, "Could you please remove her from my body before she squashes my hair. What *is* up, Marty? How many drinks have you had?"

I hold up my fingers, but they all mesh together.

"Am I embarrassing you? Should we not talk? I am a lesbian after all," I say.

Sarah looks at Alex. "Could you please do your job and not feed her any more drinks? She's going to do something she regrets."

"No regrets," I say, and shake my head until my mind spins.

"Maybe you should go home," Sarah says.

"I'm not going home." I stumble back.

"Well, I'm going inside. Watch her, please, Athlete."

"It's Alex," he says as she walks away.

I shrug my shoulders. "Band dorks."

"Maybe we should be heading home," Alex says.

"No!" I yell. We can't leave. Nothing I wanted for the night has happened. I'm not supposed to leave with Alex; I'm supposed to be with Matt. He should have looked at me and stopped everything and kissed me out in the open for everyone to see.

And Lil isn't even here. She's probably driving around blaring music out the windows and not caring that I need her. Why did Matt walk away? Why did he say he liked me and wanted to run away with me and marry me? Where did Lil go? Where's the truth in any of this? Has anything over the past few months been real?

My mind starts to swim, not in a good swimming-in-a-vat-of-wonderful-numbness way, but in the way that means

I might fall over. It makes everything inside of me want to sink to the ground. All the warm fuzziness that was clouding my brain is shifting to water and I think I might start crying.

"I need another beer," I say, and stumble over toward the keg. I can't believe Mrs. Carpenter allows this party to happen every year, but maybe it's her way of saying, *Fuck You, World,* for giving me all boys. It's her way of screaming into the night; throwing her hands up and saying, sure, yeah, wreck everything in my house. It all smells like sweat and balls anyway.

"I think maybe you've had enough," Alex says, his voice going from candy-coated to flat and serious.

"You okay, Pollyanna?" I look up from my haze. Lil is standing in front of me, her new T-shirt screaming in capital letters: GO BUCK YOURSELF. "What the hell did you do to her, Jock Strap?" she says at Alex.

"Nothing," he says and put his hands up like he's under arrest. "She's been pounding beers. I'm trying to get her to leave."

"Beers, Marty? You know you're more of a wine cooler kind of girl. Why don't you let flannel shirt here take you home."

"Why, so I can sit in my room? I'd rather be here," I slur.

"So you can sleep it off," Lil says, and grabs my arm to walk me out.

"I've been sleeping my whole life!" I yell. "Aren't you the one who told me to wake up?"

"Not with a six-pack of beer in your pint-sized stomach, Pollyanna." Lil stops and stares at me.

"Well, if it isn't Thing 1 and Thing 2," Pippa says as she passes, a red plastic cup covering her smug smile. "Finally going to admit the lesbian love between you?" She flips her brown hair over her shoulder. "Dykes."

"God, get out of here, Pippa," Alex snaps, his voice a deep growl.

I hang my head toward the ground. When did everything start to spin—and not just the usual spin in my head, but spin in reality? The green grass and red and yellow bonfire are threading together. Nickleback blares in my ear drums until I think I'll go deaf from bad lyrics about boobs and blondes. How did Nickelback become a band in the first place? Words choke the back of my throat. I'm sick of swallowing them down.

"You know what, Pippa? You suck," I say. I point to someone else in the crowd. "And you suck, too. Everyone at this party sucks!" I scream and look at Alex and Lil. "Except you two. You don't suck."

"Thanks." Alex shrugs his shoulders.

"Maybe it's time this town hears the truth." My voice is hitting decibels I didn't know it could reach, not even when I played Sarah Brown and had to hit a high A. But I can't stop it. All the pain and confusion and words I've held in are on the tip of my tongue and I need to get them out or I'll throw up. "Maybe being nice is for suckers. I mean, what has it ever gotten me? One lousy make out session and some stupid pictures in a yearbook."

"Keep your voice down, Marty," Lil says. "Forget about Pippa. She's a fucking ass wipe." Her eyes are daggers on mine, but I don't feel the prick. I'm too numb.

"No. She needs to know. You taught me to tell the truth and that's what I'm doing. I'm screaming for everyone to hear!" I take a breath and push everything out at once. "You're all a bunch of penguins. Penguins! You huddle around each other and mate for life instead of thinking about what else might be out there. Maybe living in Antarctica sucks! And God forbid someone drops an egg."

"Stop it now, Marty." Lil barks.

And then it comes out without warning. For me, for Lil, for the entire party to hear, like a sideswiping car crash. "No. You tell them. Tell them the truth about your mom! Tell them how it hurts you. Scream at the top of your lungs!" I yell.

Lil looks at me with cold black fear in her eyes. It's not the veil I normally see when she's mad. My words have cracked open her soul and exposed the bruises that form my best friend, clear down to the roots of her. And *everyone* can see.

"Screw you," Lil says.

The veil drops as quickly as it lifted and Lil runs away from me and the crowd and the truth I was about to lay bare.

I look at Alex, my head spinning, tears about to burst from so deep in my gut they may never stop raining down my cheeks.

"I think I'm going to puke," I say. And seconds later, I do. All over Alex's red Converse.

CHAPTER 18

"That was quite a performance," Alex says after I vomit the entire contents of a six-pack all over the Carpenter's lawn.

"Oh my God." Panic drops in my stomach. I look around to see how many people are staring at me. Did I just say the words I think I did, or is the beer making me hallucinate? I didn't think it could do that, but maybe it was spiked with acid or mushrooms or whatever Lil took that night at Lake Loraine. Oh shit, Lil! *Shit.* Only a few wandering eyes are left looking at my puke-covered dress. I want to curl up into a ball and forget myself and this night and Matt. I look at Alex. "I'm a terrible person. Like the worst. I'm not nice at all."

"I'm not sure I got the part about the penguins." Alex puts a finger to his chin, like he's trying to solve an equation. "You might have to say it again."

"I'm sorry," I say, my head still spinning.

"Don't be. I mean, I hate these shoes."

I wipe off the front of my puke-stained gold dress. The words I just said feel fake. Like I was living in a movie and watching myself. Marty Hart would never say those things out loud—and yet, I did. For everyone to hear. Or at least, for some people to hear over the awful guitar-stylings of Nickelback. Now, my life's soundtrack is ruined.

"I need to go find Lil," I say. Alex nods, because that's the type of person he is. He'll call me beautiful and stare at me and ask me out even though I like someone else and let me vomit on his shoes. My soul sinks into the ground, so deep I'm going to need grave diggers to find it.

I go into the house, replaying the words I said in front of everyone. How I took the one secret Lil told me and put it into the air for people to breathe in and twist to their own liking. I'm pond scum. The lowest of the low. I'm a country song with bad lyrics and bouffant hair.

I walk around the house, pushing past people, trying to find my best friend. The girl dressed in an awesome fuck you T-shirt, Mrs. Grim Reaper. How could I do this to her? I should give her every one of my poems so she can paste them all over the school for people to see.

I check the whole first floor. No Lil. Heading upstairs, my chest pinches. What if she left? What if she's upset and gets in a car accident? My words will be the last thing she hears. I start looking in the bedrooms. There are too many. Too many doors. Too many gross-smelling boy tube socks. Too many places she could be hiding. Maybe she's tucked herself into the corner of one of the closets and plugged her ears with music so she can't hear me yelling her name.

I fling open the last bedroom door. *Keep out, dickweed*, is written across the front. The lights are off, but I hear people. Not caring if I walk in on someone having sex, because I need to find my best friend, I need her to know that I love her, that I think she *is* Juliet and I'm the asshole Rosaline, that I was wrong, all wrong, I flip on the light.

My eyes go splotchy trying to adjust, but when they do, my entire world turns upside down. I think I'm not on the same planet anymore. I'm in an alternate universe where everything that could be bad gets worse.

Matt sits up on the bed, his blonde hair disheveled,

red lipstick across his cheeks and neck. I look for Meghan Whitlock, but she's not here.

Instead, Lil moves to pull her shirt back down over her stomach. GO BUCK YOURSELF. I look back and forth at their faces and the wrinkles in their clothes and the smell of heavy breathing in the air.

"Marty," Lil says as she stands up. "This isn't what you think."

I blink. What I think? I don't know what I think anymore. I stare at Matt, the boy who kissed me with so much depth I thought I might break in two. Is that what he was doing to Lil when I walked in?

"Say something," Lil says, and walks over toward me.

"I was coming to tell you that you're still a Juliet." I blink a thousand times to try and erase what I just saw. "I'll go now."

"Marty, wait," Lil tries to grab my hand, but I yank it away. I don't want her skin, the skin that was just pressed against Matt's, touching mine. Then I might forgive her. Then I might remember what it felt like for us to lie on my bed with my poetry all around us and know what true friendship is.

I tear the black jelly bracelet from my wrist and drop it on the ground. I can't believe I was stupid enough to keep it, to think it meant something.

I run down the stairs and back out to the bonfire, never looking back.

"Did you find her?" Alex asks.

"Please take me home," I say.

"Are you ..."

I cut him off, tears welling in my eyes. "Take me home!"

"Okay," he says, grabs the keys from his pocket, and puts

his arm around my waist. When his hand holds my side like I'm a doll that might break, I let everything go. Tear after tear falls down my face until I'm covered and I fall into Alex's side and let him practically carry me to the car.

He doesn't ask me what happened as we drive home. He doesn't even turn the radio on. Instead, he rolls down the windows and lets the breeze blow across my face to dry my tears.

Every few seconds, I live that moment again. The sound of kissing, the tousled clothes, my best friend and my life-size crush on the bed. Together. And then I want to puke all over again. Not from beer. From the stabbing pain in my heart. From it breaking into a million jagged pieces.

"Can I walk you inside?" Alex asks as we pull up my driveway.

"I'd rather be alone." I get out of the car without saying goodbye, without giving him a polite thank you, without making sure his Converse aren't stained with my puke. I walk in the front door without taking off my shoes and straight up to my room. I think I hear my parents say something from the couch in the family room, but I don't respond. The only noise in my head is that of two lips smacking together. The lips of Matt and Lil.

&

Danger is the close friend of excitement,
Why else would someone stand on a bridge,
Fling themselves off,
And soar through the air with wind in their hair,
Because they know the cord will pull them back,
That danger and excitement can live together,

As long as in the end,
Safety wins.
But what happens when it breaks.
What happens when you launch yourself,
Without ever tying the cord to your ankle.

∾

I don't want to get out of bed the next morning. My entire body hurts from the wrecking ball that was Matt and Lil. Every time a body part moves, I relive the scene. The hair and lipstick and heavy air. *There are people like you and then there are people like me and Matt.* I say Lil's words over and over until my heart hurts so bad I start to cry again and I have to roll over and stuff my face in the pillow to muffle the sound.

I'm mid meltdown when my phone rings on the nightstand. It's Lil. Even seeing the name pop up makes my gut so twisted and angry I want to toss my phone across the room. Instead, I stuff it under the mattress so I don't have to hear or see it.

I stare at my grandma and wonder what she would say. If everything has a season, why does it feel like I'm dying in the middle of summer? *Life comes from dirt, Marty. Some people sweep it under the rug; some people plant things in it. Don't sweep. Dig. But always remember to bring a change of underwear. No one likes dirt in their ass.*

"Marty, there's someone here for you," my mom says through my closed door.

"I don't want to see anyone," I bite out.

"Now, don't be rude, honey. He's waiting downstairs." And then she whispers more quietly, "and don't forget to shave your legs."

I sit up in bed. She said *he*. Matt? I race to the shower, take my mom's advice about the legs, and then throw on jeans and a white T-shirt. Staring at my face in the mirror, I look drained. Worse than drained. Dead. My eyes are puffy and rimmed red all the way around. I dab cover-up on the bags, but it's no use. Not even mascara will help my cause today.

I bound down the stairs, my heart fighting itself, part of me mad that Matt did what he did, but part of me happy he's here to apologize.

I stop short when I see Alex sitting in the living room.

"Hi," he says.

I try to force a smile, but the ends of my lips tug down into a frown. "What are you doing here?" I ask in a flat tone.

"I thought I might take you out today," he says.

"I'm not really in the mood." I start to make my way back up to my room, to the duvet in my bed that was cradling me so nicely a few minutes ago.

"Come on. It'll be fun." Alex moves closer to me. "You owe me." He holds out his red Converse. The ones still stained with my puke.

"Fine," I grumble.

"You two have fun!" my mom yells from the kitchen. *Ugh.* I want to go back up to my room and mope. I should have never gotten out of bed.

"Where are we going?" I ask once we're in Alex's car.

"It's a surprise," he says.

"Look, Alex, I'm not really in the mood."

"Maybe some music would help." He flips on the radio.

"Please not country. I can't handle that today," I say, but then the music starts.

"*Grease?*" I say.

"I figure you need to start getting ready for your big au-dition this week." Alex's face twinkles with excitement over his good deed.

The audition. Rizzo. After getting dumped and cheated on, I want to play the part even more. Okay, maybe not *officially* cheated on because Matt didn't *officially* ask me to be his girlfriend, but he did ask me to marry him in ten years. That's practically the same thing.

Alex and I drive though town, listening to *Grease*, until he pulls up in front of The Batter's Box.

"Batting cages?" I ask, raising an eyebrow.

"I figure you have some stuff to work out and instead of banging back beers, you could bang around some balls."

"I know we've never been in gym together, thank God, but my hand-eye coordination is seriously lacking."

"And you hate sweat, I know, but just try it. If you get hit in the face or something, we'll leave." Alex cuts the en-gine and walks around to my side to open the door.

"I could get hit in the face?" I ask, and cover my nose.

He shakes his head and smiles. "Thank goodness you're cute."

Alex grabs two bats and helmets and pays the pimple-faced boy behind the front desk. The sound of bats cracking balls echoes around the park as we walk over to one of the empty cages.

"Now, the key is to stand with your feet shoulder-width apart and watch the ball," Alex says, imitating the stance.

"I'm going to look ridiculous." I say as I put on the hel-met, a pout to my voice.

"More ridiculous than last night?"

I look at him, the memories flooding back into my brain. Matt and Lil. Lil and Matt. Wrinkled clothes. Lips smacking.

"Give me that bat."

I walk into the cage and adjust my stance to mimic Alex's. Legs shoulder-width apart. Eyes on what's to come. But who knows what that will be? Never in a million years did I think Lil would do this to me. I thought I knew her like I know myself. But maybe I was lying, the way I always have. Lil told me she wasn't a Juliet and I convinced myself she was.

Now, I'm back walking through my internal maze, not knowing which direction is the right turn and which path will lead me back to the beginning.

Maybe the straight path that I thought was wrong isn't so bad.

The ball shoots out of the sling. I swing and miss.

"That's okay," Alex claps from behind me. "Stay focused."

But I don't think I could ever go back to who I was. To lock things away instead of breathing and living and being. I can't make myself an X. My internal wiring would backfire and I'd end up a vegetable with good manners and boxes full of useless Christmas decorations.

The next ball flies through the air. I swing and miss.

"That's okay, too," Alex yells.

"Stop saying it's okay!" I yell back at him. "It's not okay! None of this is okay!"

But why does it have to hurt? Like, the worst hurt of my life. My guts are tangled and my limbs are broken and I can't call my best friend to talk to her about it because she's the one that ran me over.

The next ball comes shooting out of the sling. I watch it soar straight at me. Why did Lil have to make out with Matt? Why didn't he want me? Why don't I deserve someone who wants to kiss me and have sex with me and love me? I swing at the ball. CRACK! It pops up into the air.

"I did it!" I scream and look at Alex.

"Yeah, baby!" He jumps up and down.

"I can't believe I did it!"

"Now focus again and get this next one," he says.

One by one, I swing the bat at the fast-moving balls, and each time they connect and I hear the crack of the collision, I feel lighter. Soon sweat is dripping down my face and my shirt is rimed with salty water and I don't even smell it. All I know is that I might never leave this batting cage. I might swing my arm until it falls off and last night is erased from my mind.

We get double scoops of chocolate ice cream when all of Alex's money runs out and he can't pay for any more balls. Between the sugar and the exercise, I'm buzzing. My arm hurts like it was run over by a Mack truck, but I don't care. I might come back tomorrow and crush some more balls.

"Thanks," I say as we walk back to Alex's truck. I take my napkin and wipe away the chocolate outlining Alex's mouth. "I needed this today."

"I'm glad." he says, licking his lips. He pauses and his nose curls up.

"What?" I ask.

"I won't ask you what happened last night, if you promise me one thing."

"One thing?" I say.

"That maybe we could do this again?"

It's a punch in the gut. One Alex doesn't know he even swung. Matt's voice rings in my ears and I feel his finger graze my forehead. *Maybe we can do this again?* It brings the pain back. The pinpricks turn into a gash, bleeding all over the ground.

And I have to find a way to clean it up.

I muster a smile, but can't bring myself to say anything.

CHAPTER 19

I toss and turn all night until the pain radiating down my arm and into my chest gets so bad, I can't sleep. All I can see is *them*. All I can feel is Matt. And all I want to do is call Lil. I get out of bed and sit at my desk. Pulling the box of poems from my bottom drawer, I rifle through the pages. How many were inspired by Lil? And Matt? I want to burn them all, but I know it wouldn't solve anything. Because once something is out in the ether it's there. I could burn my entire house to the ground and the earth would still hold its memory.

Dear Grandma,
When you lost your mind,
Did you know?
Could you look in the mirror,
And see bits of yourself,
Trailing behind you,
Like a path of breadcrumbs?
And when it was all over,
Did you follow that path home?
Or did you walk a new one,
Leaving the bits behind,
So I could remember you.

❧

My knees rattle so badly as I walk into English class that I think they might break off on their own and run in the opposite direction. Everyone is talking about my outburst, but I've lived with their words all year and they're nothing compared to seeing Lil. I erased every last one of her voice-mails and texts. I can't decide if I don't care what she has to say or if I'm not ready to hear it. I know I don't want her to sit next to me. I don't want to see my best friend and know we could sit in class and send texts about boners and thongs and internally laugh until I'm smiling on the outside, too.

I walk into the room and see Alex sitting in Lil's seat. I breathe for maybe the first time today and go to my desk.

"Hi," he says out of the corner of his mouth.

"Sick of sitting in the back?" I ask.

"I thought it's time I take back what's mine." He smiles. "And I wanted to give you this."

He places a card on my desk. I stare at it, half intrigued by what's inside, half worried I might not deserve whatever it is. Alex made me feel so much better yesterday, but when I went home I was swallowed again by Matt and his empty words and Lil with her mouth on his.

I grit my teeth, not because I don't care about Alex, but because I'm not sure I deserve him caring about me the way he does, and open it.

Break a leg, but don't break an arm. You owe me another date to the batting cages. Love, Alex.

"Thank you," I say, fighting to find the right reaction. Happy. Sad. Cute. Not Matt. Beautiful. Not Matt. Sleeveless Undershirts. Not Matt. And he signed it *love*. Matt never said that once, and here Alex has written it like it's as easy as breathing.

But Matt did say he wanted to marry me and that he

liked me and thought I was really pretty. And then he made out with my best friend.

At that moment, Lil walks into the room. I sink into the ground, below my desk, below the school, into the pits of hell. A fiery, prickly feeling overtakes my entire body and I want to jump out of my desk and attack her or I want to scream at her or hug her because she's the one person who can make me feel better. Except she's the one who did this to me.

She walks past Alex and me, straight to the back of the class. I can barely breathe as she passes. I don't dare look up at her.

"So," Miss Everley says as she stands at the front of the classroom, her hot pink bra strap sticking out from her black lacy top. "Who can tell me why Jane Austen named the book *Pride and Prejudice?*"

I hope Ms. Everley doesn't call on me. I couldn't care less about Jane Austen today. Elizabeth didn't have to deal with Mr. Darcy making out with her sister Jane because no one kissed back then. They all sat around looking pretty and sewing things and waiting for a hot, loaded guy to come sweep them off their feet. Everyone was just a bunch of X's waiting for their Y's.

My phone buzzes in my bag and I pick it up.

Lil: Good luck 2day. U'll make the perfect Pink Taco or Frizzo or whatever pube-perm treatment that character is named after. And I'm sorry.

Damn it. Why did I have to pick up? Why did she have to be funny and make my stomach rumble with the idea of laughing? My finger hangs over the reply button. I want to go back to the way thing were. I want to go to her house after the audition and lie on her couch and listen to the Ramones. I want to watch her smoke and wish she would stop and think that we were placed on this earth to be in this moment together. I want to hear her sing again.

But we can't. Nothing can erase what she did.

I delete the message, just like I did all the others.

&

"Marty Hart. You're up next," Mr. Spector, Minster High School's drama coach, yells onto the stage. He's sitting in the audience, a clipboard propped on his beer belly.

I clutch my sheet music in my hands and walk out into the lights.

"You signed up for Rizzo?" he asks.

"I sure did," I smile. It's one of the main rules of auditioning. Always smile. Even if your life has been smashed to pieces. That, and never wear baggy clothes. Stage lights add pounds. I opted for tight black pants and a hot pink T-shirt.

"Well, get on with it." He waves his hand in the air. "I've got to meet my wife at the Inn Between in twenty minutes. It's fried chicken night."

I take a few deep breaths as I hand Ronny Whipple, the short sophomore accompanist, my music. I picked the song weeks ago; filing through Lil's record collection, I pulled out an album with a girl on the cover. She was dark and serious and covered in leather. *Joan Jett and the Blackhearts*, Lil said over my shoulder. *Nice choice*. I downloaded the album when I got home.

Closing my eyes, I imagine Rizzo. I think about the poetry she probably has stashed in her room and the tears she won't let herself cry. And right before the song starts, I think of Matt.

I hate myself for loving you.

I don't move as I sing, just close my eyes and let the song talk for itself. I don't know if I love Matt or like him or hate him. All I know is that I hate how I feel right now, like my heart is bleeding and no Band-Aid or stitch or patch could heal it. I clench my fists so hard with every note I sing that my nails pinch my skin.

I hate myself for loving you.

Every word comes from the deepest place in my soul, and as I sing my thoughts into the air, I'm lighter. Like when Lil cut my hair and I knew beauty had nothing to do with what I look like. Like when I wrote my first poem and understood the quiet person silently screaming in my mind. Like the first day I met Lil and she saw me, the real me, and wanted to be my friend.

When Ronny hits the last chord of the song, I breathe. From the back of the auditorium, someone starts clapping.

"That was an interesting song choice," Mr. Spector says as he packs up his clipboard. "The cast list will be up on Friday."

I squint my eyes to see past the stage lights and find Alex in the back row, his hands smacking together and a smile as big as the moon on his face.

And in this moment, I think Shakespeare and Jane Austen were wrong. Maybe love isn't about torture or pain. Maybe I shouldn't want to be a Juliet. After all, Lil *is* right; she ends up dead in the end.

❧

After my audition I go home exhausted, half of me wanting to break down in tears and the other half lighter than ever because I told the world how I feel about Matt and now I can let it go. I gave my last breath on the stage and now all I want to do is close my eyes and wait for the next sunrise. I stare at the TV and watch a show on the Discovery Channel about a man who lived with bears. He even dresses like one and tries to talk in a growl. I'm pretty sure I've seen this one before and the bears eat him in the end. For some reason, animal instinct or something, they turn on him and the friends he thought he had become his enemy.

I stare at his worn-out face and stringy shaggy hair. He wants to look like a bear. He wants to *be* a bear. But what he doesn't understand is that he will never be something he's not, no matter how much, even in the depths of his soul, he believes he is. His skin and eyes and hair tell a different story and maybe if he looked in the mirror and tried to find himself in himself, he wouldn't have ended up dead, eaten by the thing he thought he was.

You're better, Marty. Lil's voice comes through the confusion and I think I understand now. She's right. I've been healed, and now I am better.

My mom walks in the back door wearing her Shady Willows golf shirt and khakis. I wonder if she's a bear man, dressed to look like a volunteer but really a vulture. Maybe if she admitted she's a vulture, we'd get along better.

"How did the audition go, honey?" she asks. She sets her keys on the key holder and hangs her black Kate Spade handbag on the same hook she always does right by the back door.

"I think I got the part."

"Well, you were born to play Sandy." She takes off her penny loafers and puts on her slippers.

"Actually, I auditioned for Rizzo." I wait for my words

to sink in. For my mom to realize that I think I was born to play a different part in this world than the one she expects.

"No matter what part you get, I'm sure you'll be wonderful."

I sit up on the couch and look at her, sitting at the granite island she had put in the kitchen so she could have proper cooking space. Something's not right. Mom's back is hunched and she's rubbing her temples like her brain hurts. *Posture tells people how you feel about yourself, so sit up straight*, her words ring in my ears.

"Are you okay, mom?" I ask as I walk into the kitchen.

She shakes her head, hair falling in her face. "Mrs. Schneider was admitted to the hospital. She's not doing well. I'd be surprised if she makes it through the weekend."

"Oh," I say. "I'm sorry." She might be a mean, smelly old lady, but death sucks, no matter who you are.

"It's not easy working at a place where people come and go," my mom says. "I hated watching your grandma all alone, but she insisted on living there. She knew we couldn't take care of her. But that doesn't change the fact that people shouldn't die alone."

I stare at my mom, sitting looking so lost in her beautiful kitchen, and realize she started volunteering at the retirement home after my grandma passed away. In that moment, my world tilts and spins and twirls so much that all of a sudden I see things clearly.

"You do it for her?" I ask.

My mom looks at me. "Everyone copes with death differently, Marty. I miss your grandma as much as you do. Maybe more."

"Why didn't you ever say anything?"

"Would it bring her back?" my mom asks. "The best

thing I can do for her is help others." She gets up and walks over to me. With her perfectly polished fingers, she tucks the mahogany strands of hair that are falling in my face behind my ears. "Just promise me you'll pull your hair back so people can see your face when you play Rizzo."

I breathe and smell the lilac candle my mom bought last week. It's sitting on the counter, flame flickering gently. And then I hug my mom because she needs it, because she loves my grandma, because maybe she isn't a vulture. Maybe she's sad and trying to find her way in the dark just like I am.

"Thank you," she whispers in my ear.

ᘜ

When they put you in the ground,
And said you were buried,
I didn't really believe it.
How can you bury something,
That lives above the earth,
Or inside the wind?
Maybe you run with angels now,
Or dance with the devil,
Or watch from the tree tops in No-Nana Land,
Hoping the pieces of you,
The pieces they said were buried,
Got caught in people,
Not walls.
Crazy is for those,
Who don't understand,
Life only has four seasons,
And eventually everything ends.
Only leaving behind,
The words we once uttered.

246

CHAPTER 20

When the cast sheet goes up and when I walk to my first rehearsal as Rizzo and when I stand on stage opening night, Alex is there with me. And he tells me I'm beautiful again. Only this time he kisses me afterward. And I let him. His mouth moves with mine; I feel the sweet taste of our lips coming together, and I know my grandma would be proud. Alex knows me, inside and out, because he took the time to care.

Lil told me I should find someone like Alex. Someone who'd be there for me and want me and know me. And she was right about Matt. My stomach still flip-flops when I see him in the halls, but then I remember that I want someone who says words that mean something because I'm someone who speaks words that mean something.

Lil never takes her seat back and eventually she stops calling and texting. A hole settles in my heart then, but for some reason, I can't bring myself to fill it with her again. Maybe it's the memory of what she did, maybe it's that I've learned only she can love herself; I can't do it for her. Maybe it's that I'm scared to be friends with her again.

I walk down the hall and greet people after the final performance of *Grease*. My heart swells with pride at all the compliments. *You were great! I couldn't even believe it was you up there!* And I deserve them, not because I was acting, but because I left my heart and soul on the stage with every word

Rizzo said.

I see Alex and Sarah talking with my parents and smile. He's wearing a sleeveless undershirt with the words *Rizzo's Boyfriend* written across the front.

"Nice shirt," I say as I poke him in the side.

"Thought I'd wear your favorite outfit." He smiles and I melt inside. A gooey, warm, confident-he-wants-me melt. I'm not sure if I love Alex or like him, but that's okay. I've got time to figure it out. I know he's not going anywhere.

"You were wonderful, honey." My dad kisses me on the forehead.

"I'm just glad they didn't make you wear a hideous curly black wig like the chick in the movie." Sarah gags herself. "I mean, am I supposed to believe John Travolta, pre-fat and old, would ever date that person?"

I giggle. "Some things never change," I say.

Sarah looks at me with raised eyebrows. "What? It's the truth."

I roll my eyes. She still puts on lip gloss and makes shallow comments, but then again, I'm not sure I could imagine Sarah being any deeper than a baby pool. And that's okay, too.

"Can I have a minute with the star?" Alex asks.

"We'll see you at home." My mom kisses me on the forehead and they head for the door.

Alex pulls me over to a corner of the hallway. "What is it?" I ask.

"You just look so cute in that costume."

"You look terrible in that shirt, country boy," I say.

"It's all for you, baby," Alex says in a terrible Southern twang. And then he bends down to kiss me. His lips are warm and kind and his arms hold me tight, like he might never let go. I fall into him and think I might never let go either. My body tingles from head to toe, the kind of tingles I've waited seventeen years to have.

"Someone else came to see you tonight," he says as he pulls back.

"Who?"

"I never asked you what happened and I promised I won't, but I can tell you miss her. Just give her a chance," Alex whispers in my ear before walking away.

I turn and see Lil propped up against the wall, holding the playbill for *Grease*. She's wearing her leather jacket over a long black dress that hangs to the floor, but her face is clear of anything dark. She doesn't even have on her red lipstick.

"Why would they name that character Rizzo? She's way cooler than that suggests."

My breath catches at the sound of her voice. Alex is right. I have missed her. I shrug my shoulders and walk to meet her.

"So you and Jock Strap? Are you guys doin' it?" Lil raises one eyebrow.

"Do I smell different?" I ask.

She leans in and takes a whiff, then shakes her head. She pauses and her eyes get soft around the edges. The blue clears of any darkness to reveal the color of the sky on a clear summer day. "Do you love him?"

"I don't know," I say. "I like him. Maybe that's better than love."

"Marty, about that night," Lil starts, but I cut her off.

"It's over. I think we both did things we regret that night."

It's what I realized when the smoke and anger cleared. I forgot about what I said, about how I exposed Lil's soul when she didn't want that. I may have wanted her to scream, for her to show the world who she is, but I should've waited for her to find her own voice.

"I told you I wasn't a Juliet," Lil says, and pulls a cigarette from her bag.

"Who wants to be Juliet? She's an idiot." Lil laughs and lights the cigarette. It takes a second to register that we're in the school and not on her grandpa's barn in the open air. My mouth falls open. "What are you doing?"

"You're such a Pollyanna," she smiles and exhales a cloud of smoke into my face. "Maggie and I are finally leaving this town. She got a job in California."

My brain takes a second to comprehend what Lil just said. How in one fell swoop, she's pulled herself out of my life and I didn't even have the opportunity to grab hold of her or try to make her stay. My knees buckle and sink and every part of me wants to cry at the same time.

"You're leaving?" I whisper. I never imagined she'd go. I knew our friendship would never be the same, but I always thought she'd be there to remind me of who I am, of what I want my life to be. To scream with me.

Lil takes a long drag of her cigarette, but I can see the corners of her mouth pull down. She can't hide from me.

"We've outgrown the trailer. I need my own room. How am I supposed to get laid with my mom right next to me?"

I grab her in a hug, one I should have given her months ago, one she's needed since the day her father walked out and her grandpa walked away. I know I did the same thing. I told her I would never leave and that's exactly what I did.

"I'm so sorry," I say in her ear. I won't let go now. My soul sings because she showed me the power I could find in being myself.

Lil whispers, "You were the best part of this place. The best part of me."

And then she turns and walks down the hallway, a trail of smoke following behind her.

❧

Black is the night,
Black is the day,
Black is the path,
Where we find our way,
Into the light,
Into the sun,
Where we hold out our arms,
And scream freedom.

❧

Alex drives me home as I cry in the front seat. Tear after tear streams down my face like rain on the windshield. My heart is heavy with so many words I want to say to Lil, with months of wasted time, with love for her and Maggie and their trailer.

I go up to my room and pull out my box of poetry. The notebook Lil gave me sits on top. I haven't written much lately. I've been saying my words instead of writing them, but even still, almost every page is full. I don't have time to give Lil everything that I want, but maybe, just maybe, she can take me with her.

❧

I drive over to her house, my hand clutching Lil's gift. I even wrapped it in black paper with a red bow. It took days to make, the cutting and pasting and constant glue on my fingers that stuck to everything. I practically bought out Hobby Lobby. But now it's done.

I knock on the trailer door and Maggie opens it.

"Marty!" she yells, and throws her arms around me. "I was afraid I wouldn't see you before we left."

I'm afraid of what life will be without you. I'm afraid I won't be able to breathe knowing you're so far away.

"Never," I smile. "Is Lil here?"

Maggie motions inside and I walk in. Everything's packed up, all Lil's records and blankets and clothes, but the walls feel the same, like I'm cradled and safe. I swallow the lump in my throat and twist the skull ring on my finger. This is the last time I'll stand here. This is the last time I'll be alive in this moment with Lil.

"Hey, Pollyanna," she says. "I wasn't sure I'd see you."

"I wanted to give you this." I hold out the gift and Lil takes it.

"You didn't need to," she says.

"Yes, I did." *I needed to give you so much more.* "Open it."

She looks at me with apprehension in her eyes. She knows this is goodbye and part of me thinks she hoped I wouldn't come, that I would walk out on her without saying a word. But she means more to me than that. She means more to me than every word I've ever written.

Lil pulls the paper back corner by corner, and reveals the book I made. The title sparkles in gold and silver sequins on the cover. "We Are Dancer". She opens it up and starts to read.

"Your poems?" she asks. I nod. "I can't." She tries to shove the book back into my arms, but I won't take it. I don't need them. Those words live inside me and around me, like the bits of my grandma I find sparkling in my soul.

"Yes, you can."

Lil's flips through the pages of every poem I've ever written, every word I locked in the box in the bottom drawer of my desk.

"I have something for you, too." She moves over to a stack of papers sitting on top of her record player. "Here."

She hands me a heavy folder and I open it. University of California, Berkeley is written across the top. "A college application?"

"Don't stay here. Be a writer, Marty."

I look up at Lil, at her eyes as clear as the sky. Eyes that altered me before I knew I needed it. She deserves the moon and stars and a wild heart-pounding-love-filled life. We should be dancing in a universe filled with music and words and friendship, not saying goodbye.

"Please don't leave," I say and grab her in another hug, squeezing until our bodies are so close together I feel like we could mesh into one.

"Everyone leaves," Lil's quivering voice whispers in my ear.

"I love you," I say.

Lil takes a breath. Time stops and the trailer is filled with the memories of the past and the weight of the present and the brightness, like sunrise over a barren field, of the future.

"I love you, too, Pollyanna."

☙

I get in my car after saying goodbye to Maggie and toss

the folder with the application Lil gave me on the front seat. As I pull away from Addison Farm, away from Lil and her mom and all my soul-consuming, painfully alive moments of the past year, I smile. Rolling down the windows, I turn on the stereo. Only one song can be played right now. One song to remember I'm breathing and feeling and screaming with every bit of my life. As the summer sun starts to fade over the horizon, I turn up "Human" as loud as it will go and swerve my car until the road is marked with so many curved lines the next person to travel down it will have to make their own path.

When I get home, I toss the University of Michigan application that's been on my desk for two years into the garbage and replace it with Lil's gift.

California doesn't sound so bad. I hear it's summer there all year round.

THE END

ACKNOWLEDGMENTS

First, I want to thank my husband, Kyle. Without his grace, dedication, and utter belief in me, this book would not have been possible. Thank you for letting me read you page after page of the manuscript. For being my cheerleader. For being the love of my life. For being a father and a mother at times to our two girls. For believing in me. It's easy to write about love because I have you.

I want to thank Saira Rao and Carey Albertine for reading *Playing Nice* in its infancy and loving it. For believing Marty and Lil had a story to tell. For constantly coming back to the words on the page and loving them more and more. Thank you for your guidance and laughter. You never doubted that this book was meant to be shared with people. I hope I've made you proud.

Thank you, Anna Weber, for sending me an email demanding I make the phone call that changed my life.

Thank you to Allison Williams and Julie O'Connell for watching my kids so I could pursue a dream.

Thank you to Genevieve Gagne-Hawes for reading *Playing Nice*, loving it, and then telling me how to make it better. Your guidance made Marty and Lil soar. (And your copy edits corrected my terrible habit of forgetting commas.)

Thank you to all the great musical influences in my life: The Avett Brothers, The Decemberists, Cat Stevens, Bob Seger, Simon and Garfunkel. Every musical ever written. Music is pure joy. Life cannot be experienced unless a great soundtrack accompanies it.

To all the teachers from my past who molded who I am. To all the teachers I worked with in the schools I called home: New York City, Boston, Columbus. To all the teachers who stood up and said they'd read my book. I thank you from the bottom of my heart. I took a class in college called Young Adult Literature with a professor named Dr. Jackie Glasgow and I fell in love with books all over again. But it wasn't the genre that changed my life; it was the teacher who exposed it to me.

Thank you to my daughters, Drew and Hazel. I wrote this for you. I hope you see the true potential of life. That you can drive with the windows down, screaming at the top of your lungs, blaring music, and think life doesn't get any better than this. Then know that it does. I am because you are.

Thank you, Susan— for answering my phone calls at 2am, for loving me from the day my family became yours. You inspired this story. I never met your mom, but I hope you see her in the pages of this book.

From the time I was small, my parents taught me that dreams matter. That if I wanted to sing on stage or write a book or be CEO, I could. I've had many dreams in my life, some came true, others not so much. I'm still waiting for the day I'm called on stage to play Eponine in Les Miserables. Because of my parents, I never stopped wondering what might come next. Thank you, Russ and Sydney Schnurr, for raising a dreamer.

Words matter, from the dark to the funny. Marty believed that if she chose the right words, they could heal. I hope *Playing Nice* heals. That people read this book and share the power of healing with others, through words on a page or words out of your mouth. This book is me hanging out the car window and screaming at the top of my lungs for everyone to hear. Thank you, reader, for joining in the chaos.

Lil's Playlist

Words – Givers

One Love – Bob Marley

Blister in the Sun – Violent Femmes

I Wanna be Sedated – The Ramones

Over the Hills and Far Away – Led Zeppelin

We are Young - Fun.

I Hate Myself for Loving You - Joan Jett and the Blackhearts

California Bound – Carolina Liar

Human - The Killers

Ho Hey - The Lumineers

Follow Lil on Twitter @LilHatfield

Together Book Clubs:
Questions for Discussion

1. Marty tells the story from the first-person perspective which gives the reader her view of the world. How might the story be different if told from Lil's? Sarah's? Marty's mom?

2. Lil's favorite book is *One Flew Over the Cuckoo's Nest*, by Ken Kesey. Why do you think she identifies with this novel, particularly the character R. P. McMurphy?

3. Who is your favorite character and why?

4. Alex's brother says, "People are assholes." Do you agree and why? Do you think Marty agrees with that philosophy or not?

5. Marty has a connection with her grandmother that is all her own. Who are you connected with in a way that is truly yours and why?

6. Lil says, "Truth is subjective. If I told you this [rock] was a bird every single day for the next ten years, eventually you'd start calling it that." Do you think Lil's actions throughout the book are her own or a reaction to how people view her? Why? What about Marty?

7. What is your favorite line from one of Marty's poems? Why?

8. Lil and Marty identify themselves through song lyrics. What song lyrics do you identify with?

9. One of Marty's poems says, "In kindergarten we learn to get in line, Walk straight, Follow the leader, Earn a yellow star, But where does that line lead? To the same place everyone else goes. What if I went in another direction? Would I find new people to follow? Would I be the leader then? Or would I be alone?" What are the challenges to branching out on your own? Are there perks to being a follower? Are there downfalls to being a leader? What would you do if you found yourself alone?

10. Lil tells Marty, "There are people like you and there are people like me." Do you agree with Lil? Are Marty and Lil truly different?

11. Lil has some zinger lines. What is your favorite?

12. Marty and Lil battle bullying. Has the novel changed your view on bullying? What advice would you give to someone being bullied?

13. Do you think Marty and Lil ever see each other again? What would they be like as adults?

14. Are we human or are we dancer?

About Rebekah Crane

Rebekah Crane fell in love with YA literature while studying Secondary English Education at Ohio University, but it wasn't until ten years and two daughters later that she started to write it. Inspired by her past students, growing up in Cleveland with its fabulous musical theater community, and music of all kinds (particularly the Avett Brothers), she created *Playing Nice*. It is her first published novel, but having an unbridled imagination, it's not the only fantasy world she's lived in (just ask her husband). She now lives in Colorado, where the altitude only enhances the experience.

Connect with Rebekah:

http://www.rebekahcrane.com
http://rebekahcrane.tumblr.com/
https://twitter.com/rebekahcrane
https://www.facebook.com/rebekah.crane

Other Books by In This Together Media:

Soccer Sisters: Lily Out of Bounds by Andrea Montalbano
http://www.amazon.com/Lily-Bounds-Soccer-Sisters-eb-ook/dp/B008NMIDIA/

Mrs. Claus and The School of Christmas Spirit by Rebecca Mun-sterer
http://www.amazon.com/Claus-School-Christmas-Spirit-ebook/dp/B00A2DWCSS/

Connect with us!
www.inthistogethermedia.com
https://twitter.com/intogethermedia
https://www.facebook.com/InThisTogetherMedia

Made in the USA
Lexington, KY
25 January 2015